THE WORLD'S CLASSICS

EUGÉNIE GRANDET

HONORÉ BALZAC was born in 1799 at Tours, the son of
a civil servant. Put out to nurse and sent later to boarding
school, he had, except between the ages of four and eight,
little contact with home. In 1814 the family moved to Paris,
where Honoré continued his boarding-school education for
two years, and then studied law at the Sorbonne. From 1816
to 1819 he worked in a lawyer's office, but having completed
his legal training he knew he wanted to be a writer. While
his family gave meagre financial support he wrote a play,
Cromwell, but it was a complete failure. He also collaborated
with other writers to produce popular novels. During the
1820s he dabbled in journalism, and tried to make money in
printing and publishing ventures, whose lack of success laid
the foundation for debts that plagued him for the rest of his
life.

In 1829 Balzac published his first novel under his own
name, *Le Dernier Chouan* (later *Les Chouans*), and the
Physiologie du mariage. In 1830 came a collection of six
stories called *Scènes de la vie privée*. Self-styled 'de Balzac',
he became fashionable in the literary and social world of
Paris, and over the next twenty years, as well as plays and
articles, wrote more than ninety novels and stories. In 1842
many of these were published in seventeen volumes as the
Comédie humaine. Important works were still to come, but
ill-health interfered with his creativity and marred the last
years of his life.

In 1832, in his extensive fan-mail, Balzac received a letter
from the Polish Countess Hanska, whose elderly husband
owned a vast estate in the Ukraine. The next year he met
Madame Hanska in Switzerland, and in 1835 the couple
agreed to marry after Count Hanski's death. For seventeen
years, with intermissions, they conducted a voluminous
correspondence, until their marriage finally took place in
March 1850. Balzac died three months later in Paris.

SYLVIA RAPHAEL taught French language and literature at
the universities of Glasgow and London, specializing in
nineteenth-century literature. Her translations include
Balzac's *Cousin Bette* and Said's *Indiana* and *Manprat* for the
World's Classics.

CHRISTOPHER PRENDERGAST is a Fellow of King's College, Cambridge

EUGÉNIE GRANDET

HONORÉ BALZAC was born in 1799 at Tours, the son of a civil servant. Put out to nurse and sent later to boarding school, he had except between the ages of four and eight little contact with home. In 1814 the family moved to Paris, where Honoré continued his boarding-school education for two years, and then studied law at the Sorbonne. From 1816 to 1819 he worked in a lawyer's office, but having completed his legal training, he knew he wanted to be a writer. While his family gave meagre financial support he wrote a play, Cromwell, but it was a complete failure. He also collaborated with other writers to produce popular novels. During the 1820s he dabbled in journalism, and tried to make money in printing and publishing ventures, whose lack of success laid the foundation for debts that plagued him for the rest of his life.

In 1829 Balzac published his first novel under his own name, Le Dernier Chouan (later Les Chouans), and the Physiologie du mariage. In 1830 came a collection of six stories called Scènes de la vie privée. Self-styled 'de Balzac', he became fashionable in the literary and social world of Paris, and over the next twenty years, as well as plays and articles, wrote more than thirty novels and stories. In 1842 many of these were published in seventeen volumes as the Comédie humaine. Important works were still to come, but ill-health interfered with his creativity and marred the last years of his life.

In 1832, in his extensive fan-mail, Balzac received a letter from the Polish Countess Hanska, whose elderly husband owned a vast estate in the Ukraine. The next year he met Madame Hanska in Switzerland, and in 1835 the couple agreed to marry after Count Hanski's death. For seventeen years, with interruptions, they conducted a voluminous correspondence, until their marriage finally took place in March 1850. Balzac died three months later in Paris.

SYLVIA RAPHAEL taught French language and literature at the universities of Glasgow and London, specializing in nineteenth-century literature. Her translations include Balzac's Cousin Bette and Sand's Indiana and Mauprat for the World's Classics.

CHRISTOPHER PRENDERGAST is a Fellow of King's College, Cambridge.

THE WORLD'S CLASSICS

HONORÉ DE BALZAC

Eugénie Grandet

Translated by

SYLVIA RAPHAEL

With an Introduction by

CHRISTOPHER PRENDERGAST

Oxford   New York

OXFORD UNIVERSITY PRESS

Oxford University Press, Great Clarendon Street, Oxford OX2 6DP

Oxford New York

Athens Auckland Bangkok Bogota Bombay
Buenos Aires Calcutta Cape Town Dar es Salaam
Delhi Florence Hong Kong Istanbul Karachi
Kuala Lumpur Madras Madrid Melbourne
Mexico City Nairobi Paris Singapore
Taipei Tokyo Toronto Warsaw

and associated companies in
Berlin Ibadan

Oxford is a trade mark of Oxford University Press

Introduction © Christopher Prendergast 1990
Translation, Note on the Text, Select Bibliography, Chronology
and Explanatory Notes © Sylvia Raphael 1990

First published as a World's Classics paperback 1990

British Library Cataloguing in Publication Data

Data available

Library of Congress Cataloging in Publication Data

Balzac, Honoré de, 1799-1850.
[Eugénie Grandet. English]
Eugénie Grandet / Honoré de Balzac; translated by Sylvia Raphael;
with an introduction by Christopher Prendergast.
p. cm. — (The World's classics)
Translation of: Eugénie Grandet.
I. Title II. Series.
PQ2166.A37 1990 843'.7—dc20 90-6896
ISBN 0-19-282605-0

3 5 7 9 10 8 6 4

Printed in Great Britain by
Caledonian International Book Manufacturing Ltd
Glasgow

CONTENTS

CONTENTS

INTRODUCTION

I

'At this very hour', Flaubert wrote in support of the claim that the heroine of *Madame Bovary* had her counterparts in contemporary life, 'my poor Bovary no doubt suffers and weeps in twenty villages of France.' Since the greater part of Emma Bovary's tragedy takes place after the move from Tostes to Yonville, we can presumably include provincial towns as well as villages in the catchment area of this declared overlap of fiction and fact. A Bovary suffering, weeping and perhaps dreaming her life away in, for instance, Saumur? And what if we further complicate the fact-fiction scenario with the calculation that, by the time Flaubert writes the above, in Saumur one Madame de Bonfons, *née* Grandet (and by now perhaps Marquise de Froidfond) would be, or rather 'is', fifty-seven years old? Back in 1833 she 'is' a widow, and rumour has it that she is contemplating a second marriage. The use of the present tense is in fact Balzac's, introduced on the last page of his novel to narrow the gap between 'fact' and 'fiction' by closing the gap between the time of narrative and the time of narration. Moreover, the question who Eugénie Grandet is to marry is one that appeared to exercise her creator in a quite radically absorbing way. The story famously runs—though sceptics say it is apocryphal—that, in the course of an evening spent with his friend Jules Sandeau, Balzac suddenly accorded ontological priority to fiction over fact by declaring that the subject of Sandeau's conversation (his sick mother) was of little importance alongside the pressing question of his heroine's marital arrangements: 'That's all very well,' Balzac is alleged to have said after several minutes of absent-minded listening, 'but let's get back to reality. Who is going to marry Eugénie Grandet?'

This anecdote explains why Balzac would doubtless have

loved to have seen Eugénie included in Flaubert's list of 'real-life' Bovarys. It would not have been essentially because of the situational and psychological resemblances between the two heroines; though they are considerable, there are also fundamental differences (Eugénie has been described, perhaps a little primly, as the 'moral antithesis' of Emma). Nor—despite the 'paternal' fantasies at work in his own self-image as novelist—would Balzac's pleasure have derived primarily from the knowledge of some putative 'influence' on Flaubert (it is, however, no accident that *Eugénie Grandet* was one of the few Balzac novels Flaubert prized highly). The point of our otherwise absurd speculative fable is that it catches something fundamental in the nature of Balzac's artistic energies and commitments —namely, an intensity of identification which not only blurs the distinction between imagination and reality, but also questions the hierarchy whereby the former is made subordinate to the latter. Not the least of the paradoxes of Balzac is that he is the great 'realist' who lived his creations as if they were themselves more real than reality. This way madness lies, on a spectrum from delirium to megalomania. But it is also the sort of madness which is close to what Henry James called the 'fine frenzy' of the artist. Baudelaire was among the first to sense the full force and significance of this when he described Balzac as a 'visionary, a passionate visionary' (the description has since, alas, become something of a tired academic cliché). James, in an essay entitled 'The Lesson of Balzac'—along with Proust's essay 'Sainte-Beuve et Balzac' arguably the best thing ever written on the subject—spoke of Balzac's 'saturation with his idea', of 'orgies and debauches of intellectual passion' and of a 'passion . . . that had ridden him like an infliction of the gods.' Balzac himself put it like this: 'Sometimes it seems to me as if my brain were on fire and as if I were fated to die on the ruins of my mind.'

This is, of course, strong stuff, and a reader less susceptible to the rhetoric of the Romantic conception of the artist will want to take it all with a pinch of salt. Indeed

Balzac himself wrote much that was scornful of the idea of the artist as a demonically possessed and self-destructively compulsive being. It would be more accurate to represent Balzac's conception as an odd mixture of, on the one hand, the robustly industrious bourgeois with a tendency to the workaholic and, on the other hand, the Faustian dreamer close to the crazy, self-abstracting world of some of his major characters, including Frenhofer, the wildly passionate painter of *Le Chef-d'œuvre inconnu*. The two images come together in the celebrated routines and accoutrements of Balzac's working habits: the nocturnal regime, the monk's robe and, above all, the coffee (specially prepared by Balzac himself, as a thick concoction of Bourbon, Martinique, and Mocha, and consumed in vast quantities). The first account we have along these lines of Balzac at work—though the caffeine intake is curiously reduced to a single cup—is in a letter to his friend Zulma Carraud:

I must tell you that I am submerged in excessive labour. The mechanics of my life have altered. I go to bed at six or seven in the evening, like the hens. I am awakened at one o'clock in the morning and work till eight. At eight I sleep for an hour and a half. Then I have something light to eat, and a cup of black coffee, and harness my wagon until four. I receive callers, I take a bath or I go out, and after dinner I go back to bed. I have to live like this for months on end if I am not to be overwhelmed by my obligations.

This letter was written in 1833. It was, even by Balzac's extraordinary standards (what James called his 'twenty years of royal intellectual spending'), a year of prodigious activity. More important, 1833 is the year in which we find Balzac taking, in his characteristically whirlwind way, a number of decisive steps towards the formulation of that gigantic and quite implausible artistic project, the *Comédie humaine*. He signed a contract with the publisher, Madame Béchet, for the publication of his works (minus the juvenilia and the so-called *Romans et contes philosophiques*) in twelve volumes, under the general heading *Études de mœurs au XIX siècle*, and divided into three groups, *Scènes de la vie privée*, *Scènes de la vie de province*, and *Scènes de la vie parisienne*. This is one of the first manifestations of the idea of a coherent novelistic enterprise laid out in terms of a system of classificatory categories. (The other interconnecting device—the technique of recurring characters—will be developed the following year, in 1834 during the writing of *Le Père Goriot*.) It is not, however, until 1841 that the project is explicitly named *La Comédie humaine*; there follows in 1842 a general preface (the 'Avant-propos') in which the project is intellectually justified through an analogical appeal to the disciplines of history and science. The *Comédie humaine* is to be, in the terms of fiction, a form of social history (what Balzac calls the 'histoire des mœurs'), whose diversity and complexity are to be grasped not only according to the classificatory scheme of the different *Scènes*, but also by analogy with the taxonomic models of zoology: just as nature forms the animal world into 'espèces zoologiques', so—the logic of this 'so' of course begs important questions—culture and history form the human world into 'espèces sociales'; the latter (or at least their early nineteenth-century French varieties) are to be the stuff of which the *Comédie humaine* is made.

Balzac will have recourse to analogies with science on other occasions and in other contexts, most notably in the appropriation to his descriptive methods of the 'physiognomic' theories of Lavater (or, more exactly, of their adaptation by Moreau de la Sarthe to the interpretation of social life). This claiming of the 'authority' of science should not be taken too seriously (although the analogy will persist, in different guises, throughout the whole of the nineteenth century). The interesting question here lies not in determining whether Balzac's work is 'scientific' (a fruitless endeavour) but in understanding the purposes to which the comparison with science is put. Oddly, Balzac's way with science returns us to what we have called his form of madness, and in particular to its megalomaniac dimension. The perspective of science implies—at least in the early nineteenth century—a perspective of mastery, especially in the emphasis on the possibility of a systematic fictional taxonomy of the social world. Balzac's abiding concern with classification is indeed fuelled by a 'passion', and if, as James suggests, the passion sometimes appears as 'an infliction of the gods', it can also appropriately be understood as a challenge to the gods (Balzac was exceedingly fond of comparing himself to Prometheus). Balzac will rival the gods by lording it over a vast imaginative creation; or, in more modestly secular moods, he will be the rival of mere emperors, in particular of course Napoleon: 'What he [Napoleon] was unable to achieve by the sword', wrote Balzac in one of his most celebrated megalomaniac declarations, 'I shall achieve by the pen.'

These bold and bizarre projections would seem perhaps to be of interest only as pointers to Balzac's colourful fantasy life. They do, however, also express one of the deepest impulses of the Balzacian novel and, more generally, of what we have come to know as the aesthetic of 'realism'. Realism means many different things, according to the critical or theoretical vantage-point from which it is discussed. Under one—increasingly influential—description, it is characterized as 'imperialist' in its aims. Realism, so the argument runs, is, like any representation, always a representation of the real from a point of view. Realism, however, also seeks to privilege that point of view, even to mask the fact that it *is* a point of view, in order to propose its particular version of the real as the Real *tout court*. Realism is therefore imperialist in that it aims to be all-inclusive, but from a perspective which also functions as a point of exclusion and subordination. Like Napoleon exporting enlightenment to benighted alien cultures, the realist novel imaginatively 'colonizes' reality by virtue of its 'totalizing' aspirations; it wants to get everything in, to 'cover' reality, while subjecting it to the terms of a unified and grounded interpretative schema. The schema can then be read as a 'scheme', in the sense of an ideological ruse as well as that of an ordering pattern. Certainly, Balzac's belief that he could incorporate the totality of contemporary French life in his network of taxonomic categories, themselves made intelligible by virtue of the author's grasp of the underlying 'laws' of history and society (what in the 'Avant-propos' Balzac called the 'hidden meaning' of the modern world), looks like a case of the imperialist imagination running riot. But, if this is a useful, and even essential, way of describing Balzac, it is also polemical and one-sided. Balzac's identifications with gods, emperors, and patriarchs are of course highly eligible candidates for ideological and 'deconstructive' critique. But the fantasies are also enabling as well as disabling. Without them, or rather the creative energy and self-confidence which underlie them, we would not have had that most spectacular of narrative productions, the *Comédie humaine*. Styling himself as a kind of literary conqueror may have been (along with his many dreams of fame and fortune) an indispensable condition of what was in fact, and paradoxically, the profound unworldliness of Balzac's creative endeavour, that retreat, via monk's robe, coffee and so on, from the world in order fully to make and inhabit *his* world. When Henry James called Balzac 'the master' he did not mean the sort of mastery or masterfulness which our modern critical orthodoxies have come to stress; he meant rather the inward absorption, the total dedication, the way Balzac 'lived and breathed in his medium'.

II

If the year 1833 is the time when Balzac's sense of his monumental project starts to come into focus, it is also the year in which *Eugénie Grandet* was written. The two things are connected. *Eugénie Grandet* is of quite capital importance in the formation of the *Comédie humaine*. It was one of the first of Balzac's novels to be accorded the aura of 'classic' status, and has often been seen—though in some respects misleadingly—by subsequent critical opinion as *the* representative work of the *Comédie* as a whole. In terms of both subject matter and method the novel certainly reflects major developments in Balzac's art, and indeed of the art of the modern novel in general (the critic Maurice Bardèche has seen inscribed in *Eugénie Grandet* half a century of European narrative). It was originally conceived as an addition to the *Scènes de la vie privée*, and the opening portion of the novel was first published as such in the journal *L'Europe littéraire*. But, on its completion and inclusion in the Béchet edition, it had become one of the *Scènes de la vie de province*. This was not merely the result of a mechanical reclassification, but rather the index of an internal transformation whereby what was initially conceived as a story of private life—the enclosed family world of the Grandet household—came to be mapped out on the more public canvas of the social life and historical experience of a provincial town in post-Revolutionary France. The sense of the interconnectedness and interdependence of public and private is at the very heart of Balzac's mature work. So too is the belief that the prosaic forms of everyday life are worthy of the most scrupulous and exacting literary attention; as Auerbach put it in his magisterial *Mimesis*, central to Balzac's originality is his ability to see ordinary life as invested with 'existential and tragic seriousness'.

The point applies with particular force to the novel of provincial life. In the introduction which accompanied the text's first publication, Balzac himself acknowledged the challenge to the novelist's powers of a subject that, on certain expectations, must have appeared extremely low in narrative potential. Provincial life in Balzac's France was perceived by many (usually from Paris) as the last word in the irredeemably prosaic. The provinces were a backwater of stagnation and immobility, disconnected from the rhythm of a rapidly modernizing history whose centre was the capital. In many ways Balzac shared this view, and a great deal of *Eugénie Grandet* turns on the consecrated, not to say stereotyped, opposition of Paris and the provinces. Paris commonly operates in the *Comédie humaine* as the magnetic and magnetizing centre drawing all to it (both *Le Père Goriot* and *Illusions perdues* are novels built around a departure from the provinces and an arrival in Paris), and the 'Parisian' point of view will sometimes be adopted as the perspective through which we are introduced to the provincial scene (Stendhal adopts the same procedure in *Le Rouge et le Noir*). On the other hand, both the artist and the historian in Balzac see beyond the often condescending and inaccurate simplifications of the stereotype to a richer set of connections and processes. Grandet, for example, is unintelligible without reference to his grasp of the forces at work in the emergence of a modern commercial society (reflected in his ability to exploit this very stereotype in outplaying the Parisians at their own financial game). Many of Balzac's other novels of provincial life (*Les Paysans*, *La Vieille Fille*, *Le Cabinet des antiques*) stage complex struggles between the old and the new in which it is invariably the forces of the latter which win out. History in the *Comédie humaine* does not discriminate; if it moves faster in the capital, it nevertheless touches everything with its inexorable laws.

This includes the houses, with the description of which *Eugénie Grandet* begins ('The whole history of France is there' is the narrator's somewhat extravagant assertion). Balzacian beginnings are for the most part peculiarly laden affairs, often extremely long and densely packed with various kinds of information. Readers are often tempted to skip these pages and thereby make the Balzacian mistake of their lives. The elaborate 'exposition' (as Balzac called it) serves to frame and contextualize the narrative proper, to provide it with a principle of intelligibility. The intelligibility is sometimes of a causal sort, especially in the use of the 'flashback' device to supply a historical explanation of present narrative circumstance (part of the exposition of *Eugénie Grandet* is devoted to this purpose, mainly in connection with the historical antecedents of Grandet). Sometimes the causal claims are extended to the description of places and faces, on the 'physiognomic' model of the instant readability of character from physical particulars. This code is signalled in the very title of the opening sequence of *Eugénie Grandet*, 'Physionomies bourgeoises', and is active elsewhere in the text, for instance in the observation that Grandet's gold-flecked eyes are somehow in organic relation to his obsession with gold coins ('the old fellow's eyes . . . seemed to have taken on some of the glints of the yellow metal'). All this, however, is best thought of less as a causal language of representation than as a form of symbolic and metaphorical shorthand. Thus, the opening sentence of the novel, with its characterization of the provincial house as arousing 'a melancholy as great as that of the gloomiest cloisters, the most desolate moorland, or the saddest ruins', adumbrates the key theme of Eugénie's personal story as the story of a death-in-life, an unending imprisonment of body and soul. The novel begins in one of these house-tombs, and also ends there, in the desperate circularity of a no-exit entrapment.

But, whether as causal or symbolic language, the protracted introductory sequence of *Eugénie Grandet* serves to give weight to what might otherwise strike us as relatively flimsy narrative material. The close focus on the minutiae of façades, rooms, furniture locks us aesthetically into the world of the novel in a manner parallel to the way the characters are psychologically and socially locked in (this is perhaps why some readers experience a feeling of suffocation on entering Balzac's world, even in those novels where the narrative pace is more rapid). Here time has been slowed down to virtual immobility. Nothing of any significance happens until we are so saturated by the terms of life in Saumur that, although we can never forget just how monstrously reduced those terms are, we are nevertheless prepared to accept a new hierarchy of narrative values; what will count as, precisely, 'significant' has been challenged and modified by our immersion in these opening pages (a gesture, a look, a turn of the head, a muttered exchange will reverberate with all kinds of anticipation and consequence). Change, of course, has to occur, otherwise there can be no narrative, and this is provided by the unexpected arrival in Saumur of the 'outsider', Charles Grandet, the stranger from Paris. This event is crucial: it will precipitate all the great crises and confrontations of the novel—Eugénie's blossoming into sexual love, her rebellion against her father's authority, the death of her mother, and her own eventual disillusion. But we can experience these crises and confrontations *as* 'great' only by virtue of Balzac's careful art of preparations (as one critic has described Balzac's technique). It is the art which enables us to feel non-condescendingly that an argument over sugar lumps (in the famous breakfast scene) is as resonant with passion, danger, and violence as the Napoleonic battlefield or the Parisian jungle (the animal analogy forms a major strand of the metaphorical texture of *Eugénie Grandet*).

For this is a drama of passion, danger, and violence, and it is important to grasp the many human levels at which the drama is played out; to return once more to James's magnificent essay, '[Balzac's] subject is again and again the complicated human subject or human condition.' That subject and that condition are, however, thoroughly historicized. This is particularly so in the case of Grandet (the women characters have a more tenuous connection with 'history', are excluded from its main areas of opera- tion, and that is of course a fact of some considerable significance). Grandet is generally traced back to Molière's Harpagon, and thus analysed according to the language of the so-called 'classical' passions and types (the type of the Miser). But this overlooks Balzac's systematic efforts, in both the introductory sequences and the main body of the plot, to make of Grandet's relation to money something distinctively modern. Grandet is not merely a hoarder, he is also a maker of money, a brilliantly inventive entrepreneur. Thus, the flashback shows us how his acquisition of wealth is bound up with the fortunes of the provincial bourgeoisie during the Revolution of 1789 and after. This is not just a matter of a series of particular commercial transactions but also of a new general culture governing the commercial transaction. In the opening pages Balzac talks of a time when provincial communities were 'transparent', when there was 'no sharp practice' and a 'quality of simplicity which the French way of life is losing daily'. This is a version of what Raymond Williams called the 'knowable community', set against the shifting, mobile, and opaque nature of modern commercial society. It unquestionably idealizes *ancien régime* community, but does so in order to throw into relief the changing times to which Grandet belongs: Grandet is all sharp practice, wheeler-dealing, manipulation of markets, prices, and bonds, his actions covered with 'a mantle of gold' and so rendered mysterious, impenetrable, untouchable. In short, Grandet is not just a miser but also a capitalist, and his private dealings bear the imprint of a whole history producing a new capitalist class.

The figure of Grandet is thus a key point in the novel for Balzac's preoccupation with the interpenetration and mutual inflection of public and private. But this also means —it is part of the greatness of Balzac, the way everything in his work hangs together in a deeply unifying conception —that the relevant history is relativized to a psychology. Grandet the miser-capitalist is also Grandet the miser-fetishist. Grandet's secret passion for gold, and above all for *looking* at gold ('For Grandet, the sight of gold . . . had become his monomania'), reflects what in our post-Freudian vocabularies we know as the displacements and fixations bound up with a self-mutilating libido. From the reduction of all relation with the world and others to the calculus of exchange-value, Grandet's eros has turned to pure abstraction. His pathological frugality extends to movement ('he seemed to economize on everything, even on movement') as well as to food, light, and warmth (the business with the sugar, the candles, and the firewood); his house is the place of an anti-eros, of the immobilization and death of desire. By contrast, the 'sterile' light of gold is a source of intense excitement (in the night Grandet 'would come in order to cherish, caress, embrace, gloat over, glory in, his gold'). Balzac's metaphors here visibly show gold as an object of displaced libidinal attachment, and the sexualization of that attachment becomes explicit in Grandet's own prophetic account of the 'life' of modern capital: 'For truly, money lives and breeds like men; it comes and goes, it toils, it begets more of its kind.'

Finally, along with the capitalist schemer and the sexual neurotic, there is Grandet the patriarch, the figure of terrible power. This of course also brings us to the figure of Eugénie, who stands in opposition to her father, first by way of contrast and eventually in the stronger sense of rebellion. Much of the contrast is best skated over—Eugénie as written in the imagery of the 'angelic' and the painfully embarrassing analogies with Raphael's madonnas and so on. Innocence is notoriously a very difficult literary topic, and in the context of the nineteenth-century novel it was well managed perhaps only by James and Dostoevsky (who was a great fan of *Eugénie Grandet* and even did a translation of it). Eugénie's story is primarily of interest as the tale of a *rite de passage* from innocence to experience, ignorance to knowledge, illusion to disenchantment. First there is, through the encounter with Charles, the awakening to the knowledge of sexual desire and its complex emotional consequences. Here we find Balzac in masterly exploitation of his artistic resources. He picks up, for example, on the structuring motifs of light and warmth and rearticulates them through his topographical material—in the opposition of the House (site of the death of desire) and the Garden (site of its blossoming). The Grandet garden, initially presented as an extension of the enclosing gloom of the house, is now posited as the place of 'good' enclosure, light-filled, warm, nurturing, engendering 'that sensation of vague, inexplicable happiness which envelops the soul just as a cloud might envelop the body'. The garden thus becomes that which 'envelops' and protects the life of desire, in a manner entirely different from the enveloping force of Grandet's 'mantle of gold'. But it also envelops with illusion. Balzac's use of a restricted economy of symbolic means is highly flexible but never merely opportunistic. The shifting value accorded the garden is made relative to changing circumstance, point of view, and affective atmosphere; more precisely, what is described as the 'charm' of the garden is in direct proportion to the magical properties the mind can project on to the world when the body has been aroused to desire.

The magic in question is of course the web of illusion Eugénie spins around the object of her love, Charles Grandet. The latter is essentially 'device', though not pure device. Here too is a study in a *rite de passage*, from the unconscious corruption of the spoilt young Parisian to the conscious and ruthless egoism of the mature adult. But this is traced quickly and from a distance. We are interested less in what we have to learn about Charles as such than in what such knowledge implies for Eugénie's own movement into self-understanding. This process involves another kind of 'light', the harsh light of day by which we see things as they are. Balzac will use the latter as the cliché that it is, but will also link it to far subtler and more sophisticated moves. For example, around the figure of Charles the text plots further variations on the theme of 'gold'—not just in the exchange of Charles's gold dressing-case and Eugénie's gold coins which will bring about the shattering confrontation with her father, but also in the myriad details of Charles's dress and toiletries (the gold-braided waistcoats, the gold collar buttons, the gold knob on the cane, the gold chain, the dressing-gown embroidered with gold flowers, the scissors and razors inlaid with gold). These are, of course, the indices of the elegant young man about town, the Parisian 'dandy'. But there is also a persistence here which clearly exceeds mere naturalistic description, and invites us to track the motif into more interesting configurations. In particular it takes us back to Grandet's gold, by way of a reversal. At certain levels (including naturally that of Eugénie's perceptions), Grandet and Charles face each other across the divide of a series of antitheses: young/old; Parisian/provincial; father/lover; hoarder/spendthrift; avarice/luxury. It is, however, clearly part of Balzac's intention to demystify what was in the period a widespread cult of the aristocratic-romantic dandy, and he does so in large measure by lifting the barrier of antithesis separating Charles and Grandet: if Charles differs from Grandet by his willingness to spend money, he shares with him his unwillingness to give out emotion; where Eugénie's heart warms to the rays of the sun falling on the back wall of the garden, Charles remains in thrall to the glittering sterilities represented by the golden knick-knacks of his dressing table.

This is what Eugénie eventually comes to see, and *see* is the relevant verb. If, with Grandet, seeing is related to the scopic regime of the fetish, with Eugénie it is at once the means and the metaphor of knowledge. Seeing, according to one of the characters in Balzac's earlier novel, *La Peau de chagrin*, is a mode of both knowledge and power, and the Balzacian narrator often aligns himself with propositions of this sort. As a subject of knowledgeable (in)sight Eugénie often comes to take the place of the narrator. Towards the end of the novel she sees what basically only he can know: she 'foresaw her whole destiny at a glance.' Crucially, she comes to understand the depths of her father's passion through a devastating visual revelation, in that extraordinary nocturnal scene where she stumbles across Grandet lost in a trance and yoked like a beast of burden to the stick on which, with his servant Nanon, he carries his barrels of gold. This is the sort of moment Balzac was to become famous for, that moment of an intoxicated, self-absenting and self-undoing mania that figures as a kind of literary signature through to the late novels (Baron Hulot of *La Cousine Bette* is its final and most dramatic incarnation).

Here, from the point of view of Eugénie, what is witnessed is roughly the equivalent of seeing the father naked, a sudden removal of the trappings of power. This also corresponds to one of Balzac's major themes. It is often said—today with a great deal of theoretical panache—that the novel as a genre is constitutively implicated in family matters, that its fundamental and formative plots are 'family plots'. Balzac's novels, from the early *Scènes de la vie privée* onwards, are recurringly preoccupied with stories of families falling apart; Balzac, the great ideologue of 'order' and apologist for conservative social values, in his actual narrative practice is the chronicler of dissolution and collapse. In many of the novels, the agent of such dissolutions is adultery. But in others, it is rebellion by children—and importantly daughters—against the arbitrariness of paternal authority. This will assume many forms in the *Comédie humaine*. In *La Femme de trente ans* (which Balzac started to write just two years before *Eugénie Grandet*), the heroine of one of the stories rejects and violates paternal rule in the most stridently melodramatic manner imaginable, transgressing not only the codes of social decorum but also—here the criticism is of course directed against Balzac himself—the elementary laws of narrative verisimilitude. This can, however, cut both ways. We can say that this mode of literary 'excess' is exactly the point, that it is not only social forms of authority that are in question but also the complicity of the novel and its characteristic terms of representation in those forms. On the other hand, it could just as plausibly be argued that this tells us rather about Balzac's restricted capacity for imagining the space of female autonomy (or, less personally, about the terms the contemporary culture makes available for such imaginings).

Imagining spaces for the exercise of autonomy is very much an issue for *Eugénie Grandet*. The terms are different, more modest; the area of possible action is drastically reduced—disputes over sugar lumps and then, in the great set-piece of the novel, over savings. But the stakes and outcomes are no less momentous. Eugénie's awakening to the knowledge of her desire is also an awakening to the knowledge of a potential freedom. All of Balzac's art is directed towards securing this weight of significance for the decisive confrontation between father and daughter. It is, while maintaining an absolutely rigorous consistency of tone, the moment when this quiet novel of provincial life, geared to the rhythms of an endlessly self-reproducing world, explodes into the horror of a Gothic novel. Grandet runs amok, in an orgy of emotional violence and mental cruelty; the carceral metaphor becomes literal, as Eugénie is confined to her room; Madame Grandet, mortally traumatized, takes to her bed and dies. In the small world of Saumur a wildness has taken over, and we understand the force of Balzac's own analogy when he describes his story as 'a bourgeois tragedy without poison, dagger, or bloodshed, but, as far as the actors were concerned, more cruel than all the tragedies enacted in the renowned house of Atreus'.

Eugénie's rebellion, however, provides no way out; there is in fact no 'beyond', of either the space of society or the space of the novel. And this in turn raises questions and difficulties for the interpretation of the novel's ending. In many respects, it returns in conclusion to its point of departure. With the obstacle to the object of Eugénie's desires removed (the death of Grandet), the object itself (Charles) disappears for ever, under a blanket of cynical excuses. This is for Eugénie the bitterest knowledge she has to acquire, the incurable wound to the psyche inflicted by desire frustrated and betrayed (the image of the 'wound' appears in the account of Eugénie's conflicts with her father). It generates a retreat, inwards and backwards, into the 'cold, dark house', the routines and economies of the past, the scheming intrigues of her provincial suitors, and a marriage that is unwanted and unconsummated. Some critics have managed to see not only consolations in this outcome but even the occasion for a spiritual transfiguration: Eugénie resigns herself stoically to her 'fate', casts off the things of this world (the last phrase of the text is 'the corruptions of the world') and, in the words of one editor of the novel, 'marches to heaven accompanied by a procession of good deeds'. It has to be conceded that certain features of Balzac's text lend support to this fatuous observation, and this is why the novel's ability to conceive what might be both due to and possible for the female estate is a question for its critical interpretation. At the end of the novel Balzac refers to Eugénie's embroidery as a 'Penelope's web' and this takes us back to another aspect of the novel's beginning—Eugénie and her mother sitting in the corner knitting and sewing by the exiguous light. This is, of course, an archetypal image of 'feminine' passivity and relates to a female world entirely determined and controlled by men—husbands, fathers, suitors, lovers, lawyers, and finally priests urging upon the womenfolk the virtues of obedience and submission.

Where does Balzac 'stand' here? There is much tiresome rhetoric about it being in the nature of women to show 'angelic patience' in the face of misfortune (the closest Balzac gets to the idiom of his editor is in the claim that 'women have in common with angels the special care of suffering beings'). But this is a case where we do better to trust the tale rather than the teller. For example, we might cast our minds back to the fate of the long-suffering Madame Grandet. She is described by Balzac as a woman of 'angelic gentleness' and 'exceptional religious feeling', a virtue directly harnessed by the representatives of the church to the requirements of patriarchy (her appalling husband is 'a man whom her confessor represented to her as her lord and master'). But we are perhaps tempted to say of Madame Grandet what Zola said of another of Balzac's angelic women (Adeline Hulot in *La Cousine Bette*), that she was a 'mouton sublime'; certainly when Balzac writes 'she expired without uttering the slightest complaint' and comments that 'she was all soul', we may be inclined to remark: 'and look where it got her'. This must in turn bear on how we read the ending. It is true that Balzac speaks of Eugénie in terms of 'the saintliness of one whose soul is unsullied by contact with the outside world'. But he also speaks of 'the rigid outlook of the old maid', of the 'narrow vision', of the way the house 'sunless, devoid of warmth, gloomy, and always in the shade, reflects her life'. This is Balzac's 'realism' in the straightforward sense of a long hard look at the worst; an account of a life dried up and out, of immurement, loneliness, and waste. Balzac does not, at least in *Eugénie Grandet*, see or hypothesize a 'beyond', a space of different possibility, for 'woman' in the society. Indeed even his positive terms for what the fulfilled life might look like remain to the end defined in relation to men: 'Such is the story of a woman who, made to be a magnificent wife and mother, has neither husband nor children nor family.' The implication, then, is that, having none of these, she has nothing at all. But, by the same token, nor does Balzac take the conventional evasive action of referring us to another 'beyond' to which the female 'soul', purified by suffering, has special access. What we carry away from the novel is above all the memory not of purified submissiveness, but of Eugénie's brief though abortive rebellion. The rest is pure loss and hopelessness. There are no metaphysical or sentimental consolation prizes here.

III

Balzac is an acquired taste, and some never fully acquire it. A common reaction is to feel oppressed by him, not because he is a bringer of bad narrative news, telling stories of inconsolable life, but because of his manner or—in a broad sense of the term—his 'style'. Gide, for example, did not admire *Eugénie Grandet*, and for reasons to do with a difficulty he had with Balzac in general. He found Balzac's manner of writing somewhat cramping, imposing its own modes of closure and enclosure, rather like the world of *Eugénie Grandet* in that it left insufficient room in which to breathe and move. This view of Balzac is normally specified in the form of two interrelated complaints. The first is that Balzac is too explicit. This is a feeling which can unite an otherwise highly divergent set of critical positions, on a spectrum from humanist preoccupations with 'character' in fiction to poststructuralist interest in the workings of more impersonal systems of signification. The shared view here is that Balzac says too much, that there are no gaps and enigmas, no surplus or remainder for interpretation. Consider the claim, for instance, from the point of view of the question of 'character'. Balzac exercises the rights of omniscience to take us inside the consciousness of his characters, what in *Eugénie Grandet* is called their 'secret inner lives'. In many ways this is a strength, corresponding to what James called Balzac's 'love of each seized identity'. It is particularly important in connection with Eugénie: Balzac's method ensures that we see the inflections of an inner world that many of the surrounding characters never see (for example, the rival clans in Saumur see Eugénie only in terms of the stereotype of the Heiress). The complaint, however, has it that the strength is also a weakness, that, once inside his creation, Balzac cannot leave until every recess has been exhaustively explored and named. The alleged consequence is that Balzac's characters never swim free of the clutches of their creator; they remain utterly predictable, without the capacity to surprise us. Thus, of Eugénie, one critic has remarked that, in whatever set of narrative circumstances Balzac might imagine for her, she would always be found doing the 'right thing' (in the sense of the predictably expected thing).

The second complaint is that he is too insistent, that it is not only Balzac's characters who cannot escape the author's clutches but also his readers; that the 'seizing' of which James speaks becomes a grabbing, as we are buttonholed and manipulated by a garrulous, confident voice issuing instructions on how to read not only the novel but pretty well everything else as well. This is the dimension of Balzac's manner which tends to turn his novels into machines for spewing out generalizations, maxims, quasi-proverbial utterances on virtually every conceivable subject. Most readers find this platitude-generating rhetoric difficult to stomach (Roland Barthes, in his immensely influential avant-garde reading of Balzac, claimed that it actually made him sick). This is not just because the utterances are platitudinous, nor even because many of them are false or just inadequate to the complexity of experience, but rather because of the apparently unbreakable self-assurance with which they are offered. Consider the following from *Eugénie Grandet*, yet again on the subject of 'woman': 'To feel, to love, to suffer, to be devoted, will always be the theme of women's lives.' There is not much point in dwelling on this; the truly objectionable feature is of course the 'always'. This is the language of 'ideology', converting culture into nature, opinion into fact, local arrangements into universal truths, claiming to see the universe from the point of view of the universe. The tempting option is just to disregard this aspect of Balzac's text, especially when we note the brazenly *ad hoc* way in which such statements are mustered to serve particular narrative needs, only later to be contradicted. But simply turning away is too easy. The problem is that, while we can up to a point trust the tale at the expense of the teller, we cannot do so systematically. For the narrator's ideological discourse is not just a marginal textual accretion which we can neatly excise; it also serves as a frame for the intelligibility of the narrative, and so brings us back to the description of the realist novel as 'imperialist'. The rhetoric, in its very form, proclaims the text as the home of Truth in which dissenting voices will not be welcome. Confronted with that kind of implication, we naturally want to go somewhere else, into a world that is less controlled, more open to ambiguity and indeterminacy, where there are some silences and some surprises.

But the account of Balzac represented by these complaints, although valid, is by no means complete. Proust —one of Balzac's most sensitive readers—spoke of certain 'beautiful effects of silence' in the *Comédie humaine*. Proust's example is from *Le Père Goriot*, but he could just as well have taken *Eugénie Grandet*. Let us recall, for instance, that other occasion in the garden when Grandet is to be found furtively looking through the window at his daughter in her bedroom combing her hair, while she, without betraying her knowledge that she is being looked at, furtively watches her father in the mirror. This is, of course, immensely rich in potential implication. The point, however, is that Balzac leaves the implications to us; he himself maintains a scrupulous and exemplary silence. Then there is Balzac's consummate use of the figure of chiasmus. Chiasmus is the reversal and redistribution of terms across the divide of an antithesis; it destabilizes apparent fixities and thus has a high yield of surprise. Antithesis is commonly thought of as the central structuring device of Balzac's writing, powerful but crude. We have considered several instances, chiefly the opposition father/daughter in the great confrontation scene. But what we have not said about that scene is that, as it stages opposition and conflict, it also blurs that stark dividing line by intimations of sameness: Eugénie nowhere resembles her father more than when she resists him (Grandet himself reflects: 'She's more of a Grandet than I am'). This theme is pursued to the end, where, in the closing moments, we find Eugénie regressing to the attitudes and practices of her father. This chiastic pattern complicates the novel and accordingly our responses to it; while it obeys a logic, it is a logic subtler and more surprise-laden than the more rigid system of expectancies which go with a simple antithetical design.

Lastly, there are simply those 'moments' which one would never have predicted, which perhaps even go unnoticed on a first reading but which stay unforgettably in the mind once they have registered. I do not necessarily mean the well-known moments, what are now virtually anthology pieces and which have assured for *Eugénie Grandet* the status of a 'classic'. *Eugénie Grandet* is of course a classic (indeed a 'World's Classic'). It was, as previously mentioned, the first Balzac novel to acquire canonical status. This can be given a precise date: in 1889 *Eugénie Grandet* was admitted to the programme of the university *agrégation*. But the history leading to that admission tells us that the constitution of a book as a 'classic' is a complex and problematical cultural process; as historians of critical opinion have shown, Balzac was received into the official culture only after having been submitted to a kind of cleansing ritual; to be made a 'classic', Balzac had to be made respectable, and it was therefore something of an ambiguous compliment to *Eugénie Grandet* when it was chosen to represent this 'safer', domesticated Balzac.

Furthermore, even if, after exposure to such histories, we still think there is good reason to retain the label 'classic', this does not mean that the text thereby becomes something fixed once and for all, monumentalized, petrified, effectively buried in a canonical mausoleum as gloomy as Grandet's house. A better way of construing the 'identity' of the classic would be to see it as that which is porous to multiple reading, hospitable to changing interpretations, in which something can always be found which hasn't been noticed or stressed before. This can apply to the re-readings of individuals over time as well as to shifts of taste and preoccupation across generations of readers. Here, for example (to conclude on a personal note), are just a few of the 'moments'—either forgotten from or perhaps never noticed in previous readings—which took me completely by surprise on re-reading *Eugénie Grandet* this time round. They are moments of varying, sometimes zero, narrative consequence, and moreover are entirely consistent with the novel's ground plan and guiding themes. At the same time, they are moments so extreme, bizarre, outrageous as to create a feeling of utter stupefaction. What surprises, even amazes, is their sheer extravagance, part comic, part terrible, as testimony to what I have wanted to call the 'delirious' as distinct from the 'megalomaniac' side to Balzac's imaginative madness. For instance, the sort of imagined world that can contain the following priceless exchange between Eugénie and the parish priest: '"Monsieur le Curé, would it be a sin to remain a virgin while being married?" asked Eugénie with a dignified composure inspired by the thought she was about to express. "That's a question of conscience to which I don't know the answer. If you want to know what the illustrious Sanchez thinks about it in his treatise *De Matrimonio*, I can tell you tomorrow"'; or the spectacle of Grandet not economizing but *amusing* himself by cutting up sugar lumps into even smaller lumps, as if this were some kind of hobby; or his ability to astonish his lawyer as well as us when, in his dying days, he is so paranoically alerted to the security of his gold that 'to the lawyer's great amazement he would hear his dog yawning in the courtyard'; or finally and most outrageously of all, the gold-obsessed Grandet looking at his ailing wife and remarking with what appears entirely unintended but quite incredible malevolence: 'You are just a bit yellow today, but I like yellow.'

CHRISTOPHER PRENDERGAST

NOTE ON THE TEXT

Eugénie Grandet was first published by Mme Béchet in
1833–4 as the first volume of *Études de mœurs au XIXᵉ siècle,
Scènes de la vie de province*, and divided into six chapters. In
1839 it was published separately by Charpentier with, for
the first time, the dedication to Maria and with no division
into chapters. In the publication by Furne of the *Comédie
humaine* in 1843, *Eugénie Grandet* is in volume 5 as the first of
the *Scènes de la vie privée*. Balzac's own copy of the Édition
Furne is corrected in his own hand and is known as the
Furne corrigé. It is this text which is followed in modern
French editions and which has been translated here. The
division into chapters with titles and some of the divisions
into paragraphs were suppressed in the 1842–3 publication
of the *Comédie humaine* in order to save space, but they
have been reintroduced in this translation for the greater
convenience of the reader.

SELECT BIBLIOGRAPHY

(i) *Biography*

André Maurois, *Prometheus: the Life of Balzac*, Bodley Head, London, 1965

H. J. Hunt, *Honoré de Balzac: a Biography*, Athlone Press, London, 1957; reprinted and updated, Greenwood Press, New York, 1969

(ii) *General studies*

P. Bertaut, *Balzac and the Human Comedy*, New York University Press, 1963

H. J. Hunt, *Balzac's 'Comédie humaine'*, Athlone Press, London, 1964

E. J. Oliver, *Honoré de Balzac*, Weidenfeld and Nicholson, London, 1965

F. W. J. Hemmings, *Balzac: an interpretation of la Comédie humaine*, Random House, New York, 1967

F. Marceau, *Balzac and his World*, W. H. Allen, London, 1967

V. S. Pritchett, *Balzac*, Chatto and Windus, London, 1973

D. Festa-McCormick, *Honoré de Balzac*, Twayne's World Authors Series, Boston, 1979

(iii) *On 'Eugénie Grandet'*

Arnold Saxton, *Honoré de Balzac: Eugénie Grandet*, Penguin Masterstudies, Harmondsworth, 1987

A CHRONOLOGY OF
HONORÉ DE BALZAC

1799   Born at Tours, the son of Bernard-François Balzac and
        his wife Anne-Charlotte-Laure Sallambier. Put out to
        nurse till he is four.

1804   Sent as a boarder to the Pension Le Guay, Tours.

1807–13 A boarder at the Oratorian college in Vendôme.

1814   Restoration of the Bourbon monarchy in France with
        the accession of Louis XVIII. The Balzac family moves
        to Paris, where Honoré continues his education.

1815   Flight of Louis XVIII on Napoleon's escape from Elba,
        but second Restoration of the Bourbons after Napoleon's
        defeat at Waterloo.

1816   Honoré becomes a law student and works in a lawyer's
        office.

1819   Becomes a Bachelor of Law. The family moves to
        Villeparisis on the retirement of Bernard-François Bal-
        zac. Honoré stays in Paris, living frugally at the Rue
        Lesdiguières, in an effort to start a career as a writer.
        He writes a tragedy, Cromwell, which is a failure.

1820–5 Writes various novels, some in collaboration, none of
        which he signs with his own name.

1822   Beginning of his liaison with forty-five-year-old Laure
        de Berny, who remains devoted to him till her death in
        1836.

1825–8 Tries to make money by printing and publishing ven-
        tures, which fail and saddle him with debt.

1829   Publication of Le Dernier Chouan, the first novel he
        signs with his own name and the first of those to be
        incorporated in the Comédie humaine. Publication of the
        Physiologie du mariage.

1830   Publication of Scènes de la vie privée. Revolution in France
        resulting in the abdication of Charles X and the accession
        of Louis-Philippe.

1831	Works hard as a writer and adopts a luxurious, society life-style which increases his debts. Publication of *La Peau de chagrin* and some of the *Contes philosophiques*.
1832	Beginning of correspondence with Madame Hanska. Publication of more 'Scènes de la vie privée' and of *Louis Lambert*. Adds 'de' to his name and becomes 'de Balzac'.
1833	Meets Madame Hanska for the first time in Neuchâtel, Switzerland, and then in Geneva. Signs a contract for *Études de mœurs au XIXe siècle*, which appears in twelve volumes between 1833 and 1837, and is divided into 'Scènes de la vie privée', 'Scènes de la vie de province', and 'Scènes de la vie parisienne'. Publication of *Le Médecin de campagne* and the first 'Scènes de la vie de province', which include *Eugénie Grandet*.
1834	Publication of *La Recherche de l'absolu* and the first 'Scènes de la vie parisienne'.
1834–5	Publication of *Le Père Goriot*.
1835	Publication of collected *Études philosophiques* (1835–40). Meets Madame Hanska in Vienna, the last time for eight years.
1836	Publication of *Le Lys dans la vallée* and other works. Starts a journal, *La Chronique de Paris*, which ends in failure.
1837	Journey to Italy. Publication of *La Vieille Fille*, the first part of *Illusions perdues*, and *César Birotteau*.
1838	Publication of *La Femme supérieure* (*Les Employés*) and *La Torpille*, which becomes the first part of *Splendeurs et misères des courtisanes*.
1839	Becomes president of the Société des Gens de Lettres. Publication of six more works, including *Le Cabinet des antiques* and *Béatrix*.
1840	Publication of more works, including *Pierrette*.
1841	Makes an agreement with his publisher, Furne, and booksellers for the publication of the *Comédie humaine*. Publication of more works, including *Le Curé de village*.
1842	Publication of the *Comédie humaine*, with its important

introduction, in seventeen volumes (1842–8); one post-humous volume is published in 1855. Publication of other works, including *Mémoires de deux jeunes mariées*, *Ursule Mirouet*, and *La Rabouilleuse*.

1843 More publications, including *La Muse du département*, and the completion in three parts of *Illusions perdues*. Visits Madame Hanska (widowed since 1841) at St Petersburg.

1844 Publication of *Modeste Mignon*, of the beginning of *Les Paysans*, of the second part of *Béatrix*, and of the second part of *Splendeurs et misères des courtisanes*.

1845 Travels in Europe with Madame Hanska and her daughter and future son-in-law.

1846 Stays in Rome and travels in Switzerland and Germany with Madame Hanska. A witness at the marriage of her daughter. Birth to Madame Hanska of a still-born child, who was to have been called Victor-Honoré. Publication of *La Cousine Bette* and of the third part of *Splendeurs et misères des courtisanes*.

1847 Madame Hanska stays in Paris from February till May. Publication of *Le Cousin Pons* and of the last part of *Splendeurs et misères des courtisanes*.

1848 Revolution in France resulting in the abdication of Louis-Philippe and the establishment of the Second Republic. Balzac goes to the Ukraine to stay with Madame Hanska and remains there till the spring of 1850.

1849 His health deteriorates seriously.

1850 Marriage of Balzac and Madame Hanska on 14 March. He returns with her to Paris on 20 May and dies on 18 August.

1869–76 Definitive edition of the *Œuvres complètes* in twenty-four volumes, published by Michel-Lévy and then by Calmann-Lévy.

EUGÉNIE GRANDET

To Maria.*

Your portrait is the loveliest ornament of this work. May your name in this place be like a branch of holy boxwood, for ever green, taken from some unknown tree, but assuredly sanctified by religious feeling and renewed by pious hands, to protect the house.

DE BALZAC

some poor working-girl's pinks and roses are shooting up. Further on there are doors studded with enormous nails, where our ancestors' skill has inscribed domestic hieroglyphics whose meaning will never be discovered. Oft one of them a Protestant has left a symbol of his faith,

Portraits of Bourgeois

IN certain provincial towns there are houses whose appearance arouses a melancholy as great as that of the gloomiest cloisters, the most desolate moorland, or the saddest ruins. There is perhaps, in these houses, a combination of the silence of the cloister, the desolation of moorlands and the sepulchral gloom of ruins. In them life is so still and uneventful that a stranger would think them uninhabited, if his eye did not suddenly meet the pale, cold look of a motionless figure whose almost monk-like face appears above the window-ledge at the sound of an unknown step. These melancholy characteristics are to be found in the appearance of a house in Saumur, at the end of the steep street which leads to the château through the upper part of the town. This street, not much used nowadays, is hot in summer, cold in winter, and dark in parts; it is noteworthy for the resonance of its little cobbled roadway, which is always clean and dry, for the narrowness of its winding path, and for the peace of its houses that are part of the old town and are dominated by the ramparts. Dwellings there, three hundred years old, though built of wood, are still sound, and their varied exteriors contribute to the unusual appearance which commends this part of Saumur to the attention of antiquaries and artists. It is difficult to go past these houses without marvelling at the enormous beams, whose ends are carved with strange faces and which form a protruding bas-relief above most of the ground floors. In some places cross-beams are covered with slates and make blue lines on the rickety walls of a house topped by a half-timbered roof, sagging with age, and with rotting shingle warped by the alternating action of the rain and the sun. Further along you can barely see the delicate carvings on worn, blackened window-sills, that seem too flimsy to bear the weight of the brown clay pot where some poor working-girl's pinks and roses are shooting up. Further on there are doors studded with enormous nails, where our ancestors' skill has inscribed domestic hieroglyphics whose meaning will never be discovered. On one of them a Protestant has left a symbol of his faith, on another a member of the League* has cursed Henri IV.* On yet another a citizen has engraved the insignia of the nobility conferred by his position as a magistrate, the pride of his long-forgotten period of office. The whole history of France is there. Next door to the rickety house with roughcast walls, in which the artisan has set a graven image of his plane, stands a nobleman's house. Over the semicircular arch of its stone doorway, one can still see traces of his coat of arms, half-destroyed by the various revolutions which have disturbed the country since 1789. In this street, the ground-floor commercial premises are neither shops nor warehouses; in them devotees of the Middle Ages will recognize our forefathers' workshops in all their crude simplicity. The low rooms, with no shop fronts, display cases, or windows, are deep and dark, and have no decoration either external or internal. Their doors, crudely barred with iron, open in two solid parts; the upper one folds back to the inside, and the lower one, equipped with a mechanical bell, swings to and fro continually. Air and light reach this kind of damp cave either through the top of the door or through the space between the arch, the ceiling, and the little breast-high wall with its strong built-in shutters, which are taken down in the morning and are put back and secured with iron bolts in the evening. This wall is used to display the shopkeeper's wares. Here there is no sharp practice. According to the kind of business, the samples on show consist of one or two barrels of salt and salt-cod, a few bales of sailcloth, coils of rope, brass strips hanging from the rafters, hoops for barrels along the walls, or some lengths of cloth on the shelves. You go in. A neat girl, glowing with youth, wearing a white kerchief and with ruddy arms, leaves her knitting, calls her father or her mother, who comes and sells you what you

4

want, phlegmatically, obligingly, or arrogantly, according to his or her nature, whether it be for two sous' or twenty thousand francs' worth of goods. You will see a dealer in barrel-staves sitting in his doorway, twiddling his thumbs as he chats with his neighbour. He appears to have only a few inferior pieces of shelving for bottles and two or three bundles of laths. But on the quay, his well-stocked timber-yard supplies all the coopers of Anjou. He knows, down to a stave, how many barrels he can dispose of if the harvest is good. A heat-wave makes him rich, a wet spell ruins him. In a single morning, casks can rise to eleven francs or fall to six. In this region, as in Touraine, the vicissitudes of the weather dominate commercial life. Winegrowers, land-owners, timber-merchants, coopers, innkeepers, bargemen are all on the look-out for a ray of sunshine. When they go to bed they are fearful that next morning they might hear there has been a frost during the night. They dread rain, wind, and drought; they want water, heat, or cloud according to their needs. There is a perpetual duel between celestial power and terrestrial interests. As the barometer goes up or down, faces lengthen or brighten and become cheerful. From one end to the other of this street, the old Grand'rue of Saumur, the words 'What golden weather!' are passed from door to door and translated into figures. And so everyone remarks to his neighbour, 'It's raining gold louis', for they know how much money a ray of sunshine or a timely shower can bring them. After about midday on a summer Saturday you won't be able to buy a sou's worth of goods from these worthy businessmen. Each of them has his own vineyard, his own patch of land, and goes off to spend the week-end in the country. Since they know beforehand what they are going to buy and sell and how much profit they will make when they are there, they find themselves with ten out of twelve hours free to spend in convivial parties and in continually observing, commenting, and spying on their neighbours. A housewife cannot buy a partridge without the neighbours asking her husband if it was done to a turn. A girl cannot put her head

5

out of the window without being seen by every group of idlers. So every conscience, there, is open to the light of day, just as these silent, dark, impenetrable houses contain no mysteries. Life is nearly always lived in the open air. Every household sits at its front door, where it lunches, dines, and quarrels. There is not a passer-by in the street who is not closely examined. And so it is like olden times when a stranger, arriving in a country town, used to be subjected to mocking remarks from door to door. That is the source of some good stories and of the nickname 'banterers' given to the inhabitants of Angers who excelled in such communal teasing. The former mansions of the old town are at the top of the street, where the local gentry used to live. The melancholy dwelling where the events of this story took place was, in fact, one of those houses. They are the venerable remnants of a century when men and things had that quality of simplicity which the French way of life is losing daily. If you follow the windings of the picturesque street, its slightest features arousing memories and its general appearance tending to send you into an involuntary day-dream, you will notice a gloomy recess. In the middle of it is concealed 'the house where Monsieur Grandet lives'. It is impossible to understand fully what these words mean to the local people unless you are told the story of Monsieur Grandet's life.

In Saumur, Monsieur Grandet enjoyed a reputation whose causes and effects can be fully understood only by people who have lived, however briefly, in a provincial town. In 1789 Monsieur Grandet (still called Père Grandet in 1816 by some elderly people, but their number was perceptibly declining) was a prosperous master cooper, able to read, write, and do accounts. When the French Republic put church property* in the Saumur district up for sale, the cooper, then aged forty, had recently married the daughter of a rich timber-merchant. Armed with his own ready money and with his wife's dowry, two thousand gold louis in all, Grandet went to the district office, where, with the help of two hundred double louis slipped by his father-in-law into the hand of the grim Republican who was looking after the sale of national property,* he obtained legally, if not legitimately, for the price of a scrap of bread, the finest vineyards of the region, an old abbey, and a few farms. Since the inhabitants of Saumur were not very revolutionary, Père Grandet was considered to be a daring man, a Republican, a patriot, a man who fancied the new ideas, whereas, quite simply, the cooper fancied vines. He was nominated a member of the Saumur district administration and exercised a moderating influence both politically and commercially. Politically, he protected former aristocrats and did all he could to prevent the sale of émigrés'* property; commercially, he provided the Republican armies* with one or two thousand casks of white wine and took as payment some superb meadow-land which had belonged to a community of nuns and which had been held back for a final sale. Under the Consulate,* the worthy Grandet became mayor, was a sound administrator and an even better winegrower; under the Empire,* he became Monsieur Grandet. Napoleon had no love for Republicans and he replaced Monsieur Grandet, who was said to have sported the revolutionary colours, by a great landowner, a man with 'de' before his name,* who was to become a baron of the Empire. Monsieur Grandet relinquished his civic honours without any regret. In the interests of the town, he had constructed excellent roads which led to his property. He paid modest sums in tax on his house and land, which were assessed very reasonably. Since the valuation of his different vineyards, his wines, thanks to unremitting care, had become 'head of the region', a technical expression used to indicate vineyards which produce top-quality wine. He was in a position to request the cross of the Legion of Honour.* The assessment took place in 1806. Monsieur Grandet was then fifty-seven years old and his wife about thirty-six. Their only daughter, born of their legitimate union, was aged ten. In the same year Monsieur Grandet, whom Providence no doubt wished to console for his fall from administrative

7

grace, was the heir, in quick succession, first of Madame de la Gaudinière, *née* La Bertellière, Madame Grandet's mother, then of old Monsieur La Bertellière, the deceased lady's father, and then of Madame Gentillet, his maternal grandmother. That made three inheritances whose value was not known to anyone. These three old people were such inveterate misers that for a long time they had been hoarding their money so that they could contemplate it in secret. Old Monsieur La Bertellière thought that to invest money was to throw it away and that to look at his money gave him a higher rate of interest than to lend it. And so the people of Saumur estimated the amount of savings on the basis of the income from the landed property. Monsieur Grandet then obtained the new noble title that our mania for equality will never abolish—he became the biggest taxpayer in the district. He cultivated one hundred acres of vines, which, in years when the harvest was abundant, would give him seven to eight hundred casks of wine. He owned thirteen farms and an old abbey, where, for reasons of economy, he had walled up the traceries, the vaulting, and the stained glass, and that preserved them. He also owned twenty-seven acres of meadow-land, where three thousand poplars, planted in 1793, grew and flourished. Finally, the house he lived in was his own. It was thus possible to judge the amount of his visible assets. As for his invested capital, only two people could hazard a guess at its size. One of them was Monsieur Cruchot, the lawyer in charge of Monsieur Grandet's investments, the other was Monsieur des Grassins, the richest banker in Saumur, in whose profitable dealings the winegrower shared secretly when it suited him. Although old Cruchot and Monsieur des Grassins maintained that absolute discretion which in the provinces engenders confidence and wealth, they showed such great respect for Monsieur Grandet in public that observers could measure the amount of the former mayor's capital by the extent of the obsequious consideration shown to him. There was no one in Saumur who was not convinced that Monsieur Grandet had a private hoard, a hiding-place full of louis, and that every night he gave himself the ineffable pleasures to be obtained from the sight of a great mass of gold. The other misers of the town felt almost certain of this when they saw the old fellow's eyes, which seemed to have taken on some of the glints of the yellow metal. Like the eyes of a gambler, of a libertine, or of a courtier, the gaze of a man who is used to deriving an enormous profit from his capital investments is bound to acquire certain indefinable habits, a furtive, greedy, shifty flicker, which do not escape those who worship the same gods. This, in a way, constitutes the freemasonry of the passions. So Monsieur Grandet inspired the respectful esteem due to a man who owes nothing to anyone, who, as an old cooper and winegrower, could tell with astronomical precision whether he had to make a thousand casks for his harvest or only five hundred; who did not lose on a single speculation, always had barrels to sell when the barrel was worth more than its contents, could put his vintage in his cellars and wait for the moment to sell his casks for two hundred francs each when small proprietors had been obliged to sell theirs for five louis.* His famous harvest of 1811, prudently held back and slowly sold, had brought him in more than two hundred and forty thousand livres. Financially speaking, Monsieur Grandet had the qualities both of a tiger and a boa-constrictor. He had the art of lying in wait, hidden, studying his prey for a long time, and finally jumping on it; then he would open the jaws of his purse, gulp down a load of coins, and lie down again quietly to digest, like a serpent, impassive, cold, and methodical. No one saw him go by without mingled feelings of respect and terror. Had not everyone in Saumur been politely ripped by his steel claws? For one man, Maître Cruchot had obtained the money required for a land purchase, but at eleven per cent; for another, Monsieur des Grassins had discounted bills, but at an appalling rate of interest. Few days passed without Monsieur Grandet's name being mentioned in the townsfolk's gossip either in the market-place or at evening social gatherings. For some people, the old winegrower's fortune was an object of patriotic pride. And so, more than one businessman or innkeeper would say to strangers, with a certain satisfaction: 'Monsieur, we have two or three millionaire establishments here. But as for Monsieur Grandet, he doesn't know himself how much he's got!' In 1816 the ablest mathematicians in Saumur valued the old fellow's landed property at nearly four million. But since, on average, from 1793 to 1817, he must have earned a hundred thousand francs annually from his land, it could be presumed that he owned in cash an amount almost equal to the value of his property. So when, after a game of boston or some conversation about vines, someone happened to mention Monsieur Grandet, knowledgeable people would say: 'Père Grandet? . . . Père Grandet must have five or six million.'

'You are cleverer than I am, I could never find out the total,' Monsieur Cruchot or Monsieur des Grassins would reply, if they heard the remark.

If some Parisian talked of the Rothschilds* or of Monsieur Laffitte,* the people of Saumur would ask whether they were as rich as Monsieur Grandet. If the Parisian replied with an amused smile in the affirmative, they would look at each other, shaking their heads incredulously. So much money covered all Grandet's actions with a mantle of gold. If, initially, some of his idiosyncratic ways gave rise to ridicule or mockery, the mockery and ridicule had become stale. His most trivial acts carried the weight of a judicial decision. His words, his clothes, his gestures, the flicker of his eyelids were looked on as authoritative in the district, where everyone had studied him in the way naturalists study the workings of instinct in animals, and so had been able to appreciate the profound, unspoken wisdom of his slightest movements.

'It will be a hard winter,' they would say. 'Père Grandet has put on his fur-lined gloves. We must harvest the grapes.' Or, 'Père Grandet is buying a lot of cask wood; there'll be plenty of wine this year.'

Monsieur Grandet never bought meat or bread. Every week his tenant farmers brought him an adequate supply of capons, chickens, eggs, butter, and corn as part of their rent. He owned a mill, whose tenant was obliged, over and above paying the rent, to come and collect a certain amount of grain and bring back the bran and flour he obtained from it. Although she was no longer young, his only servant, Big Nanon, herself baked the bread required by the household every Saturday. Monsieur Grandet had an arrangement with market gardeners who were his tenants that they should supply him with vegetables. As for fruit, his own trees produced so much that he had a lot of it sold at the market. His firewood was cut from the hedges or taken from the half-rotten old tree-stumps which he was clearing from alongside his fields. His farmers carted it, all chopped up, into town for him, stacked it obligingly in his wood-shed, and received his thanks. His only known expenses were consecrated bread, clothes for his wife and daughter, and their chair rentals in church; candles, Big Nanon's wages, and the relining of her saucepans; the payment of taxes, the repair of his buildings, and the costs of cultivating his land. He had recently bought six hundred acres of woodland, which was looked after for him by a neighbour's keeper, whom he promised to reward for his trouble. Only when he had acquired this property did he eat game.

Grandet's manners were very simple. He spoke little. Usually he expressed his ideas in brief sententious phrases, uttered in a low voice. Since the Revolution, a period when he was in the public eye, the old fellow stammered tiresomely whenever he had to talk at any length or take part in a discussion. This stammer, his incoherent speech, the flood of words in which he drowned his thought, his apparent lack of logical reasoning, were all put down to a defective education, but they were assumed, and will be adequately explained by some of the events of this story. Moreover, he usually employed four phrases, as precise as algebraic formulae, to deal with all the difficulties of life and

11

business. 'I don't know, I can't, I don't want to, we shall see.' He never said *yes* or *no* and he never put anything in writing. If anyone spoke to him, he listened dispassionately, held his chin in his right hand, and supported his right elbow on the back of his left. Whatever the business, he never changed his mind once it had been made up. He thought a long time about even the smallest transactions. When, at the end of a skilfully conducted conversation, his opponent, thinking that he had won the day, revealed the secret of his intentions, Grandet would reply, 'I cannot decide anything till I have consulted my wife.' His wife, whom he had reduced to a state of absolute submission, was his most convenient screen in matters of business. He never paid visits, as he did not want to receive guests or have people to dinner. He went about noiselessly and seemed to economize on everything, even on movement. He never touched anything belonging to others out of an unshakeable respect for the rights of property. Nevertheless, in spite of his soft voice and discreet behaviour, one could see traces of the language and ways of a cooper, especially in his own house, where he restrained himself less than elsewhere.

Physically, Grandet was five feet four inches tall, thick-set, and squarely built, with thirteen-inch calves, gnarled knee-caps, and broad shoulders. He had a round, sunburnt, pock-marked face, a straight chin, uncurving lips, and white teeth. His eyes had the calm, voracious expression which is popularly attributed to the basilisk, and his well-furrowed brow was not without significant bumps. His sandy, greying hair was sometimes called 'silver' and 'gold' by young men who did not know how serious it was to make a joke about Monsieur Grandet. His squat nose had a veined wen on it, popularly said, and not without reason, to be full of malice. His face revealed a dangerous cunning, a cold-blooded honesty, the selfishness of a man used to concentrating his feelings on the pleasures of avarice and on the only being he really cared about, his daughter and sole heiress, Eugénie. Everything about him, his bearing, manners, and gait indicated the self-confidence that stems from unbroken success in every enterprise. So, although apparently gentle and easy-going, Monsieur Grandet was as hard as steel. He was always dressed in the same way, and if you saw him today you would see him as he had been since 1791. His heavy shoes were tied with leather laces; in all weathers he wore thick woollen stockings, silver-buckled breeches of heavy brown cloth, a double-breasted velvet waistcoat with alternate yellow and puce stripes, a loose brown coat with full skirts, a black necktie, and a Quaker hat. His gloves, as strong as a policeman's, would last him for twenty months, and to keep them clean he would always put them systematically in the same place on the brim of his hat. Saumur knew nothing more about this eminent person.

Only six of the townsfolk had the right of entry into Grandet's house. Of the first three of these, the most important was Monsieur Cruchot's nephew. Ever since he had been appointed president of the county court at Saumur, this young man had added the name of Bonfons to that of Cruchot and had been working hard to make Bonfons supersede Cruchot. He already signed himself C. de Bonfons. If any litigant was ill-advised enough to call him Monsieur Cruchot, he soon became aware of his blunder in court. The magistrate favoured those who called him 'Monsieur le Président' but he bestowed his most generous smiles on the flatterers who said 'Monsieur de Bonfons'. Monsieur le Président was thirty-three years old and owned the estate of Bonfons (*Boni Fontis*), which brought in an income of seven thousand livres a year. He expected to inherit from his uncle the lawyer and from his uncle the Abbé Cruchot, a dignitary of the Chapter of Saint-Martin-de-Tours, both of whom were said to be quite rich. These three Cruchots, supported by numerous cousins and connected with twenty families in the town, formed a party as the Medici used to do in Florence and, like the Medici, the Cruchots had their Pazzi.* Madame des Grassins, the mother of a twenty-three-year-old son, used to come very regularly to play cards with Madame

Grandet, in the hope of arranging a marriage between her dear Adolphe and Mademoiselle Eugénie. Monsieur des Grassins, the banker, energetically backed up his wife's tactics by repeatedly doing the old miser favours, and he always turned up at the right moment to support his wife on the battlefield. The three des Grassins, too, had their adherents, their cousins and their faithful allies. On the Cruchot side, the Abbé, the Talleyrand* of the family, well supported by his brother the lawyer, hotly contested the ground with the financier's wife and tried to keep the rich inheritance for his nephew the President. The secret struggle between the Cruchots and the des Grassins for the prize of Eugénie Grandet's hand was a source of passionate interest to all sections of society in Saumur. Would Mademoiselle Grandet marry Monsieur le Président or Monsieur Adolphe des Grassins? To this question some replied that Monsieur Grandet would give his daughter to neither the one nor the other. The former cooper, they said, was eaten up with ambition and was looking for some peer of France as a son-in-law, a peer who, for an income of three hundred thousand livres a year, would overlook all Grandet's casks, past, present, and future. Others replied that Monsieur and Madame des Grassins were from a noble family, extremely rich, that Adolphe was a very charming young gentleman, and that unless they had a Pope's nephew up their sleeve, so suitable a match ought to satisfy a family of nobodies, a man whom all Saumur had seen with a cooper's adze in his hand, and who, moreover, had once sported the red cap of the Revolutionaries.* The more judicious pointed out that Monsieur Cruchot de Bonfons could visit the house at any time, while his rival was received only on Sundays. Some maintained that Madame des Grassins, who was more friendly with the women of the Grandet household than were the Cruchots, might implant certain ideas in their heads which, sooner or later, would bring her success. Others replied that the Abbé Cruchot was the most persuasive man in the world and that a duel between a woman and a priest was one between

14

equals. 'They are running neck and neck,' said one Saumur wit. The older inhabitants of the region, better informed, claimed that the Grandets were too sharp to let the property go out of the family; Mademoiselle Eugénie Grandet of Saumur would be married to the son of Monsieur Grandet of Paris, a rich wholesale wine-merchant. To these the Cruchot party and the Grassinites would reply: 'In the first place, the two brothers have not seen each other for thirty years. Next, Monsieur Grandet of Paris has high ambitions for his son. He is a district mayor, a deputy, a colonel in the National Guard, and a judge in the commercial court. He denies all connection with the Grandets of Saumur and aspires to a match with the family of some Napoleonic duke.' What was left unsaid about an heiress who was talked about for twenty miles around, even in public vehicles going as far as Angers in one direction and Blois in the other?

At the beginning of 1818, the Cruchot party scored an outstanding victory over the Grassinites. The Froidfond estate, renowned for its park, its beautiful château, its farms, river, ponds, and woodland, and worth three million, was put up for sale by the young Marquis de Froidfond, who had to realize his capital. Maître Cruchot, President Cruchot, and the Abbé Cruchot, helped by their supporters, were able to prevent its being sold in small lots. The lawyer concluded a splendid bargain with the young man, persuading him that he would have to embark on countless lawsuits against the purchasers before he could get the money for the different lots; it was better to sell to Monsieur Grandet, who was solvent and, moreover, able to pay for the estate in ready money. So the marquis's fair lands were ushered along towards Monsieur Grandet's gullet, and when the formalities had been completed he paid for it, less discount for cash, to the great astonishment of all Saumur. This transaction caused a stir as far away as Nantes and Orléans. Monsieur Grandet went to see his château, taking advantage of a lift on a cart that was returning there. After casting an owner's eye over his

15

property, he came back to Saumur, certain that that he would get five per cent return on his investment and fired with the magnificent idea of rounding off the marquisate of Froidfond by joining all his property to it. Then, to replenish his depleted coffers, he decided to cut down his woods and forests completely and to sell the poplars from his meadows.

It is now easy to understand the full significance of the words, 'the house where Monsieur Grandet lives', that pale grey, cold, silent house at the upper end of the town, under the shadow of the ruined ramparts. The two pillars and the arch framing the front door had, like the house, been built of a white chalk stone peculiar to the banks of the Loire and so soft that on average it lasted barely two hundred years. The inclemencies of the weather had pitted the stone with numerous irregular holes of various sizes, and this gave the arch and the sideposts of the porch the appearance of the vermiculated stone of French architecture and some resemblance to the doorway of a gaol. Above the arch was a long bas-relief carved in hard stone, with figures, already worn and quite black, representing the four seasons. Above the bas-relief was a projecting ledge, on which were growing a number of wild plants, yellow pellitory, bindweed, convolvulus, plantain, and a little cherry tree already grown quite tall. The brown, solid oak door was weatherbeaten and cracked all over, but though it looked shaky it was strongly secured by bolts, systematically arranged in a symmetrical pattern. In the middle of the oak door a smaller door contained a square grating, not very big, but with close-set bars. These were red with rust, and they served as a kind of background decoration for a door-knocker, which hung from the grating by a ring and struck against the grinning head of a huge iron stud. This knocker, oblong in shape and of the kind that our ancestors called Jacquemart, looked like a large exclamation mark. An antiquary, examining it carefully, would have found on it some traces of the typical jester's face which it had once represented and which had been worn away

16

by long use. Through the little grating, intended for the recognition of friends at the time of the Civil Wars,* curious eyes could glimpse, beyond a dark, greenish archway, a few dilapidated steps leading to a garden picturesquely enclosed by thick, damp walls, which oozed moisture and were covered with clumps of sickly shrubs. These were the walls of the château ramparts, on top of which could be seen the gardens of some of the neighbouring houses. On the ground floor of the house, the most important room was a living-room, whose door was under the arch of the main entrance. Few people know how important a living-room is in the little towns of Anjou, Touraine, and Berry. The living-room is the hall, the drawing-room, the study, the sitting-room, the dining-room, all in one. It is the theatre of domestic life, the centre of the home. There the local barber would come twice a year to cut Monsieur Grandet's hair; there he would receive his tenant farmers, the parish priest, the sub-prefect, and the miller's boy. The room, whose two windows gave on to the street, had a wooden floor. Grey, wooden panelling with antique moulding lined the walls from top to bottom. The ceiling consisted of exposed beams, also painted grey, the spaces between them being filled with a yellowing mixture of whitewash and sand. An old copper clock, inlaid with tortoiseshell arabesques, adorned the white, badly carved, stone chimney-piece. Above it hung a greenish mirror, whose edges, bevelled to show its thickness, reflected a thin stream of light along an old-fashioned pier-mirror of damascened steel. The two candelabra of gilded copper which ornamented each end of the chimney-piece served two purposes; if you removed the branch roses which served as sconces, the main rose-stem, set in a bluish marble pedestal with old copper fittings, made a candlestick for ordinary days. The old-fashioned chairs were upholstered in tapestry depicting La Fontaine's fables, but you had to know this to recognize the subjects, for the faded colours and much darned figures were barely discernible. In each corner of the room stood a corner cupboard, a kind of sideboard with grimy shelves above. An old marquetry card-table, whose top was used as a chess-board, was placed in the space between the two windows. Above the table was an oval barometer set in a black frame decorated with gilded wooden ribbons, on which the flies had sported so freely that it was difficult to see the gilt. On the wall opposite the fireplace were two pastel portraits, said to be pictures of Madame Grandet's grandfather, old Monsieur de la Bertellière, as a lieutenant in the French Guards, and the late Madame Gautillet as a shepherdess. On the windows hung curtains of red Tours fabric, looped back by silk cords with church tassels. This ornamental luxury, so little in keeping with Grandet's ways, together with the pier-mirror, the clock, the tapestried chairs, and the rosewood corner cupboards, had been included in the purchase of the house. At the window nearest the door was a straw-bottomed chair, raised on wooden blocks, so that Madame Grandet could sit high enough to be able to see the passers-by. A bleached cherrywood worktable filled the window-bay and Eugénie Grandet's little armchair stood right beside it. For fifteen years mother and daughter had spent peaceful days, from April to November, sitting in this spot constantly at work. On the first of November they could take up their winter positions by the fireplace. Only on that day did Grandet allow a fire to be lit in the room and he had it put out on the thirty-first of March, taking no account of either the cold of early spring or of autumn. A footwarmer, supplied with embers from the kitchen fire ingeniously kept for them by Big Nanon, helped Madame and Mademoiselle Grandet to get through the coldest mornings and evenings of April and October. The mother and daughter kept all the household linen in repair and spent their days so conscientiously at this work, which was real working-woman's toil, that if Eugénie wanted to embroider a little collar for her mother she was forced to take time off her sleep, deceiving her father so that she could have a light. For a long time the miser had been giving out candles to his daughter and Big Nanon, just as, first thing in the morning, he had been giving out bread and the necessary supplies for the day's consumption.

Big Nanon was perhaps the only human being capable of putting up with her master's tyranny. The whole town envied Monsieur and Madame Grandet for having her. Big Nanon, so called because of her great height of over six feet, had been in Grandet's service for thirty-five years. Although her wages were only sixty livres, she was reported to be one of the richest servants in Saumur. The sixty livres, which had mounted up over thirty-five years, had recently enabled her to invest four thousand livres in an annuity with Maître Cruchot. The result of Big Nanon's long, steady saving seemed enormous. Every servant, seeing that the poor sixty-year-old had bread for her old age, was jealous of her, without thinking of the hard slavery by which it had been acquired. At the age of twenty-two, the poor girl's looks were so unattractive that she could not get a job anywhere. This feeling was, to be sure, unfair, for her face would have been much admired had it been on the shoulders of a Grenadier Guardsman. But, as they say, everything in its proper place. Having had to leave a burnt-down farm where she had looked after the cows, she came to Saumur; there, spurred on by the kind of steadfast courage which is willing to take on anything, she looked for a job. At that time Père Grandet was thinking of getting married and was already wanting to set up house. He noticed this gir' who was sent away from door to door. As a cooper he was a judge of her physical strength and he was aware of the use to be made of a female built like Hercules, planted as firmly on her feet as a sixty-year-old oak on its roots, with powerful hips, a broad back, a carter's hands, and a sturdy honesty as unassailable as her untarnished virtue. Not the warts scattered on Nanon's soldierly face, nor her brick-red complexion, nor her sinewy arms, nor her rags dismayed the cooper, who was then at the age when the heart is easily moved. So he clothed, shod, and fed the poor girl, gave her wages, and employed her without ill-treating her too much. Seeing herself received in this way, Big Nanon wept secretly for joy and became sincerely attached to the cooper, although he exploited her like a feudal overlord. Nanon did everything. She did the cooking and the washing, she took the bed-linen to wash in the Loire, carrying it back on her shoulders. She got up at daybreak and went to bed late; she prepared all the meals for the grape-pickers at harvest-time and supervised the gleaners. She defended her master's property like a faithful dog and, filled with a blind trust in him, obeyed his most absurd whims without a murmur. In the famous year of 1811, when the harvest required an exorbitant amount of work and Nanon had served him for twenty years, Grandet decided to give her his old watch; it was the only present she ever received from him. Although he let her have his old shoes (they fitted her), it was impossible to look on the quarterly bonus of Grandet's shoes as a present, for they were so worn. Necessity had made the poor girl so miserly that, in the end, Grandet had come to love her as one loves a dog and Nanon had let a collar be put round her neck, a spiked collar which did not prick her any more. If Grandet cut the bread a little too sparingly, she did not complain. She shared cheerfully in the benefits to health which followed from the strict diet of the house, where no one was ever ill. And then Nanon was a member of the family. She would laugh when Grandet laughed, would become sad, freeze, get warm, and work with him. How many sweet compensations there were in this equality! The master had never reproached his servant with taking wild apricots or peaches or plums or nectarines, which she ate under the trees. 'Go on, help yourself, Nanon,' he would say to her in the years when the branches bent with the weight of the fruit which the farmers had to give to the pigs. To a field labourer who, in her youth, had harvested only ill-treatment, to a poor girl taken in out of charity, Père Grandet's dubious laugh was a real ray of sunshine. In any case, Nanon's simple heart and limited intelligence could contain only one feeling and one idea.

After thirty-five years she could still see herself arriving at Père Grandet's timber-yard, barefoot and in rags, and could still hear the cooper saying to her, 'What do you want, my dear?' And her gratitude was as fresh as ever. Sometimes, as Grandet reflected that the poor creature had never been paid a single compliment, that she was unaware of the tender feelings women inspire, and might one day appear before God more chaste than the Virgin Mary herself, he would be seized with pity and, looking at her, would say, 'Poor Nanon!' His exclamation was always followed by an indescribable look from the old servant. These words, uttered from time to time, had over a long period formed an unbroken chain of friendship to which every exclamation added a link. This pity, coming from Grandet's heart and gratefully accepted by the old maid, had something indefinably revolting about it. The ghastly miser's pity, which brought great pleasure to the old cooper's heart, was Nanon's total sum of happiness. Who will not repeat 'Poor Nanon!'? God will recognize his angels by the tones of their voices and their hidden sorrows. In Saumur there were a great many households where the servants were better treated but where, for all that, the masters received no satisfaction. Hence this other remark, 'What do the Grandets do to their Big Nanon to make her so attached to them? She would go through fire for them!' Her kitchen, whose barred windows looked on to the courtyard, was always clean, tidy, and cold, a real miser's kitchen where nothing was to be wasted. When Nanon had washed the dishes, put away the remains of the dinner, and extinguished the fire, she would leave her kitchen, which was separated from the main room by a passage, to come and spin hemp beside her employers. One single candle was enough for the family for the evening. The servant slept at the end of the passage in a tiny closet with no direct lighting. Her robust health enabled her to live unharmed in this hole where, in the profound silence which reigned throughout the house day and night, she could hear the slightest sound. Like a watchdog, she must have slept with one ear open and rested while keeping watch.

The other parts of the house will be described as the story unfolds, but, in any case, the sketch of the living-room, where all the luxury of the household was displayed, may give an advance idea of the bareness of the upper floors.

At the beginning of an evening in the middle of November 1819, Big Nanon lit a fire for the first time. The autumn had been very fine. The day was a day of celebration well-known to the Cruchot party and the Grassinites, and so the six antagonists were getting ready to come fully armed to an encounter in the living-room and to vie with each other in manifestations of friendship. In the morning, all Saumur had seen Madame and Mademoiselle Grandet, accompanied by Nanon, going to mass at the parish church and everyone remembered that that day was Mademoiselle Eugénie's birthday. So, calculating the time when dinner would be finished, Maître Cruchot, the Abbé Cruchot, and Monsieur C. de Bonfons hurried to arrive before the des Grassins to congratulate Mademoiselle Grandet. All three brought enormous bunches of flowers from their little hothouses. The stems of the flowers which the President was intending to present were skilfully wrapped in a white satin ribbon with a gold fringe. In the morning, following his custom for the noteworthy days of Eugénie's birthday and saint's day, Monsieur Grandet had come to her room before she got up and had solemnly given his paternal present, which for thirteen years had been a rare gold coin. Madame Grandet usually gave her daughter a winter or summer dress, according to the season. These two dresses and the gold coins which she received on New Year's Day and on her father's birthday gave Eugénie a little income of about a hundred écus, which Grandet loved to see her accumulate. Was it not putting his money from one box into another and, as it were, carefully fostering his heiress's avarice? Now and again he asked for an account of her treasure, which at one time used to be increased by the La Bertellières, saying to her: 'It will be your marriage dozen.'

The 'dozen' is an ancient custom still in force and piously observed in a few areas of central France. In Berry and Anjou, when a girl gets married, her or her future husband's family has to give her a purse containing twelve, or twelve dozen, or twelve hundred, silver or gold coins, according to their means. The poorest herd-girl would not get married without her dozen, even if it were only of copper coins. At Issoudun they still talk of some dozen or other given to a rich heiress, containing a hundred and forty-four Portuguese gold pieces. When Catherine de Médicis* married Henri II, her uncle gave her a present of a dozen, extremely valuable, antique gold medals.

During dinner, the father, delighted to see his Eugénie looking more beautiful than usual in a new dress, had exclaimed, 'Since it's Eugénie's birthday, let's make a fire! It will be a good omen.'

'Mademoiselle will get married in the course of the year, that's for sure,' said Big Nanon as she cleared away the remains of a goose, the cooper's equivalent of a pheasant.

'I don't see any match for her in Saumur,' replied Madame Grandet, giving her husband a timid glance which, given her age, proclaimed the total conjugal servitude under which the poor woman suffered.

Grandet looked at his daughter and declared cheerfully, 'The child is twenty-three today. We'll soon have to do something about her future.'

Eugénie and her mother silently exchanged a look of mutual understanding.

Madame Grandet was a thin, withered-looking woman, yellow as a quince, awkward and slow-moving—one of those women who seem made to be tyrannized. She had big bones, a big nose, a big forehead, and big eyes, and at first sight she was vaguely like one of those cottony fruits which have no flavour or juice. Her few teeth were discoloured, her mouth was wrinkled, and her chin was of the long, thin type popularly called nut-cracker. She was an admirable woman, a true La Bertellière. The Abbé Cruchot managed to find a few opportunities of telling her that she had not been too bad-looking and she believed him. An angelic gentleness, the submissiveness of an insect tortured by children, exceptional religious feeling, an unfailing evenness of temper, and a good heart made her universally pitied and respected. Her husband never gave her more than six francs at a time for her personal expenses.

Although it seems absurd, this woman, whose dowry and inheritance had brought Père Grandet more than three hundred thousand francs, had always felt so deeply humiliated by a dependence and slavery against which the gentleness of her heart forbade her to rebel that she had never asked for a penny nor made any comment on the documents for signature which Maître Cruchot set before her. This foolish, secret pride, this nobility of heart which Grandet never understood and constantly wounded, dominated her behaviour. Madame Grandet always wore a dress of greenish levantine silk, which she had become used to making last for almost a year. She wore a white cotton shawl and a stitched straw hat, and hardly ever took off a black taffeta apron. As she rarely went out of doors, she wore out her shoes very little. In short, she never wanted anything for herself. So Grandet, sometimes touched by a twinge of remorse when he recalled how long it was since he had given his wife six francs, always stipulated that there should be a little pin-money for her when he sold his annual harvest. The four or five louis given by the Dutch or Belgian buyer of the Grandet vine-harvest formed the steadiest part of Madame Grandet's annual income. But often, when she had received her five louis, her husband would say to her, as if they shared a common purse, 'Could you lend me a few sous?', and the poor woman, happy to be able to do something for a man whom her confessor represented to her as her lord and master, handed over to him a few crowns from her pin-money in the course of the winter.

When Grandet drew out of his pocket the five-franc piece allotted monthly for his daughter's personal expenses of dress, needles, and thread, he never failed to say to his wife, when he had buttoned up his pocket again, 'And what about you, mother, do you want anything?'

'My dear,' Madame Grandet would reply with maternal dignity, 'I'll think about it.'

Her sublime attitude was totally lost upon Grandet. He thought he was very generous to his wife. Philosophers who come upon people like Nanon, Madame Grandet, and Eugénie are surely entitled to think that irony is the basic characteristic of Providence. After the dinner when Eugénie's marriage was discussed for the first time, Nanon went to fetch a bottle of blackcurrant cordial from Monsieur Grandet's room and nearly fell as she was coming downstairs again.

'Clumsy creature,' said her master, 'are *you* going to fall, like anyone else?'

'Monsieur, it's that step on the staircase which is loose.'

'She's right,' said Madame Grandet. 'You ought to have had it mended a long time ago. Yesterday Eugénie nearly sprained her ankle on it.'

'Well,' said Grandet to Nanon, seeing that she had turned quite pale, 'since it's Eugénie's birthday and you nearly fell, take a little glass of blackcurrant cordial. That will set you to rights.'

'Indeed, I well deserve it,' said Nanon. 'In my place, many people would have broken the bottle. But I would rather have broken my elbow, so as to keep it up in the air and out of harm's way.'

'Poor Nanon!' said Grandet, pouring out the blackcurrant cordial for her.

'Did you hurt yourself?' asked Eugénie, looking at her with concern.

'No, I broke my fall by managing to land on my back.'

'Well,' said Grandet, 'since it's Eugénie's birthday, I'll mend the step for you. You people don't think to put your foot on the corner where it is still firm.'

Grandet took the candle, left his wife, his daughter, and his servant with no light except for what came from the bright, darting flames of the fire, and went to get wood, nails, and his tools from the washhouse.

'Do you need any help?' called Nanon when she heard him hammering on the staircase.

'No, no! I'm an old hand at this,' answered the former cooper.

Just as Grandet was mending his rickety staircase himself and whistling loudly as he remembered the days of his youth, the three Cruchots knocked at the door.

'Is that you, Monsieur Cruchot?' asked Nanon, looking through the little grating.

'Yes,' replied the President.

Nanon opened the door and, by the light of the fire reflected under the entrance arch, the three Cruchots could grope their way to the living-room.

'Oh, you've come to celebrate the birthday,' said Nanon, smelling the flowers.

'Excuse me, gentlemen,' called Grandet, recognizing his friends' voices, 'I'll be with you shortly. I'm not proud. I'm just patching up a step in my staircase, myself.'

'Carry on, carry on, Monsieur Grandet. *A charcoal burner is mayor in his own house*,'* said the President sententiously, laughing all by himself at his allusion which no one understood.

Madame and Mademoiselle Grandet stood up. Then the President, taking advantage of the dim light, said to Eugénie:

'Will you allow me, Mademoiselle, to wish you today, the day of your birth, a succession of happy years and the continuation of your present good health?'

He proffered a large bouquet of flowers of a kind rarely seen in Saumur; then, gripping the heiress's elbows, he kissed her on both sides of her neck with a complacency that embarrassed Eugénie. The President, who looked like a big rusty nail, thought that this was the way to conduct his courtship.

'Don't stand on ceremony,' said Grandet as he came back into the room. 'How you do go on when it's a day of celebration, Monsieur le Président!'

'But, with Mademoiselle,' said the Abbé Cruchot, armed with his bouquet, 'every day would be a day of celebration for my nephew.'

The Abbé kissed Eugénie's hand. As for Maître Cruchot, he kissed the girl squarely on both cheeks and said, 'How our little girl is growing up! Twelve months older every year.'

As he put the light back in front of the clock, Grandet, who never liked to let a joke go and would repeat it *ad nauseam* if he thought it amusing, said, 'Since it's Eugénie's birthday, let's light the torches!'

He carefully lifted off the branches of the candelabra, put the socket in each pedestal, took a new candle wrapped in a twist of paper from Nanon's hands, stuck it in the hole, made sure it was firmly fixed, lit it, and went and sat down beside his wife, looking in turn at his friends, his daughter, and the two candles. The Abbé Cruchot, a plump, chubby little man, with a flat, red wig and the face of a card-playing old woman, stretched out his feet, well-shod in strong shoes with silver buckles, saying, 'Haven't the des Grassins come yet?'

'Not yet,' said Grandet.

'But will they be coming?' asked the old lawyer, twisting his face into a grin, a face as full of holes as a kitchen strainer.

'I think so,' answered Madame Grandet.

'Is your grape-harvest completed?' President de Bonfons asked Grandet.

'Yes, everywhere,' said the old winegrower, getting up and walking up and down the room, proudly throwing out his chest as he said 'everywhere'. Going past the door of the passage that led to the kitchen, he caught sight of Nanon, sitting by her fire with a light and getting ready to spin there so as not to intrude on the birthday party. 'Nanon,' he said, going out into the passage, 'put out your fire and your light, and come and sit with us. Goodness me! The room is big enough for us all.'

'But, Monsieur, you're going to have distinguished visitors.'

'Aren't you just as good as they are? They all come from Adam's rib, just like you.'

Grandet came back into the room and, turning to the President, said, 'Have you sold your harvest?'

'Indeed, no. I'm hanging on to it. If the wine is good now, in two years' time it will be better. As you well know, the growers have sworn to stick to the agreed price and this year the Belgians won't get the better of us. If they go away, oh well, they'll come back.'

'Yes, but we must stand firm,' said Grandet in a tone that sent a shudder through the President.

'Could he be negotiating a deal?' thought Cruchot.

Just then a knock at the door heralded the arrival of the des Grassins family and this interrupted a conversation between Madame Grandet and the Abbé. Madame des Grassins was one of those lively, plump, pink and white little women who, thanks to the seclusion of provincial life and blameless habits, are still young at forty. They are like the last roses of late summer, which are pleasant to look at but whose petals have something chilly about them and whose scent is fading. She dressed quite well, had fashionable clothes sent from Paris, was the leader of society in Saumur, and gave evening parties. Her husband, a former quartermaster in the Imperial Guard, had been badly wounded at Austerlitz* and pensioned off. In spite of his respect for Grandet, he retained the superficial bluntness of the military man.

'Good evening, Grandet,' he said, holding out his hand to the winegrower and assuming an air of superiority, with which he always crushed the Cruchots. 'Mademoiselle,' he said to Eugénie, after bowing to Madame Grandet, 'you are always good and beautiful; I don't really know what one can wish you.' Then he presented her with a small box which his servant was carrying and which contained Cape heather, a very rare plant recently introduced into Europe.

Madame des Grassins kissed Eugénie very affectionately, shook her hand, and said, 'Adolphe has assumed responsibility for giving you my little gift.'

A tall, fair, pale, delicate-looking young man stepped

forward. He had quite good manners and appeared to be shy, but he had just spent eight or ten thousand francs more than his allowance in Paris, where he had gone to study law. He kissed Eugénie on both cheeks and presented her with a work-box filled with silver-gilt implements. It was really a shoddy piece of work, in spite of the coat of arms, quite nicely engraved with a Gothic E.G., which gave an impression of good craftsmanship. On opening it, Eugénie experienced one of those moments of complete happiness which make girls blush, quiver, and tremble with joy. She turned her eyes to her father as if to ask whether she might accept the gift, and Monsieur Grandet replied with a 'Take it, my child', in tones that would have done credit to an actor.

The three Cruchots were dumbfounded when they saw the happy, eager look bestowed on Adolphe des Grassins by the heiress, to whom such riches seemed unprecedented. Monsieur des Grassins offered Grandet a pinch of snuff, took one himself, shook off the grains which had fallen on to the Legion of Honour ribbon in the buttonhole of his blue coat, then looked at the Cruchots as if to say, 'Parry that thrust, if you can!' Madame des Grassins' eyes fell on the blue vases in which the Cruchots' bouquets had been put, as, with the pretended good faith of a malicious woman, she looked round for their presents. In this delicate situation, the Abbé Cruchot left the company, which went to sit in a semicircle round the fire, while he joined Grandet in his walk at the other end of the room. When the two old men were in the bay of the window furthest away from the des Grassins, the priest whispered to the miser, 'Those people throw money out of the window.'

'What does it matter, if it lands in my cellar?' replied the winegrower.

'If you wanted to give your daughter golden scissors, you could certainly afford to do so,' said the Abbé.

'I give her better things than scissors,' replied Grandet.

'My nephew is an idiot,' thought the Abbé, looking at the President, whose tousled hair made his ill-favoured, swarthy face even less attractive. 'Couldn't he think up a little bit of nonsense which would look expensive?'

'We'll make up your game of cards, Madame Grandet,' said Madame des Grassins.

'But as we're all together, we can have two tables . . .'

'Since it's Eugénie's birthday, have a game of lotto* for everybody', said Père Grandet. 'The two children can join in.' The former cooper, who never played any game, indicated his daughter and Adolphe. 'Come on, Nanon, set out the card-tables.'

'We'll help you, Mademoiselle Nanon,' said Madame des Grassins cheerfully; she was delighted at the pleasure she had given Eugénie.

'I have never been so pleased in my life,' said the heiress. 'I haven't seen anything so pretty anywhere.'

'It was Adolphe who chose it and brought it back from Paris,' Madame des Grassins whispered to her.

'Go on, carry out your plan, you damned schemer,' the President said to himself. 'If you or your husband is ever engaged in a lawsuit, you'll never win.'

From the corner where he was sitting, the lawyer looked calmly at the Abbé, saying to himself, 'Whatever the des Grassins do, they won't get anywhere. My fortune, together with my brother's and nephew's, amounts to eleven hundred thousand francs. The des Grassins have, at most, only half of that and they have a daughter. They can give her what they like, the heiress and the presents will all be ours one day.'

At half past eight in the evening, two tables were set up. Pretty Madame des Grassins had managed to put her son beside Eugénie. The actors in this scene, apparently so ordinary but in reality full of interest, were provided with numbered cards of different colours and blue glass counters. They seemed to be listening to the jokes of the old lawyer, who did not draw a number without making a comment, but they were all thinking of Monsieur Grandet's millions. The old cooper, filled with self-satisfied pride, was looking at Madame des Grassins's pink feathers and fresh gown, at the banker's soldierly face, at Adolphe's, at the President, the Abbé, and the lawyer, and was saying to himself, 'They have come for my money. They come and spend a boring evening here for the sake of my daughter. Ha! my daughter will be for neither the one nor the other, and I use all these people as harpoons to fish with.'

The gaiety of the family party in the grey old sitting-room, ill-lit by two candles, the laughter to the accompaniment of the hum of Big Nanon's spinning-wheel, sincere only on the lips of Eugénie or her mother, the petty minds playing for such great stakes, the girl, who, like one of those birds, unknowing victims of the high price placed on them, was tracked down and hemmed in by manifestations of friendship which she took to be genuine, all this combined to make the scene a sad comedy. Indeed, is it not a scene of all times and places reduced to its simplest terms? The face of Grandet, who was exploiting the false affection of the two families and obtaining enormous profits from it, dominated the drama and made its meaning clear. Money, the only god that people believe in nowadays, was expressed here, in all its power, by a single countenance. The kindly feelings of life occupied only a secondary place there. They animated three pure hearts, Nanon's, Eugénie's, and her mother's. Yet how ignorant they were in their simple innocence!

Eugénie and her mother knew nothing of Grandet's fortune. They valued the things of life only in the light of their vague conceptions and neither esteemed nor despised money, accustomed as they were to doing without it. Their feelings, keen, though bruised without their realizing it, and their secret inner lives, made them strange exceptions in this gathering of people whose existences were purely materialistic. How frightful is man's condition! There is not one of his joys which does not come from some ignorance or other. At the very moment when Madame Grandet was winning a pool of sixteen sous and when Big Nanon was beaming with pleasure at seeing Madame pocket such a handsome sum, a knock resounded at the front door and was so loud that the women started in their chairs.

'No Saumur man would knock like that,' said the lawyer.

'What a way to thump!' said Nanon. 'Do they want to break our door?'

'Who the devil is it?' exclaimed Grandet.

Nanon took one of the candles and, followed by Grandet, went to open the door.

'Grandet, Grandet!' cried his wife, who, impelled by a vague feeling of fear, hurried to the living-room door.

All the players looked at each other.

'Perhaps we ought to go,' said Monsieur des Grassins. 'That knock on the door sounds ominous to me.'

Monsieur des Grassins barely had time to catch sight of the face of a young man, accompanied by a porter from the coach office who was carrying two enormous trunks and dragging travelling-bags after him, when Grandet, turning round sharply to his wife, said, 'Madame Grandet, go back to your lotto.' Then he quickly closed the door of the room, where the anxious players resumed their seats but did not continue the game.

'Is it someone from Saumur, Monsieur des Grassins?' asked his wife.

'No, it's a traveller.'

'He must come from Paris. Indeed it is *ni-ine of the clock*', said the lawyer, pulling out his old watch, which was as thick as two fingers. 'Dash it all! The mail coach from the main office is never late.'

'And is this gentleman young?' asked the Abbé Cruchot.

'Yes,' replied Monsieur des Grassins. 'He is bringing luggage that must weigh at least half a ton.'

'Nanon's still at the front door,' said Eugénie.

'It must be one of your relations,' said the President.

'Let's place our stakes,' said Madame Grandet quietly. 'I could tell from his voice that Monsieur Grandet was put out. He might not be pleased to find that we are talking about his affairs.'

'Mademoiselle, it's probably your Grandet cousin,' Adolphe said to his neighbour. 'He's a very good-looking young man, whom I have seen at a ball at Monsieur de

32

Nucingen's.' Adolphe did not go on; his mother had trodden on his foot. Then, having asked him out loud for two sous for his stake, she whispered to him, 'Hold your tongue, you big fool.'

At that moment Grandet came back into the room without Big Nanon. Her footsteps and those of the porter could be heard going upstairs. Grandet was followed by the traveller who, in the last few moments, had aroused so much curiosity and excited the minds of the company so keenly that his arrival in the house could be compared to that of a snail in a beehive or to the introduction of a peacock in some remote village farmyard.

'Sit down by the fire,' said Grandet.

Before sitting down, the young stranger bowed gracefully to the assembled company. The men got up and responded with a polite bow, and the women made a formal curtsey.

'You must be cold, Monsieur,' said Madame Grandet. 'You have perhaps come from . . .?'

'That's just like a woman!' said the old winegrower, looking up from reading a letter which he was holding in his hand. 'Let the gentleman have a rest.'

'But, father, perhaps the gentleman needs some refreshment,' said Eugénie.

'He has a tongue,' replied the winegrower sternly.

Only the stranger was surprised at the scene. The others were used to the old man's peremptory ways. Nevertheless, when these two questions had been asked and answered, the stranger got up, turned his back to the fire, lifted one of his feet to warm the sole of his boot, and said to Eugénie, 'Thank you, cousin. I had dinner at Tours. And', he added, looking at Grandet, 'I don't need anything. I am not even at all tired.'

'Have you come from the capital, Monsieur?' inquired Madame des Grassins.

On hearing a question addressed to him, Monsieur Charles (for that was the name of the son of Monsieur Grandet of Paris) took a little eyeglass that was hanging on a chain round his neck, put it to his right eye to examine what was on the table and the people who were sitting round it, unabashedly scrutinized Madame des Grassins, and, when he had surveyed everything, said, 'Yes, Madame.' Then he added, 'I see you are playing lotto, aunt. Do go on with your game. It's too amusing to leave . . .'

'I was sure it was the cousin,' thought Madame des Grassins, fluttering her eyes at him.

'Forty-seven,' called out the old Abbé. 'Mark your card, Madame des Grassins. Isn't that your number?'

Monsieur des Grassins put a counter on his wife's card. In the grip of sad forebodings she looked in turn at the Parisian cousin and at Eugénie, without a thought for the lotto. From time to time the young heiress stole a furtive glance at her cousin and it was not difficult for the banker's wife to discern in it a crescendo of astonishment and curiosity.

The Cousin from Paris

MONSIEUR CHARLES GRANDET, a handsome young man of twenty-two, provided at that moment a strange contrast to the worthy provincials, who were already rather sickened by his aristocratic manners and were all studying him carefully so as to make fun of him. A word of explanation is required here.

At the age of twenty-two, young men are still near enough to childhood to indulge in childish behaviour. So perhaps you might meet ninety-nine out of a hundred of them who would have behaved as Charles Grandet did. A few days earlier, his father had told him to go for several months to his uncle's at Saumur. Perhaps Monsieur Grandet of Paris was thinking of Eugénie. Charles, who was making his first excursion into a provincial town, had the idea of appearing there with the superiority of a fashionable young man, of driving the whole district to despair by his display of luxury, of making his stay a memorable event, and of introducing the innovations of Parisian life. In short, he wanted to spend more time in Saumur than he did in Paris on polishing his nails and displaying the studied elegance of dress that a fashionable young man sometimes abandons for casual clothes that have their own charm. So Charles took with him the prettiest hunting-costume, the prettiest gun, the prettiest knife, and the prettiest sheath in Paris. He took all his fanciest waistcoats: there were grey, white, black, and scarab-green ones: some were shot with gold, some spangled, some mottled; some were double-breasted, some had roll-collars, some had stand-up collars, and some fastened up to the throat with gold buttons. He brought with him every variety of collar and tie that was popular at the time. He brought two Buisson* coats and his finest linen. He brought his pretty gold dressing-case, a present from his

35

mother, and his dandy's trinkets, including a charming little writing-case given to him by the most amiable of women, at least in his eyes, a great lady whom he called Annette; the victim of certain suspicions, she was forced for the time being to sacrifice her happiness and to go on a boring journey to Scotland with her husband. Charles also had a quantity of pretty note-paper on which to write to her once a fortnight. In fact he had brought with him a cargo of Parisian frippery as complete as it was possible to make it. From the riding-whip that is used to start a duel to the fine engraved pistols which bring it to an end, it contained all the implements which an idle young man uses to plough through the field of life. His father had told him to travel alone and modestly, and so he had reserved the front of the coach for himself, quite pleased not to spoil a delightful travelling carriage he had ordered for his journey to meet Annette, the great lady whom . . . etc., and whom he was to rejoin next June at the spa of Baden. Charles expected to meet crowds of people at his uncle's, to ride to hounds in his uncle's forests, in short, to lead country-house life there. He did not know that he would find his uncle in Saumur, where Charles had made enquiries only to ask the way to Froidfond. But when he heard that Grandet was in town, he thought his uncle would be in a large mansion. With a view to making a suitable entry into his uncle's home, whether at Saumur or at Froidfond, he had put on his smartest travelling dress, an outfit of the most elegant simplicity, the most 'adorable', to use the word that is currently employed to express the ultimate perfection in things or men. At Tours, a hairdresser had just recurled his beautiful chestnut hair; he had changed his linen and put on a black satin cravat together with a round collar that framed his pale, smiling face becomingly. A travelling coat, close-fitting at the waist, was half-unbuttoned to reveal a cashmere waistcoat with a roll-collar, under which was a second white waistcoat. His watch, carelessly slipped into a pocket, was attached by a short gold chain to one of his buttonholes.

36

His grey trousers were buttoned at the sides and ornamented at the seams with black silk embroidery. He had a pleasing way of handling his cane, whose carved gold knob did not mar his spotless grey gloves. Finally, his cap was in excellent taste. Only a Parisian, a Parisian from the highest social sphere, could rig himself out in this way without looking ridiculous and could give a fatuous harmony to all such nonsense. Moreover, Charles carried it off with a dashing air, the air of a young man who has fine pistols, a sure aim, and Annette. Now, if you want to understand fully the surprise of the Saumur people and of the young Parisian respectively, to see clearly the bright vision formed by the traveller's elegance in the grey shadows of the room and surrounded by the figures that made up the family picture, try to imagine the Cruchots. All three of them took snuff and had long ceased to bother about their snively noses or the little black specks which were scattered on the fronts of their dingy shirts with crumpled collars and yellowed creases. Their limp cravats rolled up into ropes as soon as they were put round their necks. They had such a huge quantity of linen that they needed to have a washing done only every six months, and could keep it at the bottom of their cupboards, leaving Time to stamp it with his grey, ancient tints. They were a perfect mixture of awkwardness and senility. Their faces, as faded as their threadbare jackets, as creased as their trousers, seemed worn out, wizened, and simpering. The general slovenliness of the other outfits, all ill-assorted and dingy-looking, as clothes are in provincial towns (people there gradually cease to dress to please others and are reluctant to pay the price of a pair of gloves), fitted in with the carelessness of the Cruchots. Horror of the fashionable was the only point on which the Grassinites and the Cruchot party were in perfect agreement. When the Parisian took his eyeglass to examine the unusual features of the room, the rafters of the ceiling, the colour of the woodwork, or the marks left on it by the flies, marks so numerous that they would have been enough to punctuate the *Encyclopédie méthodique** and the *Moniteur*,* the lotto players immediately lifted their heads from their game and examined him with as much curiosity as they would have shown for a giraffe. Monsieur des Grassins and his son, to whom the appearance of a man of fashion was not unfamiliar, nevertheless joined in their neighbours' astonishment, either because they experienced the indefinable influence of a common feeling, or because they approved of it, indicating to their fellow provincials by ironical glances, 'That's what *Parisians* are like.' Moreover, they could all observe Charles at leisure, without fearing the displeasure of the master of the house. Grandet was absorbed in the long letter he was holding, and to read it he had taken the only candle from the table without considering his guests or their game. Eugénie, who had never before seen a being of such perfection either in dress or person, thought that her cousin was a seraph from some heavenly region. With delight she breathed in the perfume exhaled by that head of hair which was so glossy and so gracefully curled. She would have liked to touch the white skin of those pretty kid gloves. She envied Charles his small hands, his complexion, the freshness and delicacy of his features. It is hardly possible to sum up the impression which the young dandy made on an ignorant girl, who spent all her time darning stockings and mending her father's clothes, and whose life had been spent in the shadow of that filthy wainscoting without seeing more than one passer-by an hour in the silent street outside; the sight of her cousin awoke in her heart exquisite emotions of pleasure like those aroused in a young man by the fanciful feminine figures drawn by Westall* in English keepsakes* and so skilfully engraved by the Findens* that one is afraid of making the heavenly apparitions disappear by breathing on the vellum. Charles took out of his pocket a handkerchief embroidered by the great lady who was travelling in Scotland. When she saw this pretty piece of work, executed with love during the hours lost for love, Eugénie looked at her cousin to see if he was really going to use it. Charles's manners and gestures, the way he picked up his eyeglass, his affectation of impertinence, his scorn for the work-box which had just given the rich heiress such pleasure and which he evidently thought was either valueless or ridiculous, in fact everything which shocked the Cruchots and the des Grassins delighted her so much that, before falling asleep, her thoughts could not but dwell for a long time on this phoenix of cousins.

The numbers were being drawn very slowly, but soon the lotto was halted. Big Nanon came in and said quite audibly, 'Madame, you'll have to give me sheets to make up the gentleman's bed.'

Madame Grandet followed Nanon out of the room. As soon as they had gone, Madame des Grassins whispered, 'Let's keep our sous and stop playing.' They all took their two sous from the old chipped saucer in which they had placed them. Then the company, as a body, moved their chairs and turned towards the fire.

'Have you finished the game, then?' asked Grandet, without looking up from his letter.

'Oh, yes,' replied Madame des Grassins, going to sit beside Charles.

Prompted by one of those ideas which arise in a young girl's heart when a feeling comes to dwell there for the first time, Eugénie left the room to help her mother and Nanon. If she had been interrogated by a skilful confessor, she would no doubt have admitted that she was not thinking either of her mother or of Nanon but that she was motivated by a burning desire to inspect her cousin's room, to busy herself with the arrangements for her cousin, to put anything useful she could think of in his room, to make sure nothing was forgotten, so that it was as neat and elegant as possible. Eugénie already believed that only she could appreciate her cousin's taste and ideas. In fact, very fortunately, she arrived in time to show her mother and Nanon, who were leaving the room thinking they had done everything, that everything remained to be done. She suggested to Big Nanon that she should air the sheets with a warming-pan filled with embers from the fire. Eugénie herself covered the old table with a cloth and instructed Nanon to change it every morning. She convinced her mother of the necessity of lighting a good fire in the fireplace and persuaded Nanon to take a big pile of wood up on to the landing without saying a word to her father. She hurried to get from one of the corner cupboards in the sitting-room an old lacquer tray inherited from the late old Monsieur de la Bertellière; she also took from the cupboard a hexagonal crystal tumbler, a little tarnished gilt spoon, and an antique glass decanter engraved with cupids. All these objects she placed triumphantly on one end of the mantelpiece. More ideas had rushed into her mind in a quarter of an hour than she had had since she was born.

'Mama,' she said, 'my cousin will never be able to stand the smell of a tallow-candle. What about buying a wax one? . . .' Light as a bird, she went to get from her purse the five-franc piece she had been given for her month's expenses. 'Here you are, Nanon,' she said, 'be quick.'

'But what will your father say?' This terrible objection was made by Madame Grandet when she saw her daughter bearing an old Sèvres sugar-bowl, which Grandet had brought back from the house at Froidfond. 'And where will you get sugar from? Are you mad?'

'Nanon will buy sugar as well as a wax-candle, Mama.'

'But what about your father?'

'Would it be right if his nephew couldn't have a glass of sugared water to drink? Anyway, he won't notice.'

'Your father sees everything,' said Madame Grandet, shaking her head.

Nanon hesitated; she knew her master.

'Do go, Nanon, since it's my birthday!'

On hearing the first joke her young mistress had ever made, Nanon burst into a loud laugh and obeyed her. While Eugénie and her mother made efforts to beautify the room allotted to his nephew by Monsieur Grandet, Charles was being subjected to Madame des Grassins' flirtatious attentions.

'You are very brave, Monsieur,' she said, 'to exchange the winter pleasures of the capital for a stay in Saumur. But if we don't scare you too much, you will see that we can have quite a good time even here.'

She eyed him in a way that was unmistakably provincial, for in the provinces women are used to looking very demure and reserved but their furtive glances express the avid desire peculiar to the eyes of the clergy, to whom every pleasure seems to be stolen or sinful. Charles felt so out of his element in this room, so far removed from the huge mansion and the sumptuous life-style which he had assumed were his uncle's, that, as he looked carefully at Madame des Grassins, he came to discern a faint likeness to the faces he had known in Paris. He replied graciously to the indirect invitation addressed to him, and quite naturally slipped into a conversation in which Madame des Grassins gradually lowered her voice in keeping with the confidential nature of her remarks. Both she and Charles shared a need to confide in someone. So after a few moments of coquettish chatter and of jokes with a serious intent, the astute provincial lady could assume she would not be overheard by the others, who were talking of the wine sales, the preoccupation of all Saumur, and felt able to say: 'Monsieur, if you will do us the honour of coming to see us, my husband and I will both be delighted. Our drawing-room is the only one in Saumur where you will find important business people and the gentry gathered together. We belong to both sets, who are willing to meet only in our house, because they enjoy themselves there. My husband, I am proud to say, is highly esteemed by both groups. In this way, we shall try to relieve the boredom of your stay here. If you were to spend all your time at Monsieur Grandet's, my goodness, what would become of you? Your uncle's a skinflint who thinks only of layering his vines, your aunt is a sanctimonious bigot who can't put two ideas together, and your cousin is a common, uneducated, little nitwit, with no dowry, who spends her life mending dusters.'

41

'She's not bad at all, this woman,' thought Charles Grandet, as he acknowledged Madame des Grassins's simperings.

'You seem to want to monopolize the gentleman, my dear,' said the tall burly banker, with a laugh.

At this comment, the lawyer and the President exchanged some more or less cutting remarks, but the Abbé looked at them knowingly, as he took a pinch of snuff, and passed round his snuff-box. 'Who could do the honours of Saumur to the gentleman better than Madame?'

'Well, what do you mean by that, Monsieur l'Abbé?' asked Monsieur des Grassins.

'I mean it, Monsieur, in the sense most favourable to you, to Madame, to the town of Saumur, and to Monsieur,' replied the wily old man, turning towards Charles.

Without appearing to pay the slightest attention to it, the Abbé Cruchot had been able to guess at the gist of the conversation between Charles and Madame des Grassins.

'Monsieur,' said Adolphe at last, trying to speak in a free and easy way, 'I don't know if you remember me at all. I had the pleasure of dancing opposite you at a ball given by Monsieur le Baron de Nucingen, and . . .'

'Of course, I remember you perfectly,' replied Charles, surprised to find himself the centre of everyone's attention.

'Is this gentleman your son?' he asked Madame des Grassins.

The Abbé looked at the mother with a mocking glance.

'Yes, Monsieur,' she said.

'You must have come to Paris pretty young, then,' continued Charles, turning to Adolphe.

'That's how it is, Monsieur,' said the Abbé. 'We send them to Babylon as soon as they are weaned.'

Madame des Grassins gave the Abbé a remarkably significant look which seemed to inquire what he meant. 'You have to come to the provinces', he went on, 'to find women of thirty and over, who, with sons about to graduate in law, are as young-looking as Madame. It seems to me no time at all since the young men and ladies stood on chairs to see you dance at a ball, Madame,' added the Abbé, turning to his female opponent. 'For me, it's as if your triumphs took place only yesterday.'

'Oh, the old rascal!' said Madame des Grassins to herself. 'Could he have guessed my thoughts?'

'It looks as if I shall be a great social success at Saumur,' thought Charles, unbuttoning his frock-coat, putting a hand into his waistcoat, and looking into space so as to imitate Lord Byron's pose in Chantrey's statue.*

Père Grandet's inattention, or rather the preoccupation into which he was plunged by the reading of his letter, did not escape either the lawyer or the President, who tried to guess its contents from the barely perceptible changes in expression of the old fellow's face, which at that moment was brightly lit by the candle. The winegrower was with difficulty maintaining the usual composure of his features. Indeed, anyone can imagine what his face was like as he read the following fateful letter.

My dear brother,

It is now nearly twenty-three years since we last saw each other. My marriage was the occasion of our last meeting and we parted with both of us in happy circumstances. I would certainly have found it hard to foresee that one day you would be the sole support of the family whose property at that time gave you so much satisfaction. When you hold this letter in your hands, I shall no longer be alive. In the position I found myself in, I did not want to survive the shame of a bankruptcy. I have stood on the edge of the abyss till the last moment, retaining hope that I might survive. But now I must give up. The combined bankruptcies of my stockbroker and my lawyer Roguin deprive me of my last resources and leave me with nothing. I am in the painful position of owing nearly four million, without being able to pay more than twenty-five per cent of that. The value of my stock of wines has tumbled to rock bottom, because of the abundance and quality of your harvests. In three days' time, Paris will say, 'Monsieur Grandet was a scoundrel!' I, an honest man, shall be in a shroud of infamy. I rob my son both of his good name, which I have cherished, and of his mother's fortune. He, unhappy boy, whom I idolize, knows nothing of this. We bade each other an

43

affectionate farewell. Will he not curse me one day? Oh, my dear brother, our children's curse is a terrible thing; they can appeal against ours, but theirs is irrevocable. Grandet, you are my older brother, you owe me your protection; don't let Charles cast bitter words on my grave. Dear brother, even if I wrote to you with my blood and tears, this letter would not contain as much pain as it does, for then I should weep, I should bleed, I should be dead, I should be suffering no longer. But I am suffering and see death with dry eyes. So now you are Charles's father. He has no relatives on his mother's side, you know why. Why did I not comply with social prejudices? Why did I yield to love? Why did I marry the natural daughter of a great nobleman? Charles has now no family. Oh, my unhappy son! My son! Listen to me, Grandet. I am not imploring you to help me—in any case, your fortune is perhaps not big enough to stand a loan of three million—but to help my son. You must know, brother, that as I think of you, my hands are joined in supplication. I entrust Charles to you with my dying breath. I look at my pistols without grieving, as I think that you will be a father to him. Charles was very fond of me. I was so good to him. I never crossed him. He will not curse me. Besides, you will see, he has a gentle disposition; he takes after his mother. He will never give you any trouble. Poor boy! He is used to luxury and has no experience of the privations which we both endured during our early years of poverty. And now he is ruined and alone. Yes, all his friends will desert him, and it is I who will be the cause of his humiliations. Oh, I should like to have a strong enough arm to send him with a single blow to his mother in heaven. But that is madness. I return to my misfortunes and to Charles's. I have sent him to you so that you can tell him of my death and of his future lot, in a suitable manner. Be a father to him—a kind father. Don't tear him away suddenly from his life of idleness, you would kill him. I beg him on my knees to renounce the claims that, as his mother's heir, he could make against me. But there's no need for such a prayer. He is an honourable man and will certainly feel that he ought not to join my creditors. Make him renounce in good time his claims to my estate. Explain to him the harsh conditions of the life I am preparing for him, and if he retains his affection for me, tell him in my name that all is not lost for him. Yes, work, which has been the salvation of both of us, may give him back the fortune of which I am depriving him. And, if he will listen to the voice of his father, who for his sake would like to rise for a moment from the grave, let him leave France and go to the Indies. Dear brother, Charles is an upright, stout-hearted young man. If you give him a job lot of goods for trading, he would die rather than not repay your initial advance. For you will lend him something, Grandet; if you don't, you will lay up remorse for yourself. Oh, if my child were to get neither help nor affection from you, I would ask God throughout all eternity for vengeance on your harshness. If I had been able to rescue a few assets, I should certainly have been entitled to give him something from his mother's fortune, but the payments I had to make at the end of the month took all my resources. I wish I did not have to die uncertain of my child's fate; I should like to have felt sacred promises in the warmth of your handshake that would have comforted me. But I have no time. While Charles is on his way, I must draw up my balance-sheet. I am trying to prove by the good faith with which I conduct my business affairs that my disasters have not been caused by fault or dishonesty on my part. Isn't that to do something for Charles? Farewell, dear brother. May all God's blessings be on you in reward for the guardianship which I entrust to you and which you generously accept. I have no doubt about that. There will be a voice that will pray for you unceasingly in the world to which we must all go one day, and where I shall already be when you read this letter.

Victor-Ange-Guillaume GRANDET.

'So you're having a chat,' said Père Grandet, folding the letter carefully in its original creases and putting it in his waistcoat pocket. He looked at his nephew in a timid, humble manner which concealed his feelings and his calculations. 'Have you warmed up now?'

'Yes, thank you, my dear uncle.'

'Well, where have the womenfolk gone?' said the uncle, forgetting already that his nephew was to be put up in his house. At that moment Eugénie and Madame Grandet came back into the room. 'Is everything ready upstairs?' asked the old man, recovering his composure.

'Yes, father.'

'Well, nephew, if you are tired, Nanon will show you to your room. I'm afraid you won't have very fashionable quarters, but you must forgive poor winegrowers who

45

never have a sou to spare. Taxes swallow up all we have.'

'We don't want to intrude, Grandet,' said the banker. 'You may have things to talk about with your nephew, so we'll wish you goodnight. I shall see you tomorrow.'

At these words the company rose to go, everyone making a characteristic bow or curtsey. The old lawyer went to get his lantern from behind the front door and came back to light it. He offered to escort the des Grassins home, as Madame des Grassins had not foreseen the incident which was to make the party finish early and her servant had not come yet.

'Will you do me the honour of accepting my arm, Madame?' the Abbé Cruchot said to Madame des Grassins.

'Thank you, Monsieur l'Abbé, but my son is with me,' she replied curtly.

'Ladies couldn't compromise their reputations with me,' said the Abbé.

'Take Monsieur Cruchot's arm, then,' said her husband.

The Abbé shepherded the pretty lady along so smartly that they were soon a few steps ahead of the rest of the cavalcade.

'That's a very attractive young man, Madame,' he said, pressing her arm. '*Farewell to the baskets, the harvest's over!** You will have to say goodbye to Mademoiselle Grandet; Eugénie will go to the Parisian. Unless the cousin has taken a fancy to a Parisian girl. Your son Adolphe will find in him a rival who is the most . . .'

'Enough of that, Monsieur l'Abbé. It won't take this young man long to see that Eugénie is a faded nitwit. Did you look at her carefully this evening? She was as yellow as a quince.'

'Perhaps you have already pointed that out to her cousin.'

'Oh, I didn't hide my opinion . . .'

'Always sit next to Eugénie, Madame, and you won't need to say much to the young man against his cousin. He himself will make a comparison which . . .'

'Anyway, he's promised to come and dine at my house the day after tomorrow.'

'Oh, if you chose to, Madame, . . .' said the Abbé.

'And what would you like me to choose to do, Monsieur l'Abbé? Are you trying to give me evil advice? I haven't reached the age of thirty-nine with a spotless reputation, thank God, in order to spoil it now, even for the sake of the Grand Mogul's Empire. We are both of an age to understand what we're talking about. Indeed, for a churchman you have some very strange ideas. Shame on you. Your suggestion is like something from *Faublas*.'*

'So you have read *Faublas*?'

'No, Monsieur l'Abbé, I meant *Les Liaisons dangereuses*.'*

'Ah, that's a much more moral book,' said the Abbé with a laugh. 'But you make me out to be as corrupt as a young man of today. I simply wanted to . . .'

'Do you dare tell me that you weren't thinking of advising me to do something nasty? Isn't that quite obvious? If this young man—and I agree he is very good-looking —were to court me, he wouldn't think of his cousin. I know that in Paris some devoted mothers sacrifice themselves in this way for the happiness and well-being of their children, but we are in a provincial town, Monsieur l'Abbé.'

'Yes, Madame.'

'And', she continued, 'I would not want a hundred million bought at that price, nor would Adolphe himself.'

'Madame, I never mentioned a hundred million. The temptation would perhaps have been too much for both of us. Only I think a virtuous woman can quite honourably allow herself little harmless flirtations which are part of her social duties and which . . .'

'Do you think so?'

'Ought we not to try to be nice to each other, Madame? . . . . Excuse me, I must wipe my nose.—I assure you, Madame,' he continued, 'that the young man was eyeing you through his monocle with a much more flattering gaze than the one he bestowed on me; but I forgive him for preferring to honour beauty rather than old age . . .'

'It is obvious', the President was saying in his loud

voice, 'that Monsieur Grandet of Paris is sending his son to Saumur with extremely matrimonial intentions.'

'But in that case the cousin would not have landed on them like a bomb,' replied the lawyer.

'That doesn't mean anything,' said Monsieur des Grassins. 'The old chap is so secretive.'

'Des Grassins, my dear, I have asked the young man to dinner. You must go and ask Monsieur and Madame de Larsonnière, and the du Hautoys together with their beautiful daughter, of course. I do hope she is well dressed that day. Her mother is so jealous of her that she rigs her out abominably. I hope, gentlemen,' she added, stopping the procession to turn to the two Cruchots, 'that you will do us the honour of coming too.'

'Here you are at your own house, Madame,' said the lawyer.

The three Cruchots said goodnight to the three des Grassins and, on their way home, applied their provincials' genius for analysis to a minute examination of the evening's great event which had changed the positions of the Grassinites and the Cruchot party in relation to one another. The admirable good sense which guided the actions of these cunning schemers made both sides appreciate the necessity of a temporary alliance against the common enemy. Should they not combine to prevent Eugénie from falling in love with her cousin and Charles from thinking of Eugénie? Would the Parisian be able to withstand the treacherous insinuations, the smooth calumnies, the laudatory slanders, and the ingenuous denials which were going to surround him incessantly in order to deceive him?

When the four relatives were left alone in the living-room, Monsieur Grandet said to his nephew: 'Now it's bedtime. It's too late to discuss the business which brings you here. We'll find a suitable moment tomorrow. Here we breakfast at eight o'clock. At midday we have a snack, a piece of fruit and a morsel of bread with a glass of white wine. Then, like the Parisians, we dine at five o'clock. That's the order of the day. If you want to visit the town

48

or explore the district, you are free as air to do so. You must excuse me if my affairs do not always permit me to accompany you. Perhaps you'll hear everyone in the town saying that I'm rich: Monsieur Grandet here, Monsieur Grandet there! I let them talk; their gossip does no harm to my credit. But I haven't a sou and in my old age I toil like a young workman whose only possessions are a blunt plane and two strong arms. Perhaps you'll soon see for yourself what an écu is worth, when you have to sweat for it. Come on, Nanon, get the candles.'

'I hope you will find everything you need, nephew,' said Madame Grandet, 'but if you want anything, you can call Nanon.'

'That's not very likely, my dear aunt. I think I've brought all I require with me. Allow me to wish you and my young cousin goodnight.'

Charles took a lighted wax-candle from Nanon's hand. It was a very yellow Anjou candle, that had been a long time in the shop and looked so like a tallow-candle that Monsieur Grandet, incapable of suspecting there was such a thing in the house, did not notice its magnificence.

'I'll show you the way,' said the old man.

Instead of going out by the living-room door that led to the archway, Grandet ceremoniously went along the passage which separated the living-room from the kitchen. A swing door with a large oval glass pane closed off the passage at the staircase end so as to mitigate the blast of cold air which swept through it. But even so, in winter the north wind blew in very fiercely and, in spite of the draught-excluders fixed round the doors, the room could scarcely be kept warm enough. Nanon bolted the front door, closed up the living-room, and went to the stable to unleash an Alsatian dog with a hoarse bark which made him sound as if he had laryngitis. This animal, well known for his fierce temper, recognized no one but Nanon. The two country-bred creatures got on well together. When Charles saw the yellowing, grimy walls of the stairway with its worm-eaten banisters and the steps which were

49

shaking under his uncle's heavy tread, his disillusionment grew stronger than ever. He felt as if he were in a hen-roost. His aunt and his cousin, to whom he turned with an enquiring glance at their faces, were so used to the stairs that, unaware of the reason for his astonishment, they took it for an expression of friendliness and acknowledged it with a pleasant smile which reduced him to despair.

'Why on earth has my father sent me here?' he said to himself.

When he reached the first landing, he noticed three doors, painted a dull brownish-red, set almost imperceptibly without frames in the dusty wall, and with conspicuous iron bars ending in flame-shaped strips. This design was repeated at each end of the long keyholes. The door which was at the top of the staircase and which led to the room above the kitchen was obviously walled-up. In fact it could be entered only by going through Grandet's room and he used it as his office. The single window which let in the light was protected on the courtyard side by a grating of massive iron bars. No one, not even Madame Grandet, was allowed to enter; the old man wanted to be there on his own like an alchemist at his stove. There he had, no doubt, cleverly contrived some secret hiding-place, there were stored the title-deeds to his properties, there hung the scales for weighing his gold coins, there secretly, by night, receipts and acknowledgements were written out and calculations made, to such an effect that other businessmen, finding Grandet always well-prepared for any transaction, might have imagined that he had a fairy or a demon at his beck and call. It was there, no doubt, that, while Nanon snored loudly enough to shatter the rafters, while the Alsatian watched and yawned in the courtyard, while Madame and Mademoiselle Grandet slept soundly, the old cooper would come in order to cherish, caress, embrace, gloat over, glory in, his gold. The walls were thick, the shutters discreet. He alone had the key to this laboratory, where, it was said, he would study maps on which all his fruit trees were marked and from which he would calculate the value of his crops to the last shoot from his vines, to the last bundle of faggots. Eugénie's room was opposite the walled-up door. Then at the end of the landing were Monsieur and Madame Grandet's rooms, which occupied the whole front of the house. Madame Grandet had a room next to Eugénie's, which was accessible by means of a glass door. The room of the master of the house was separated from his wife's by a partition, and from the mysterious private office by a thick wall. Père Grandet had housed his nephew on the second floor in the lofty attic above his own room, so that he could hear if Charles took it into his head to go in and out. When Eugénie and her mother reached the middle of the landing, they kissed each other good night. Then, after saying a few parting words to Charles, words which sounded cold but, in the daughter's heart at least, were full of warmth, they retired to their own rooms.

'Here is your room, nephew,' said Père Grandet to Charles, opening the door for him. 'If you need to go out, you should call Nanon. Without her, that's the end of you! The dog would eat you up without uttering a sound. Sleep well. Goodnight. Well, well, these good ladies have made a fire for you,' he continued. At that moment Big Nanon appeared, armed with a warming-pan. 'Here's another of them!' said Monsieur Grandet. 'Do you take my nephew for a woman in labour? Take away your embers, Nanon.'

'But, Monsieur, the sheets are damp and this gentleman is really as delicate as a woman.'

'Alright, go on then, since you've set your mind on it,' said Grandet, pushing her on the shoulder. 'But take care not to set the place on fire.' Then the miser went downstairs, muttering under his breath.

Charles stood aghast among his trunks. His eyes glanced round at the walls of an attic-room, hung with the kind of yellow, flowered wallpaper that you find in riverside cafés, at a fluted limestone mantelpiece, the very sight of which was chilling, at the yellow wooden chairs, trimmed with varnished cane, which seemed to have more than four corners, at an open bedside table large enough to contain a

51

small light-infantry sergeant, at the meagre strip of carpet, at a canopied bed, whose hangings trembled as if, finished off by worms, they were about to collapse. Then he looked solemnly at Big Nanon and said, 'Well, my good girl, am I really at the house of Monsieur Grandet, former Mayor of Saumur, brother of Monsieur Grandet of Paris?'

'Yes, Monsieur, and he's a very nice, kind, perfect gentleman. Would you like me to help you unpack?'

'Indeed, I wish you would, old soldier. Haven't you served in the Marine Guards?'

'Oh! Oh! Oh! Oh!' said Nanon. 'What on earth are the Marine Guards? Are they salt-water creatures? Do they go out to sea?'

'Look, get my dressing-gown out of that case. Here's the key.'

Nanon was quite amazed to see a green silk dressing-gown embroidered with an antique design of golden flowers.

'Are you going to put that on to go to bed?' she asked.

'Yes.'

'Holy Virgin! What a beautiful altar-cloth that would make for the parish church. But, my dear, pretty young gentleman, you should give it to the church. That would save your soul, but with a gown like that, you'll lose it. Oh, how nice you look in it. I'll call Mademoiselle so that she can see you.'

'That's enough, Nanon, since Nanon's your name. Stop your chatter and let me go to bed. I'll put my things in order tomorrow. And if you like my gown so much, you can save your own soul. I am too good a Christian not to give it to you when I leave, and you can do what you like with it.'

Nanon stood rooted to the spot, gazing incredulously at Charles.

'Give *me* that beautiful gown!' she said as she left the room. 'The gentleman's dreaming already. Goodnight.'

'Goodnight, Nanon.'

'What on earth am I doing here?' Charles said to himself as he fell asleep. 'My father's not a fool. There must be some point in my journey. Oh well! Serious affairs can wait till tomorrow, as some Greek old fogey said.'

'Holy Virgin! How nice my cousin is,' Eugénie said to herself in the middle of her prayers which, that evening, were never finished. Madame Grandet had no thoughts as she went to bed. Through the communicating door in the middle of the partition, she could hear the miser walking up and down in his room. Like all timid wives, she had studied the character of her lord and master. Just as a seagull foresees a storm, she could tell, from almost imperceptible signs, that an inner tempest was raging in Grandet and, to use her own expression, she lay as still as death. Grandet was looking at the door of his study, which he had had fitted with an inner lining of sheet-iron, and was saying to himself, 'What a strange idea my brother had, to bequeath me his son! That's a pretty legacy! I haven't twenty écus to give him. But what's twenty écus to that dandy, who eyed my barometer through his glass as if he wanted to make a bonfire of it?'

As he thought of the consequences of that tragic will, Grandet was perhaps more upset than his brother was when he wrote it.

'Am I really to have that golden gown? . . .' Nanon was saying as she fell asleep, wrapped in her altar-cloth, dreaming of flowers, watered silk, and damask for the first time in her life, as Eugénie dreamed of love.

Provincial Love

In the innocent, monotonous life of a young girl there comes a day of delight when the sun's rays flood into her heart, when a flower seems to express her thoughts, and when her heartbeats convey their fertile warmth to her brain, so that all her ideas dissolve into a vague longing; it is a day of innocent melancholy and tranquil happiness. When babies begin to see, they smile; when a girl first becomes aware of the feelings of nature, she smiles as she smiled when a baby. If light is the first thing we love in life, is not love the light of the heart? The moment of seeing the things of this world clearly had arrived for Eugénie. An early riser, like all provincial girls, she got up in good time, said her prayers, and set about getting dressed, an occupation which, from that day on, was to have some meaning for her. First she brushed her chestnut hair till it shone, then she twisted the thick tresses with the utmost care into plaits on the top of her head, making sure there were no stray wisps, and arranged them with a symmetry which enhanced the timid candour of her face, the simple style being in harmony with its innocent contours. As she washed her hands several times in the pure water that made her skin rough and red, she looked at her beautiful rounded arms and wondered what her cousin did to have such soft, white hands and such well-shaped nails. She put on new stockings and her prettiest shoes. She laced herself up firmly without missing out any of the eyelets in her stays. Finally, wanting for the first time in her life to look her best, she experienced the joy of having a well-cut, new dress which made her look attractive. When she had finished dressing, she heard the church clock strike and was surprised to count only seven strokes. She was so anxious to have all the time she needed to dress properly that she had got up too early. Knowing nothing of the art of rearranging a lock of hair ten times and studying the effect,

Eugénie simply folded her arms, sat down at her window, and gazed at the courtyard, the narrow garden, and the high terrace overlooking it. It was a restricted, rather depressing view, but one not devoid of the mysterious beauties peculiar to lonely spots or to untended nature. By the kitchen was a stone-rimmed well with a pulley attached to a bent iron rod. This was overgrown by a vine that had been withered, reddened, and blighted by the late autumn weather. From this point, the twisted vine grew as far as the wall, clung to it, and, running the length of the house, finished on a woodpile, where the logs were arranged as carefully as a bibliophile's books. The passage of time had turned the flagstones of the courtyard almost black with the growth of moss and weeds and the lack of use. The thick walls were clothed in greenery streaked with long brown marks. And at the far end of the courtyard, the eight steps leading to the garden gate were broken and half-buried under tall plants like the tomb of a knight buried by his widow at the time of the crusades. Above a low wall of crumbling stones was a trellis of rotten wood, half-collapsed with age, but where rampant climbing plants were clinging. The twisted branches of two stunted apple trees encroached on either side of the wicket-gate. The garden itself consisted of square plots protected by boxwood edges and separated by three parallel gravel paths; it ended at the foot of the ramparts in a clump of limes. At one end there were raspberry canes, at the other was a huge walnut tree, whose branches bent right over on to the cooper's office. A clear light and the lovely autumn sun, natural to the banks of the Loire, began to dissipate the hoar-frost that night had left on the picturesque stones, on the walls and plants of the garden, and the courtyard. Eugénie became aware of a completely new charm in the appearance of all these things, which till then she had thought so ordinary. A thousand confused feelings were arising in her heart and they gathered strength as the rays of the sun grew stronger outside. Finally she had that sensation of vague, inexplicable happiness which envelops the soul just as a cloud might envelop the body. Her thoughts chimed in with the details of the curious scene before her, and the harmonies in her heart joined forces with the harmonies of nature. When the sun reached a stretch of wall from which maidenhair fern was hanging, with the colours on its thick leaves iridescent like those on a pigeon's breast, heavenly rays of hope lit up the future for Eugénie; she found pleasure ever after in looking at that section of the wall, at its pale flowers, its blue harebells, and its faded grasses, which were mingled with a memory as charming as those of childhood. The sound made by each leaf as it fell from its branch on to the courtyard seemed to respond to the girl's secret questionings; she could have stayed there all day without noticing the passage of time. Then she experienced a tumultuous stirring of the heart. She got up again and again, stood before her mirror, and looked at herself like a conscientious author examining his own work critically and telling himself what is wrong with it.

'I am not beautiful enough for him.' This was Eugénie's humble thought, a thought giving rise to much suffering. The poor girl did not do herself justice. But modesty, or rather a fear of being unworthy, is one of the first virtues aroused by love. Eugénie was a good example of the kind of strongly built, lower-middle-class girl whose beauty is rather commonplace, but though her figure may have resembled that of the Venus de Milo,* her appearance was refined by that gentleness of Christian feeling which purifies a woman and gives her a distinction unknown to the classical sculptors. She had a very large head, the masculine but delicate forehead of Phidias' Jupiter,* and grey eyes which sparkled with all the clarity of her chaste life. The features of her round face, at one time fresh and pink, had been coarsened by smallpox that had been mild enough not to leave scars but had destroyed the bloom of the skin; nevertheless, it was still so soft and fine that her mother's pure kiss made a fleeting red mark on it. Her nose was a little too prominent, but was in keeping with her bright red mouth, whose lips, with their thousands of little lines, seemed to express love and kindness. Her

56

throat was perfectly rounded. The curves of her bosom, carefully veiled by her dress, caught the eye and stirred the imagination. She was, no doubt, lacking a little in the gracefulness which comes from elegant clothes, but for connoisseurs her straight, tall figure must have had its own charm. So although Eugénie, tall and strong, had none of the prettiness that pleases the crowd, she was beautiful with that unmistakable beauty which arouses love only in artists. The painter who seeks a typical example of Mary's celestial purity in this world, who expects all women to have those modestly proud eyes perceived by Raphael and those pure contours which are often due to an accident of birth but which can only be preserved or acquired by a modest Christian life, such a painter, longing for so rare a creature, would immediately have seen in Eugénie's face an unconscious innate nobility. He would have seen a world of love beneath her calm brow and something divine in the shape of her eyes and in the movements of her eyelids. Her features, never, as yet, strained or wearied by expressions of pleasure, and the mould of her head, were like the soft lines of a distant horizon beyond tranquil lakes. This calm, glowing face, bordered with light like a pretty, newly opened flower, brought peace to the soul, communicated the charm of the pure conscience reflected in it, and arrested the eye. Eugénie was still at the brink of life, where childish illusions bloom and daisies are picked with a delight unknown in later years. And so, as she looked in the mirror, knowing as yet nothing of love, she said to herself, 'I am too ugly; he won't take any notice of me.'

Then she opened the door of her room, which gave on to the staircase, and craned her neck to listen to the sounds of the household. 'He's not getting up,' she thought, as she heard Nanon's morning cough and the sounds of the good woman coming and going, sweeping the room, lighting the fire, tying up the dog, and talking to the animals in the stable. Straight away Eugénie ran downstairs to Nanon, who was milking the cow.

'Nanon, be a dear, make cream for my cousin's coffee.'

'But, Mademoiselle, I'd have had to see to that yesterday,' said Nanon, who burst out into a hearty laugh. 'I can't make cream. Your cousin's a darling, a real darling. You haven't seen him in his night rig-out of gold and silk. *I* saw him. The material of his shirts is as fine as Monsieur le Curé's surplice.'

'Make pancakes for us, then, Nanon.'

'But, Mademoiselle, who's going to give me wood for the oven, and flour and butter?' said Nanon, who in her capacity as Grandet's prime minister sometimes assumed enormous importance in the eyes of Eugénie and her mother. 'Are we to rob the old man to make a treat in honour of your cousin? *You* ask him for butter, flour, and wood. He's your father, he may give you some. Look, here he is, coming downstairs to see to the food supplies . . . .'

Eugénie fled into the garden, quite terrified when she heard the staircase creaking under her father's tread. She was already feeling the effects of the sensitive modesty and special awareness of happiness which make us think, perhaps not without reason, that our thoughts are engraved on our brows and are clear for others to read. Noticing for the first time the cold bareness of her father's house, the poor girl felt a kind of irritation at her inability to make it appropriate to her cousin's elegance. She felt a passionate need to do something for him. But what? She had no idea. In her honest simplicity she followed the promptings of her angelic nature with no misgivings about her impressions or feelings. The mere sight of her cousin had aroused in her a woman's natural inclinations; they were all the more intense, as now, at the age of twenty-three, she was fully developed in body and mind. For the first time her heart was filled with terror at the sight of her father; she saw in him the master of her fate and felt guilty at keeping some of her thoughts from him. She began to walk hurriedly, surprised that the air she breathed seemed purer and the sun's rays more invigorating; she seemed to draw from them a spiritual warmth, a new life. While she was trying to think up a scheme to get pancakes, a quarrel was developing between Big Nanon and Grandet, something as rare as swallows in winter. Armed with his keys, the old man had come to measure out the supply of provisions for the day.

'Is there any bread left from yesterday?' he asked Nanon.

'Not a crumb, Monsieur.'

Grandet took a large, round, floury loaf, shaped in one of those flat baskets they use for baking in Anjou, and was about to cut it, when Nanon said:

'There are five of us today, Monsieur.'

'That's true,' replied Grandet, 'but your loaf weighs six pounds; that's more than enough. Besides, you'll see, these young men from Paris never eat bread.'

'Do they eat *frippe*, then?' asked Nanon.

In Anjou, *frippe*, a local dialect word, means what is spread on the bread, from butter, the commonest *frippe*, to apricot jam, the grandest *frippe* of all. Everyone who, in childhood, has licked off the *frippe* and left the bread will understand the significance of Nanon's question.

'No,' answered Grandet, 'they eat neither *frippe* nor bread. They are rather like girls ready for marriage.'

Having given orders for the meagre menu of the day, the old man was about to go to his fruit store (first closing his pantry, however), when Nanon stopped him and said, 'Do give me some flour and butter, Monsieur, and I'll make pancakes for the children.'

'Are you going to ransack the house because of my nephew?'

'I wasn't thinking any more of your nephew than of your dog, no more than you were thinking of him yourself. And you've only left out six lumps of sugar for me. I need eight.'

'Well, well, Nanon, I've never seen you like that before. What are you thinking of? Are you the mistress here? You will get only six lumps of sugar.'

'And what about your nephew? What will he sweeten his coffee with?'

'With two lumps. I'll do without, myself.'

'Do without sugar at your age! I'd rather buy you some from my own pocket.'

59

'Mind your own business.'

In spite of the fall in the price of sugar, in the cooper's eyes it was still the most valuable of the imports from the colonies. For him it was still worth six francs a pound. The economical use of it, a duty in the days of the Empire,* had become the most inveterate of his habits. All women, even the most stupid, can use wiles to attain their ends. Nanon dropped the matter of the sugar in order to get the pancakes.

'Mademoiselle,' she called through the window. 'Don't you want pancakes?'

'No, no,' answered Eugénie.

'Alright, Nanon,' said Grandet as he heard his daughter's voice. 'Here you are.' He opened the bin where the flour was kept, measured some out, and added a few ounces of butter to the piece he had already cut.

'I shall need wood to heat the oven,' said the implacable Nanon.

'Well, take what you need,' he said gloomily. 'But, in that case, make a fruit-tart for us and cook the whole dinner in the oven, so that you won't have to make two fires.'

'Goodness me,' cried Nanon. 'You don't need to tell me that.' Grandet gave his faithful minister an almost paternal glance. 'Mademoiselle,' the cook called out, 'we'll have pancakes.' Père Grandet came back, carrying his fruit, and arranged one plateful on the kitchen table. 'Look, Monsieur,' Nanon said, 'what lovely boots your nephew has. What good leather and how nice it smells. What should I clean them with? Should I use your egg polish?'

'I think egg would spoil that leather, Nanon. You had better tell him that you don't know how to polish morocco leather, yes, it is morocco. He'll buy something in Saumur himself to shine his boots with. I've heard that they put sugar in the polish to make it gleam.'

'So they're good to eat, then,' said the servant, putting the boots to her nose. 'Well, well, they smell of Madame's eau-de-cologne. Oh, isn't that funny!'

'Funny!' said her master. 'You think it funny to spend more on boots than the man who wears them is worth.'

'Monsieur,' she said, when her master came back from closing the fruit-store. 'Will you not put the stock-pot on once or twice a week because of your . . . .?'

'Yes.'

'I'll have to go to the butcher's.'

'Certainly not; you'll make chicken-broth for us. The tenant-farmers will see you don't lack fowls. But I'm going to tell Cornoiller to kill some crows for me. That game makes the best broth on earth.'

'Is it true, Monsieur, that they eat corpses?'

'What a fool you are, Nanon! Like everyone else, they eat what they can find. Don't we live off the dead? What are inheritances, then?' Père Grandet, having no more orders to give, pulled out his watch and, seeing that he still had half an hour before breakfast, took up his hat, went to his daughter, kissed her, and said, 'Will you come for a walk to my meadows on the banks of the Loire? I have something to do there.'

Eugénie went to put on her stitched straw hat, lined with pink taffeta; then the father and daughter walked down the winding street to the square.

'Where are you off to so early?' asked the lawyer Cruchot, meeting Grandet.

'To have a look at something,' replied the old man, not at all deceived by his friend's early morning walk.

The lawyer knew from experience that whenever Grandet went to have a look at something, there was always an advantage to be gained by going along too. And so he went with him.

'Come along, Cruchot. You are one of my friends. I am going to show you how stupid it is to plant poplars in good land,' Grandet said to the lawyer.

'So you count as nothing the sixty thousand francs you pocketed for the poplars in your meadows by the Loire?' said Maître Cruchot, opening his eyes wide with astonishment. 'Weren't you lucky? . . . To cut your trees at the very moment when there was a shortage of white wood in Nantes, and to sell them for thirty francs!'

Eugénie was listening, unaware that the most solemn moment of her life was approaching, and that the notary's remarks were to cause a sovereign, paternal decree to be pronounced upon her. Grandet had reached the magnificent meadows he owned on the banks of the Loire, where thirty workmen were employed in clearing, filling in, and levelling the ground formerly occupied by the poplars.

'Maître Cruchot, see how much land a poplar takes,' he said to the lawyer. 'Jean,' he called to a workman, 'm-measure right round the s-space with your rule.'

'Eight feet by four,' replied the workman, when he had done so.

'That's a loss of thirty-two feet,' Grandet said to Cruchot. 'I had three hundred poplars in that row, right? Now . . . three h-h-hundred times thirty-t-t-two f-feet eats up the space for f-five h-hundred bundles of hay. Add twice as much again for the spaces down the sides, that's fifteen hundred; as much again for the middle rows. Well, l-let's s-say, a thousand bundles of hay.'

'Well,' said Cruchot to help his friend, 'a thousand bundles of hay are worth six hundred francs.'

'S-s-say tw-tw-elve hundred, counting the three to four hundred francs from the second growth. Well, w-w-work out wh-wh-at the co-co-compound interest on tw-tw-twelve hundred francs at the g-g-going rate amounts to over forty years.'

'About sixty thousand francs', said the lawyer.

'I agree. That w-w-will m-m-make only sixty thousand francs. Well,' continued the winegrower, without stammering, 'two thousand poplars wouldn't give me fifty thousand francs in forty years. So there's a loss on them. I worked that out myself,' said Grandet boastfully. 'Jean,' he went on, 'fill up the holes, except those on the Loire side; plant the poplars I bought there. If they are put in the river, they will get nourishment at the government's expense', he added, turning to Cruchot, and the wart on his nose gave a slight twitch, which had the effect of a very wry smile.

'That's obvious; poplars ought to be planted only on poor soil,' said Cruchot, amazed at Grandet's calculations.

'Y-y-yes, *Monsieur*,' replied the cooper ironically.

Eugénie, who was looking at the magnificent Loire landscape without listening to her father's calculations, soon began to pay attention to what Cruchot was saying when she heard him say to his client, 'Well, you've brought a son-in-law from Paris. All Saumur is talking of nothing but your nephew. I'll soon have a marriage contract to draw up, Père Grandet.'

'You c-c-came out early t-t-to t-t-tell me that,' replied Grandet, twitching his wart as he made this remark. 'Well, my old friend, I'll be frank and t-t-tell wh-wh-what you w-w-want t-t-to kn-kn-know. I'd l-l-like you to kn-kn-know that I'd rather th-th-throw my d-d-daughter into the Loire than g-g-give her to her c-c-cousin. You c-c-can t-t-tell that to the world. But no, l-l-let them all g-g-gossip.'

Everything seemed to swim before Eugénie's eyes when she heard this reply. The faint hopes which were beginning to arise in her heart suddenly blossomed and opened out to form a nosegay of flowers which she saw rent apart and strewn on the ground. Since the previous day, she had been bound to Charles by all the ties of happiness which unite hearts; henceforth suffering was going to strengthen those ties. Is it not the noble destiny of women to be more touched by the trappings of poverty than by the splendours of wealth? How could paternal feeling have been extinguished in her father's heart? What crime was Charles guilty of? The answers to these questions were a mystery to her. Her budding love, itself so profound a mystery, was already being surrounded by mysteries. She walked home, her legs trembling beneath her. When she reached the old, dark street, which had been so full of joy for her, she thought it looked sad and she absorbed the melancholy that time and old buildings had imprinted upon it. She was spared none of the lessons of love. A few steps from the house, she went ahead of her father and, after knocking at the door, waited for him. But Grandet, who saw that there was a newspaper, still in its wrapper, in the lawyer's hand, had said, 'What's the price of government stock today?'

'You won't listen to me, Grandet,' Cruchot replied. 'Buy some, quickly. That still gives twenty per cent profit in two years, apart from the interest at an excellent rate, an income of five thousand livres for an investment of eight thousand francs. The going rate is eighty francs fifty.'

'We shall see,' replied Grandet, rubbing his chin.

'Good God!' said the lawyer.

'Why, what's the matter?' exclaimed Grandet, as Cruchot stuck the paper in front of him, saying:

'Read that.'

Monsieur Grandet, one of the most respected businessmen in Paris, blew his brains out yesterday, after having put in his usual appearance at the stock exchange. He had sent in his resignation to the President of the Chamber of Deputies and had also resigned from his office as judge of the commercial court. The bankruptcies of Messieurs Roguin and Souchet, his stockbroker and his lawyer, have ruined him. The esteem in which Monsieur Grandet was held and his creditworthiness were nevertheless so considerable that he would assuredly have found help amongst the Paris business community. It is regrettable that this honourable man has succumbed to an initial impulse of despair, etc.

'I knew about it,' said the old winegrower to the lawyer.

These words made Maître Cruchot's blood run cold. In spite of his legal imperturbability he felt a shiver down his spine at the thought that the Grandet of Paris had perhaps appealed in vain to the millions of the Grandet of Saumur.

'And his son, he was so cheerful yesterday . . .'

'He doesn't know anything about it yet,' replied Grandet in the same calm tone.

'Goodbye, Monsieur Grandet,' said Cruchot, who now understood the whole situation and went off to reassure President de Bonfons.

When he came into the house, Grandet found breakfast ready. Madame Grandet was already sitting in her raised chair and knitting sleeves for herself for the winter. Eugénie threw her arms round her mother's neck and kissed her with the sudden expression of emotion which is aroused by a secret sorrow.

'You can start breakfast,' said Nanon, coming down the stairs, four at a time. 'The boy is sleeping like a lamb. How pretty he looks with his eyes shut! I went into his room and called him. But for all that, there was no answer.'

'Let him sleep,' said Grandet. 'He'll still wake up early enough today to learn bad news.'

'What's the matter then?' asked Eugénie, putting the two tiny sugar lumps in her coffee. Goodness knows how few grams they weighed, for Grandet amused himself in his spare moments by cutting them up. Madame Grandet, who had not dared to ask the question, looked at her husband.

'His father has blown his brains out.'

'My uncle? . . . .' said Eugénie.

'Poor young man!' cried Madame Grandet.

'Yes, poor,' continued Grandet, 'he hasn't a penny.'

'Well, he's sleeping as if he were king of the earth,' said Nanon gently.

Eugénie stopped eating. Her heart was filled with anguish, in the way a woman's heart is filled when compassion, aroused for the first time by the misfortune of the man she loves, overflows her whole being. The poor girl began to cry.

'You didn't know your uncle, why are you crying?' said her father, with a look like a famished tiger's, a look, no doubt, that he would often cast at his piles of gold.

'But, Monsieur, who wouldn't be filled with pity for the poor young man, who's sleeping like a log and doesn't know what's happened to him?' said the servant.

'I wasn't speaking to you, Nanon. Hold your tongue.'

At that moment Eugénie learned that a woman in love must always hide her feelings. She made no reply.

'I hope, Madame Grandet, that you won't say anything to him about this before I come back,' continued the old man. 'I have to go and see to the straightening of the ditch by my meadows along the road. I'll be back at twelve for lunch and I'll talk to my nephew about his affairs. As for you, Mademoiselle Eugénie, if you're crying for that over-dressed dandy, that's enough, my child. He'll be off to the Indies in no time. You'll never see him again . . .'

The father took his gloves from the rim of his hat, put them on with his usual composure, and pushed them firmly into place by smoothing down the fingers of each hand with the fingers of the other. Then he went out.

'Oh, mama, I can't breathe,' cried Eugénie when she was alone with her mother. 'I have never felt pain like this before.'

Madame Grandet, seeing her daughter turn pale, opened the window to let in the fresh air. 'I feel better now,' said Eugénie a moment later.

This nervous reaction, in someone who till then had appeared calm and unemotional, upset Madame Grandet; she looked at her daughter with the intuitive sympathy mothers have for the object of their love, and guessed everything. But, indeed, the lives of the two famous Hungarian sisters,* joined to each other by an error of nature had not been more intimately linked than those of Eugénie and her mother; they were always together in the bay-window, together at church, and breathing the same air as they slept.

'My poor child!' said Madame Grandet, drawing Eugénie's head to her breast.

At these words, the girl lifted up her head, gave her mother a questioning look as if to penetrate her innermost thoughts, and said, 'But why send him to the Indies? If he's in trouble, oughtn't he to stay here? Isn't he our nearest relative?'

'Yes, dear, that would be very natural. But your father has his reasons. We must respect them.'

The mother and daughter said no more and sat down, the one on her raised chair, the other on her little armchair, and they both resumed their work. Then, overcome with gratitude for her mother's remarkable sympathetic understanding, Eugénie kissed her hand and said, 'How

66

kind you are, dear mama!' At these words, the mother's old, tired face, worn by long suffering, lit up. 'Do you like him?' asked Eugénie.

Madame Grandet replied only with a smile. Then, after a moment's silence, she whispered, 'Are you in love with him already? That wouldn't be right.'

'Why not?' asked Eugénie. 'You like him. Nanon likes him. Why shouldn't I like him? Come, mama, let's set the table for his breakfast.' She threw down her work and her mother followed suit, saying, 'You're crazy.' But she was happy to excuse her daughter's folly and even to share it. Eugénie called Nanon.

'What do you want now, Mademoiselle?'

'Nanon, you'll have cream by twelve o'clock, won't you?'

'Oh, by twelve o'clock, yes,' answered the old servant.

'Well, make his coffee good and strong. I have heard Monsieur des Grassins say that in Paris they make the coffee very strong. Put in a lot.'

'And where do you think I'll get it from?'

'Buy some.'

'And suppose I run into Monsieur?'

'He is down at his meadows.'

'I'll go right away. But, when I went for the wax-candle, Monsieur Fessard already asked if the Three Wise Men were staying with us. The whole town will learn about our lavish goings-on.'

'If your father notices anything, he is quite capable of beating us,' said Madame Grandet.

'Alright, he'll beat us. We'll go down on our knees and take his blows.'

Madame Grandet's only reply was to raise her eyes to heaven. Nanon put on her bonnet and went out. Eugénie laid a tablecloth and then went to the loft to fetch some grapes; she had amused herself by stringing them up there in bunches. She walked quietly along the corridor so as not to awaken her cousin and, when she came to his door, could not help listening to his regular breathing.

'Misfortune is awake, while he sleeps,' she thought.

She took the greenest vine-leaves, arranged her grapes as attractively as an experienced head waiter might have done, and brought them in triumph to the table. In the kitchen, she helped herself to the pears her father had counted out for lunch and arranged them in a pyramid with leaves around them. She came and went, skipped and hopped to and fro. She would gladly have ransacked every room in her father's house, but everything was locked and he had the keys. Nanon came back with two new-laid eggs. When she saw the eggs, Eugénie wanted to throw her arms round the old servant's neck.

'The farmer from La Lande had some in his basket; I asked him for some and he gave me these, the nice man, so as to keep me sweet.'

After two hours of careful work, during which Eugénie left her sewing twenty times to see to the coffee boiling or to listen to the sound of her cousin getting up, she managed to prepare a very simple, inexpensive lunch but one which was a terrible departure from the inveterate habits of the household. The midday meal was eaten standing up. Everyone took a little bread, a piece of fruit or some butter, and a glass of wine. As she looked at the table drawn up to the fire, at one of the armchairs put in front of the place set for her cousin, at the two platefuls of fruit, the egg-cup, the bottle of white wine, the bread, and the sugar piled up on a saucer, Eugénie trembled in every limb; only then did she think of the looks her father would give her if he happened to walk in at that moment. So she kept glancing at the clock, to calculate if her cousin would have time to eat before the old man came back.

'Don't worry, Eugénie, if your father comes in, I shall take responsibility for everything,' said Madame Grandet.

Eugénie could not restrain her tears.

'Oh, how kind you are, mother,' she exclaimed. 'I've never loved you enough.'

After pottering around his room for a long time, humming to himself, Charles came downstairs at last. Fortunately it was still only eleven o'clock. Like a true Parisian, he had dressed with as much care as if he had been staying at the country house of the noble lady who was travelling in Scotland. He came in with that friendly, happy expression which is so becoming to young people and which filled Eugénie with a melancholy joy. He had taken in good part the destruction of his castles in Anjou and greeted his aunt very cheerfully.

'Did you sleep well, dear aunt? And what about you, cousin?'

'Yes, thank you, Monsieur. Did you?' replied Madame Grandet.

'Oh, I slept splendidly.'

'You must be hungry, cousin,' said Eugénie. 'Come and eat.'

'But I never eat before twelve, which is when I get up. Still, I ate so badly on the way, that I'll fall in with your suggestion. Besides . . .' He took out the most charming flat watch that Bréguet* had ever made. 'Goodness me, but it's only eleven o'clock. I've got up early.'

'Early? . . . .' said Madame Grandet.

'Yes, but I wanted to unpack my things. Yes, I'd be quite happy to have a snack, nothing much, a chicken or a partridge.'

'Holy Virgin!' cried Nanon, when she heard this remark.

'A partridge,' thought Eugénie, who would, just then, have given all her savings for a partridge.

'Come and sit down,' said his aunt.

The dandy dropped into the armchair like a pretty woman taking up her position on a sofa. Eugénie and her mother brought up chairs and sat down near him in front of the fire.

'Do you always live here?' asked Charles, who thought the room even uglier in the daylight than it was by candle-light.

'Always,' replied Eugénie, gazing at him, 'except during the grape harvest. Then we go and help Nanon, and we all stay at the Abbey of Noyers.'

'Do you never go out anywhere?'

'Sometimes on Sundays after vespers, when it's fine, we walk to the bridge or go and watch the hay being mown.'

'Have you a theatre?'

'Go to the theatre to see actors!' cried Madame Grandet. 'But, Monsieur, don't you know that's a mortal sin?'

'Here you are, my fine young gentleman,' said Nanon, bringing in the eggs. 'We'll give you the chickens in the shell.'

'Oh, new-laid eggs', said Charles, who, in the way of people used to luxury, already thought no more of his partridge. 'But that's delicious; would you have any butter to go with them, my good girl?'

'Oh, butter. But then you won't get pancakes later,' said the servant.

'Go on, give him some butter, Nanon,' cried Eugénie.

The girl watched her cousin closely as he cut his bread into little pieces, and took as much pleasure in the sight as the most sentimental Paris shopgirl does when she sees the triumph of innocence in a melodrama. It is true that Charles, brought up by a charming mother, with his manners perfected by a woman of fashion, was as attractive, elegant, and dainty in his movements as any fashionable little coquette. A girl's sympathy and affection have a truly magnetic power, so that Charles, seeing himself the object of his aunt's and cousin's attentions, could not escape the influence of the feelings which were directed towards him and, as it were, flooding over him. He gave Eugénie a glance sparkling with affectionate good nature, a glance that seemed to smile. As he looked at Eugénie, he became aware of the exquisite harmony and purity of her features, of her innocent demeanour, of the magical brightness of her eyes, where young thoughts of love were shining and desire knew nothing of sensual pleasure.

'Indeed, dear cousin, if you were in a front box, in full evening-dress at the Opera, I assure you my aunt would be quite right. You would make the men commit many sins of covetousness and the women sins of jealousy.'

This compliment made Eugénie's heart miss a beat and

then throb with joy, though she did not understand a word of it.

'Oh, cousin, you're making fun of a poor little country-girl.'

'If you knew me well, cousin, you would know that I detest making fun of people. It dries up the heart, offends every feeling . . .' And he swallowed down his finger of bread and butter with enjoyment. 'No, I am probably not witty enough to make fun of others, and this failing does me a lot of harm. In Paris, they know how to ruin a man by saying, "He has a good heart." That sentence means, "The poor chap's as stupid as a rhinoceros." But as I'm rich and am known to be able to knock down a dummy first shot at thirty paces with any kind of pistol and in the open air, the mockers respect me.'

'Your words show you have a kind heart, nephew.'

'You are wearing a very pretty ring,' said Eugénie. 'Would you mind if I asked to look at it?'

Charles, taking off his ring, held out his hand; Eugénie blushed as her fingertips touched her cousin's nails.

'Look, mother, what beautiful workmanship!'

'Oh, there's a lot of gold in that,' said Nanon, as she brought in the coffee.

'What's that?' asked Charles, laughing.

And he pointed to a brown oblong jug, of glazed earthenware, lined with porcelain and surrounded by a fringe of ashes, in which the coffee was falling to the bottom and coming back to the surface of the boiling liquid.

'That's boiled coffee,' said Nanon.

'Oh, I shall leave behind at least some useful trace of my stay here, dear aunt. You are very much behind the times. I'll teach you to make good coffee in a Chaptal* coffee-pot.'

He tried to explain to them how a Chaptal coffee-pot works.

'Oh dear,' said Nanon. 'If it's such a business, I'd have to spend my whole life at it. I'll never make coffee that way, never. And who would see to the grass for our cow while I was making the coffee?'

71

'*I* would make it,' said Eugénie.

'What a child you are,' said Madame Grandet, looking at her daughter.

At these words, which recalled the trouble about to overwhelm this unfortunate young man, the three women fell silent and looked at him pityingly in a way that surprised him.

'What's the matter, cousin?'

'Sh!' said Madame Grandet to Eugénie, who was going to speak. 'You know, my dear, that your father has undertaken to tell Monsieur.'

'Call me Charles,' said young Grandet.

'Oh, your name is Charles. That's a nice name,' exclaimed Eugénie.

Expected misfortunes nearly always happen. At that moment, Nanon, Madame Grandet, and Eugénie, who could not think of the old cooper's return without a shudder, heard the sound of a familiar knock.

'That's papa,' said Eugénie.

She took away the saucer of sugar, leaving a few lumps on the tablecloth. Nanon removed the egg plate. Madame Grandet started up like a frightened deer. It was a moment of complete panic that amazed Charles, who could not understand it.

'But what's the matter?' he asked.

'My father's coming,' said Eugénie.

'What of it? . . .'

Monsieur Grandet came in, looked straight at the table and at Charles; he took in everything.

'Aha, you've made a party for your nephew; that's fine, very fine, indeed very fine,' he said without stammering. 'When the cat's away, the mice will play.'

'A party? . . .' thought Charles, quite unable to conceive the slightest idea of the diet and customs of this household.

'Give me my glass, Nanon,' said the miser.

Eugénie brought the glass. Grandet took from his pocket a horn-handled knife with a large blade, cut a slice of bread, took a little butter, spread it carefully, and began

72

to eat standing up. At that moment, Charles was putting sugar in his coffee. Père Grandet noticed the sugar lumps, looked closely at his wife, who turned pale, and took three steps forward. He leaned over and whispered into the poor woman's ear, 'Where did you get all that sugar from?'

'Nanon went to Fessard's for it; we didn't have any.'

It is impossible to imagine the profound concern aroused in the three women by this scene, enacted without a word. Nanon had left her kitchen and was looking into the room to see what would happen. Charles tasted his coffee and, finding it too bitter, looked for the sugar, which Grandet had already put away.

'What are you looking for, nephew?' he asked.

'The sugar.'

'Put some milk in, that will sweeten your coffee,' replied the master of the house.

Eugénie brought back the saucer of sugar that Grandet had already put away, and placed it on the table, looking calmly at her father. The Parisian girl who, to help her lover escape, takes the weight of a silken ladder on her weak arms, certainly shows no more courage than Eugénie did in putting the sugar back on the table. The lover will reward the Parisian girl, who will proudly display a beautiful bruised arm, but every bruise will be bathed in tears and kisses and cured by love. Charles, however, would never know the secret of the deep emotions which were breaking his cousin's heart as she stood devastated by the old cooper's look.

'You're not eating, wife.'

The poor helot came forward, miserably cut a slice of bread, and took a pear. Eugénie boldly offered her father grapes, saying, 'Taste some of my fruit, papa. You'll have some, cousin, won't you? I got these lovely bunches especially for you.'

'Oh, if they're not stopped, they'll plunder all Saumur for you, nephew. When you've finished, we'll go into the garden together. I've got some things to tell you which are not so sweet.'

73

Eugénie and her mother looked at Charles with an expression the young man could not mistake.

'What do you mean by those words, uncle? Since my poor mother's death . . .' (at these words his voice softened) 'no worse misfortune is possible for me.'

'Who can know the afflictions God sends to try us with, nephew?' said his aunt.

'Ta, ta, ta, ta,' said Grandet. 'Now the nonsense is starting. I am sorry to see, nephew, that you have such pretty, white hands.' He showed Charles the fists, rather like shoulders of mutton, that nature had affixed to the ends of his own arms. 'Those are hands fit for raking in the cash! You've been brought up to put your feet into the fine leather we use for making wallets for our bills of exchange. That's bad, very bad!'

'What do you mean, uncle? I'll be hanged if I understand a word of what you're saying.'

'Come with me,' said Grandet.

The miser snapped his knife-blade shut, drank what was left of his white wine, and opened the door.

'Be brave, cousin!'

The tone of the girl's voice sent a chill through Charles, who, a prey to deadly anxiety, followed his terrible relative. Eugénie, her mother, and Nanon went into the kitchen, impelled by an invincible curiosity to watch the two actors in the scene that was about to take place in the damp little garden. To start with, the uncle walked there in silence with his nephew. It did not embarrass Grandet to tell Charles of his father's death, but he felt a kind of compassion at knowing that his nephew was penniless and he tried to find words to soften the impact of this cruel truth. 'You have lost your father!' That was not hard to say. Fathers usually die before their children. But, 'You are quite without any means at all.' All the woes of the earth were summed up in these words. And for the third time the miser went up and down the central path, whose gravel crunched beneath his feet. In the crises of life, our feelings become strongly linked to the place where the joy or sorrow overwhelms us. And so it was with very special attention that Charles studied the boxwood edges

74

in the little garden, the pale, falling leaves, the crumbling walls, and the strange shapes of the fruit trees, picturesque details which were to remain imprinted on his mind, for ever associated with this crucial moment by the tricks of memory peculiar to strong feelings.

'It's very warm, very fine,' said Grandet, drawing a deep breath.

'Yes, uncle, but why? . . .'

'Well, my boy,' continued his uncle. 'I've bad news to tell you. Your father's very ill . . .'

'Then what am I doing here?' said Charles. 'Nanon!' he shouted, 'get post-horses! Surely I can find a carriage somewhere in the place,' he added, turning to his uncle, who stood motionless.

'Horses and carriage are useless,' replied Grandet, looking at Charles, who stared at him, speechless. 'Yes, my poor boy, you have guessed correctly. He is dead. But that's nothing; there's worse to come. He has blown his brains out . . .'

'My father?'

'Yes, but that's nothing. The newspapers gossip about it as if they had a right to. Look, read this.'

Grandet, who had borrowed Cruchot's newspaper, placed the fatal article before Charles's eyes. At that moment the poor young man, still a boy, still at the age when feelings express themselves uninhibitedly, burst into tears.

'Just as well,' thought Grandet. 'His eyes were frightening me. He is crying, so he'll be alright.' 'But that's not the worst of it, my poor nephew,' continued Grandet aloud, without knowing whether Charles was listening to him. 'That's nothing, you'll get over it, but . . .'

'Never! never! My father! my father!'

'He has ruined you. You haven't a penny.'

'What does that matter? Where is my father, my father?'

The awful sound of his tears and sobs rang out and re-echoed between the garden walls. Overcome with pity, the three women wept; tears are as infectious as laughter

75

can be. Charles, without listening to his uncle, ran into the courtyard, found his way to the stairs, went up to his room, and threw himself across his bed, burying his face in the sheets to cry undisturbed, away from his relatives.

'We must let the first shower pass,' said Grandet, returning to the room where Eugénie and her mother had hastily resumed their places and, having wiped their eyes, were working with trembling hands. 'But that young man is good for nothing. He is more concerned with the dead than with money.'

Eugénie shuddered to hear her father talk in this way about the holiest of sorrows. From that moment she began to be critical of her father. Although they were muffled, Charles's sobs could be heard throughout the resonant house and his deep moans, which seemed to come from beneath the ground, did not stop till the evening, after becoming gradually fainter.

'Poor young man!' said Madame Grandet.

It was a fatal exclamation. Père Grandet looked at his wife, at Eugénie, and at the sugar bowl. He remembered the extraordinary lunch prepared for his unfortunate relative and took up his stance in the middle of the room.

'Well, I hope, Madame Grandet, that you are not going to continue your extravagances,' he said with his usual composure. 'I don't give you MY money to stuff that young man with sugar.'

'My mother has nothing to do with it,' said Eugénie. 'It was I who . . .'

'Is it because you have come of age that you want to cross me?' continued Grandet, interrupting his daughter. 'Think, Eugénie . . .'

'Your brother's son should never lack anything in your house, father . . .'

'Ta, ta, ta, ta,' said the cooper in rising semitones, 'my brother's son here, my nephew there. Charles is nothing to us. He hasn't a farthing. His father has gone bankrupt. And when this dandy has wept his fill, he'll clear out of here. I don't want him to cause a revolution in my house.'

'What does it mean to go bankrupt, father?'

'To go bankrupt is to commit the most dishonourable of all actions that can dishonour a man,' replied the father.

'It must be a very great sin and our brother's soul may be damned,' said Madame Grandet.

'There's your usual religious language,' he said to his wife, shrugging his shoulders. 'To go bankrupt, Eugénie,' he continued, 'is a theft which unfortunately is protected by law. People gave their goods to Guillaume Grandet on the strength of his reputation for honesty and fair dealing. Then he took all they had, leaving them only their eyes to weep with. A highway robber is preferable to a bankrupt. A highwayman attacks you, but you can defend yourself and he risks his life. But the other . . . In short, Charles is dishonoured.'

These words smote the poor girl's heart with the full force of their significance. She was as upright as a flower from the depths of the forest is delicate, and she knew nothing of worldly wisdom, neither its specious arguments nor its sophistry. So she accepted the appalling explanation of bankruptcy that her father gave her on purpose, without telling her of the distinction between an involuntary and an intentional bankruptcy.

'But, father, couldn't you have prevented this misfortune?'

'My brother didn't consult me. Besides, he owes four million.'

'What's a million, then, father?' she asked with the *naïveté* of a child who thinks she can have whatever she wants immediately.

'Two million?'* said Grandet, 'but that's two million twenty-sous pieces, and you need five twenty-sous pieces to make five francs.'

'Oh, my goodness,' cried Eugénie, 'how could my uncle have had four million of his own? Can there be anyone else in France who has as many millions?' (Père Grandet stroked his chin and smiled, and his wart seemed to dilate.) '—But what will become of my cousin Charles?'

77

'He's going to leave for the Indies, where, following his father's wishes, he will try to make his fortune.'

'But has he the money to go there?'

'I'll pay for his journey . . . as far as . . . yes, as far as Nantes.'

Eugénie jumped up and threw her arms round her father's neck.

'Oh, father, how kind you are!'

She hugged him so warmly that Grandet became almost ashamed, for his conscience was pricking him a little.

'Does it take a long time to save up a million?' she asked.

'Indeed it does!' said the cooper. 'You know what a napoleon is. Well, you need fifty thousand of them to make a million.'

'Mama, we shall have novenas* said for him.'

'That's just what I was thinking,' replied her mother.

'That's right, always spending money', said her father. 'Do you think we're made of money here?'

Just then a dull moan, more mournful than all the others, could be heard coming from the loft, and it petrified Eugénie and her mother with terror.

'Nanon, go upstairs to see if he's not killing himself,' said Grandet. 'Now then,' he continued, turning to his wife and daughter, who had turned pale at these words, 'no nonsense, you two. I'll leave you now. I'm going to see our Dutch buyers, who are going away today. Then I'll go and see Cruchot and have a chat with him about all this.'

He went out. When Grandet had shut the door behind him, Eugénie and her mother breathed more freely. Before that morning the daughter had never felt constrained by her father's presence. But in the last few hours her feelings and her ideas had been changing minute by minute.

'Mama, how many louis does a cask of wine fetch?'

'Your father sells his for between a hundred and a hundred and fifty francs, sometimes for two hundred, from what I've heard.'

'When his harvest amounts to fourteen hundred casks of wine . . .'

'Really, my dear, I don't know what that comes to; your father never talks to me about his business affairs.'

'But then papa must be rich.'

'Perhaps. But Monsieur Cruchot told me that your father bought Froidfond two years ago. That will have left him short of money.'

Eugénie, not being any the wiser about her father's means, abandoned her calculations.

'He didn't even see me, the dear boy,' said Nanon, returning to the room. He's sprawled on his bed like a calf, weeping like a Magdalen, something terrible. What's distressing the poor, nice young man?'

'Let's go and comfort him quickly, mama, and if there's a knock at the door we'll come down again.'

Madame Grandet was defenceless against the tones of her daughter's voice. Eugénie was sublime, she had become a woman. With beating hearts they both went up to Charles's room. The door was open. The young man neither heard nor saw them. Immersed in tears, he was uttering inarticulate moans.

'How he loves his father,' whispered Eugénie.

In the tone of these words it was impossible not to discern the hopes of a heart unwittingly filled with love. Madame Grandet gave her daughter a concerned, maternal look and whispered, 'Take care, you may fall in love with him.'

'Fall in love with him!' replied Eugénie. 'Oh, if you only knew what father said!'

Charles turned round and caught sight of his aunt and cousin.

'I have lost my father, my poor father! If he had confided to me the secret of his misfortune, we would have worked together to repair the damage. Oh, God! my kind father! I was so sure of seeing him again that I think I kissed him goodbye rather coldly.'

Sobs choked his voice.

'We'll pray fervently for him. Resign yourself to God's will,' said Madame Grandet.

'Cousin, take heart,' said Eugénie. 'Your loss is irreparable, so think now of saving your honour.'

With that instinctive feminine tact which knows how to handle every situation, even that of comforting a mourner, Eugénie wanted to distract her cousin from his grief by turning his attention to himself.

'My honour?. . .' cried the young man abruptly, brushing his hair back from his face. And he sat up on the bed and folded his arms. '—Ah! that's right. My uncle was saying that my father had gone bankrupt.' He uttered a heart-rending cry and hid his face in his hands.—'Leave me alone, cousin. Oh God! Oh God! Forgive my father. He must have suffered greatly.'

There was something touching yet appalling in the sight of this sincere, youthful grief, quite spontaneous and uncalculating. It was a grief that needed privacy and this the simple hearts of Eugénie and her mother understood when Charles made a sign, asking them to leave him alone. They went downstairs, silently resumed their places at the window, and worked for about an hour without saying a word. In the surreptitious glance that Eugénie had cast at the young man's belongings—and a girl's glance sees everything in the twinkling of an eye—she had noticed the pretty knick-knacks of his toilet equipment, his scissors and razors inlaid with gold. This glimpse of luxury in the midst of grief made Charles even more interesting to her, perhaps by contrast. Never before had so serious an event, so dramatic a sight, struck the imagination of these two beings, whose lives hitherto had always been spent in quiet seclusion.

'Mama,' said Eugénie, 'let's wear mourning for my uncle.'

'Your father will decide about that,' replied Madame Grandet.

They fell silent again. Eugénie plied her needle with a mechanical regularity which would have revealed to any observer that many thoughts were filling her mind. This adorable girl's first wish was to share her cousin's mourning. About four o'clock a sharp knock at the door filled Madame Grandet's heart with apprehension.

'What's the matter with your father?' she said to her daughter.

The winegrower came in, in high spirits. After taking off his gloves, he rubbed his hands together so vigorously that he would have taken the skin off, had it not been tanned like Russian leather, though it did not smell of larches and incense. He walked up and down. He looked out at the weather. At last he let out his secret.

'My dear,' he said without stammering, 'I've caught the lot of them. Our wine is sold. The Dutch and the Belgians were due to leave this morning. I walked up and down the town square in front of their inn, looking rather stupid. What's his name, you know who I mean, came up to me. The owners of all the good vineyards are keeping their harvest and want to wait. I didn't stop them. Our Belgian friend was desperate. I could see that. So we made a bargain. He is taking our harvest at two hundred francs a cask, half cash down. I have been paid in gold. The promissory notes have been made out. Here's six louis for you. In three months the price of wine will go down.'

These last words were uttered calmly but with such profound irony that the people of Saumur, assembled at that moment in the square and devastated by the news of the sale that Grandet had just made, would have shuddered had they heard them. A sudden panic would have made the price of wine fall by fifty per cent.

'You have a thousand casks this year, father?' asked Eugénie.

'Yes, little girl.'

This expression revealed the highest degree of happiness in the old cooper.

'That makes two hundred thousand five-sous pieces.'

'Yes, Mademoiselle Grandet.'

'Then, father, you can easily help Charles.'

The astonishment, the fury, the stupefaction of Balthazar,* when he saw *Mene, Mene, Tekel, Upharsin* written on the wall, were as nothing compared to Grandet's cold rage when, having forgotten all about his nephew, he found the

81

young man lodged in his daughter's heart and calculations.

'That's enough. Since that young fop set foot in my house, everything's been turned upside down. You take it upon yourselves to buy sweets, to make parties and celebrations. I don't want goings-on of that kind. At my age, I know how to conduct my household, don't I? Besides, I won't take lessons from my daughter or anyone else. I shall do what is appropriate for my nephew. It's not for you to stick your nose into the business. As for you, Eugénie,' he added, turning towards her, 'don't speak to me about that again, or I'll send you to the Abbey at Noyers with Nanon, see if I don't, and no later than tomorrow, if you say any more. But where is the boy? Has he come downstairs?'

'No, dear,' replied Madame Grandet.

'Well, what's he doing, then?'

'He is weeping for his father,' replied Eugénie.

Grandet looked at his daughter and could not find a word to say. He, too, had some of a father's feelings.

After taking one or two turns round the room, he went quickly upstairs to his office to consider making an investment in government stock. The timber felled in two thousand acres of woodland had brought him in six hundred thousand francs. If he added to that amount the money from the sale of his poplars, and his income from last year and the current year, not counting the two hundred thousand francs from the bargain he had just concluded, he had available a sum of nine hundred thousand francs. The twenty per cent to be made on a short-term investment in stock quoted at seventy francs was tempting. He jotted down his calculations on the newspaper in which his brother's death was announced, hearing but paying no attention to his nephew's moans. Nanon came and knocked on the wall to ask her master to come downstairs; dinner was ready. On the last step of the staircase, as he went under the archway, Grandet was saying to himself, 'Since I'll get my eight per cent interest as well, I'll do it. In two years I'll have fifteen hundred thousand francs, which I shall withdraw from Paris in real gold.'

'Well, so where's my nephew?'

'He says he doesn't want anything to eat,' replied Nanon. 'It's not good for him to go without food.'

'That's so much saved,' replied her master.

'Well, yes,' she said.

'Bah! he won't weep for ever. Hunger drives the wolf from the wood.'

It was a strangely silent dinner.

'My dear,' said Madame Grandet, when the cloth had been removed. 'We must go into mourning.'

'Really, Madame Grandet, what will you think of next in order to spend money. Mourning is in the heart, not in clothes.'

'But mourning for a brother is obligatory and the church orders us to . . .'

'Buy your mourning out of your six louis. You can get me a crêpe band; that'll be enough for me.'

Eugénie raised her eyes to heaven without saying a word. For the first time in her life, her generous instincts, which had been dormant and repressed but were now suddenly awakened, were being constantly wounded. This evening appeared to be like a thousand others of their monotonous existence, but it was certainly the most awful. She sewed without raising her head and did not use the work-box that Charles had despised the previous evening. Madame Grandet knitted her sleeves. Grandet twiddled his thumbs for four hours, lost in the calculations whose outcome was to amaze Saumur the next day. That evening, no one came to see the family. As they sat there, the whole town was ringing with the news of Grandet's cunning transaction, of his brother's bankruptcy, and of his nephew's arrival. To satisfy the need to discuss their common interests, all the upper- and middle-class owners of vineyards in Saumur were at Monsieur des Grassins's house, where they hurled terrible curses against the former mayor. Nanon was spinning and the hum of her spinning-wheel was the only sound to be heard beneath the dingy rafters of the living-room.

'We're not wearing our tongues out,' she said, showing

83

her teeth, which were as large and white as peeled almonds.

'Mustn't wear anything out,' replied Grandet, rousing himself from his meditations. He saw before him the prospect of eight million in three years and was sailing ahead on that long sea of gold. '—Let's go to bed. I'll say goodnight to my nephew for everybody and see if he wants anything to eat.'

Madame Grandet stayed on the first-floor landing to listen to the conversation which was about to take place between Charles and her husband. Eugénie, bolder than her mother, went up two steps.

'Well, nephew, you are in distress. Yes, weep, that's natural. A father is a father. But we have to bear our troubles patiently. I have been looking after your affairs while you have been crying. Come, take heart. Would you like a little glass of wine? Wine costs nothing in Saumur. People offer wine here as they offer a cup of tea in India. —But', went on Grandet, 'you have no light. That's bad, very bad. We must see clearly what we're doing.' Grandet went to the mantelpiece. 'Well, I never!' he cried, 'here's a wax-candle. Where the devil did they unearth a wax-candle from? Those crazy women would tear up the floorboards of my house to cook eggs for this lad.'

When they heard these words, the mother and daughter returned to their rooms and scurried to their beds as quickly as frightened mice returning to their holes.

'So you've got hidden treasure somewhere, Madame Grandet?' said the husband, coming into his wife's room.

'My dear, I am saying my prayers. Wait a moment,' replied the poor mother in a trembling voice.

'May the devil take your god!' muttered Grandet.

Misers do not believe in an afterlife. The present is everything for them. This thought casts a terrible light on the present day, when, more than ever before, money dominates the law, politics, and social behaviour. Institutions, books, men, and doctrines, all conspire to undermine the belief in a life to come, which has been the foundation of the social fabric for eighteen hundred years. Nowadays people have little fear of the grave as a transition period. The future that used to await us beyond the requiem has been transferred to the present. To arrive *per fas et nefas** at the earthly paradise of luxury and vain pleasures, to harden one's heart and mortify the flesh in order to gain fleeting possessions, as in the past one endured martyrdom for the sake of eternal bliss, that is the universal ambition, an ambition, moreover, inscribed everywhere, even in our laws; the legislator is required to have regard to money rather than to justice. When this attitude to life has passed down from the middle to the lower classes, what will become of the country?

'Have you finished, Madame Grandet?' asked the old cooper.

'I am praying for you, my dear.'

'Alright! Goodnight. We'll talk tomorrow morning.'

The poor woman fell asleep like a schoolboy who has not done his homework and who is afraid of being confronted with his teacher's angry face when he wakes up. As she was burying herself in the bedclothes, in terror of hearing anything further, Eugénie, barefoot and in her nightdress, slipped in beside her mother and kissed her on the forehead.

'Oh, kindest of mothers,' she said. 'Tomorrow I'll tell him it was me.'

'No, he'll send you to Noyers. Leave it to me. He won't eat me.'

'Do you hear, mama?'

'What?'

'Well, *he*'s still crying.'

'Go to bed now, dear. Your feet will get cold. The floor is damp.'

Thus passed the momentous day which was to burden the whole future life of the poor, rich heiress, whose sleep was never again to be as sound or as untroubled as it had been up till then. Quite often certain human actions are performed in real life although, in books, they appear improbable. But that may be because we nearly always omit to cast, as it were, a psychological light on our impulsive decisions by failing to reveal the hidden causes that make them inevitable. Perhaps Eugénie's deep-seated passion should be analysed down to its minutest roots, for, as some people were to say sneeringly, it became a disease and influenced her whole existence. Many people prefer to reject the conclusions, rather than to measure the strength of the links, the bonds, and the connections which form the hidden psychological chains that lead from one event to another. So, to observers of human nature, Eugénie's past life will serve as an adequate explanation for her unreflecting *naïveté* and the impulsive expression of her feelings. Feminine pity, that most resourceful of emotions, developed in her heart all the more strongly because her life hitherto had been so calm. And so, disturbed by the day's events, she woke several times in the night to listen to her cousin, thinking that she could hear his sighs which, since the previous day, had been re-echoing in her heart. Sometimes she imagined him dying of grief, sometimes she dreamed he was dying of hunger. Towards morning she was sure she heard a terrible cry. She dressed immediately and at daybreak ran noiselessly to her cousin's room. He had left his door open. The candle had burnt down to the socket of the candlestick. Charles, overcome by natural fatigue, was sleeping, fully dressed, sitting in an armchair with his head fallen on to the bed. He was dreaming, as men do who go to bed on an empty stomach. Eugénie could weep undisturbed. She could admire the handsome young face, mottled by grief, and the eyes, swollen with tears, which, even fast asleep, still seemed to be weeping. Charles could feel Eugénie's presence. He opened his eyes and saw her compassionate look.

'I beg your pardon, cousin,' he said, obviously unaware of time or place.

'There are hearts here that feel for you, cousin, and *we* thought that you might be needing something. You ought to go to bed. You are tiring yourself out, staying up like this.'

'That's true.'

'Well, goodbye.'

86

She fled, both ashamed and happy at having come. Only innocence dares be so bold. Once it is no longer ignorant, Virtue can scheme as well as Vice. Eugénie, who in her cousin's room had not trembled, could scarcely stand when she was back in her own. Her life of ignorance had suddenly come to an end. She argued with herself, she reproached herself over and over again. 'What will he think of me? He will believe I am in love with him.' That was exactly what she most wanted him to believe. True love has an intuition of its own and knows that love begets love. What an event it was in the life of this lonely girl to have gone stealthily to a young man's room! Are there not some thoughts and actions which, in love, for certain hearts amount to a sacred betrothal? An hour later, she went into her mother's room and, as usual, helped her to dress. Then they went and sat down at their places by the window and waited for Grandet, full of the anxiety that, according to temperament, makes the blood run cold or puts one in a fever, oppresses or dilates the heart, when one is dreading a scene or a punishment. This is a very natural feeling, which even domestic animals experience to such an extent that they utter cries at the slight pain of a master's beating, though they make no sound when they hurt themselves inadvertently. The old man came downstairs but he spoke absent-mindedly to his wife, kissed Eugénie, and sat down to breakfast without appearing to think of his previous evening's threats.

'What's happened to my nephew? The boy doesn't get in the way, does he.'

'He's still asleep, Monsieur,' Nanon replied.

'So much the better; he doesn't need wax-candles,' said Grandet jokingly.

This unwonted mildness, this brittle good humour, surprised Madame Grandet, who looked very closely at her husband. The old man (the *bonhomme*)* . . . . Perhaps it is appropriate to remark here that in Touraine, Anjou, Poitou, and Brittany the word *bonhomme*, which has often been used already to indicate Grandet, is applied to the most cruel as well as to the most kindly of men as soon as they have reached a certain age. The appellation pronounces no judgement on individual benevolence. The *bonhomme*, then, took up his hat and gloves, saying, 'I'm going for a stroll round the square, so that I can see the Cruchots.'

'Eugénie, your father has certainly got something on his mind.'

In fact, Grandet, who slept little, spent half his nights in making the preliminary calculations which gave his opinions, his observations, and his plans their astonishing accuracy and guaranteed them the constant success that amazed the people of Saumur. All human power is a mixture of time and patience. Powerful men know what they want, then watch and wait. A miser's life is the unremitting exercise of every human faculty in the service of his own personality. He is sustained by only two feelings, vanity and self-interest; but since self-interest is, in a sense, a tangible form of a proper understanding of vanity, the unceasing testimony to a real superiority, vanity and self-interest are two parts of one and the same whole, egotism. Perhaps that explains the enormous interest aroused by a skilful presentation of misers on the stage. Everyone has one link with these characters who both outrage and incorporate all human feelings. Where is the man who does not want something, and how can anyone get what he wants in society without money? Grandet really had something on his mind, as his wife put it. Like all misers, he had a permanent need to compete with other men, to win their money from them legally. To get the better of others, surely that was to exercise power, to give oneself the right always to despise those weaklings who let themselves be devoured here on earth. Oh, who has properly understood the lamb lying peacefully at God's feet, that most touching symbol of all earthly victims and of their future, in short, Suffering and Weakness glorified? That is the lamb the miser allows to grow fat; he then pens it, kills it, cooks it, eats it, and despises it. The provender of misers is made up of money and contempt. During the night, Grandet's ideas had followed another course;

that accounted for his mildness. He had hatched a plot to make fools of the Parisians, to twist them round his fingers, to lick them into whatever shape he liked, and to mould them like clay, to make them come and go, sweat, hope, and turn pale, all for his own entertainment, for him, the former cooper, who lived in a dingy room and climbed a worm-eaten staircase in his house in Saumur. He had thought about his nephew. He wanted to save his dead brother's honour without it costing him or his nephew a penny. His capital was going to be invested for three years. All he had to do now was to manage his property. So he needed fodder for his mischievous activity and he had found it in his brother's bankruptcy. Having nothing to squeeze between his paws, he wanted to pulverize the Parisians for Charles's benefit and show himself to be a good brother at little cost. The family honour counted for so little in his plan that his good intentions can be compared to the gambler's need to see a game played well even though he has no stake in it. He required the Cruchots for his scheme, but he did not want to go in search of them. He had decided to make them come to him, and to make a start that very evening on the comedy he had just planned, so that the next day, without it costing him a farthing, he would be an object of admiration for the whole town.

A Miser's Promises and Lovers' Vows

In her father's absence, Eugénie had the happiness of being able to look after her beloved cousin openly, to lavish the treasures of her pity on him without fear. Pity is one of the qualities in which women are sublimely superior; it is the only one that they are willing to reveal, the only one they will forgive men for allowing them a greater share of. Three or four times Eugénie went to listen to her cousin's breathing, to find out if he was asleep or awake. Then, when he got up, the cream, the coffee, the eggs, the fruit, the plates, the glass, every detail connected with his breakfast was the object of her special care. She ran briskly up the old staircase to listen to the sounds her cousin was making. Was he getting dressed? Was he still crying? She went right up to his door.

'Cousin Charles?'

'Yes, cousin?'

'Will you come downstairs for breakfast or have it in your room?'

'Wherever you like.'

'How are you feeling?'

'My dear cousin, I am ashamed to say I am hungry.'

For Eugénie, this conversation through the door was like an episode in a novel.

'Very well then, we'll bring you breakfast in your room so as not to annoy my father.' She went down to the kitchen, as light as a bird. 'Nanon, go and do his room.'

The staircase, which she had gone up and down so often, where the least sounds reverberated, seemed to Eugénie to have lost its decrepit appearance. She saw it glowing with light, it spoke to her, it was young like her, young like the love it was serving. Her mother, her kind, indulgent mother, was willing to go along with the caprices of her love, and when Charles's room was done, they both went up to keep the unfortunate young man company. Did not Christian

90

charity command them to comfort him? The two women drew a good number of little sophistries from religion to justify their behaviour. So Charles Grandet found himself the object of the most affectionate and loving attention. His grieving heart felt keenly the gentleness of this friendship, as soothing as the touch of velvet, the perfect sympathy which these two inhibited souls could express when, for once, they were free in their natural sphere, that of suffering. Taking a liberty that their relationship permitted, Eugénie began to put away the clothes and toilet articles that her cousin had brought with him, and could admire at her leisure each costly trinket, each knick-knack of finely wrought gold or silver which she happened to pick up and which she kept in her hand for a long time under the pretext of examining it. Charles was deeply touched by the generous interest of his aunt and cousin. He was well enough acquainted with Parisian society to know that in his position he would have found only indifferent or cold hearts there. Eugénie appeared to him in all the radiance of her own special kind of beauty, and from that moment he admired the innocent ways he had laughed at the day before. So when Eugénie, naïvely showing her feelings, took from Nanon's hands the earthenware bowl full of coffee with cream, and gave the Parisian a kindly look as she did so, his eyes filled with tears. He took her hand and kissed it.

'Why, what's the matter now?' she asked.

'Oh, they are tears of gratitude,' he replied.

Eugénie turned round smartly to the mantelpiece and picked up the candlesticks.

'Nanon, take these away,' she said.

When she looked at her cousin, her face was still very red, though her look could at least dissemble and did not reveal the overwhelming joy that was filling her heart. But their eyes expressed the same feeling, just as their hearts were joined by the same thought: the future was theirs. Charles found this sweet emotion all the more delightful, in the midst of his immense grief, in that it was quite unexpected. A knock at the door made the two women hurry to their places in the living-room. Fortunately they could go downstairs quickly enough to be at their work when Grandet came in; if he had met them under the archway, that would have been enough to arouse his suspicions. After lunch, which Grandet took standing up, the gamekeeper, who had not yet received the payment due to him, came from Froidfond, bringing with him a hare, partridges killed in the park, eels, and two pike, which the millers owed for their rent.

'Aha, poor old Cornoiller, he's as welcome as fish in Lent. Are those ready for eating?'

'Yes, my good master, they were killed two days ago.'

'Come on, Nanon, get going,' said Grandet. 'Take them. They'll do for dinner. I am entertaining two of the Cruchots.'

Nanon opened her eyes wide in amazement and looked at everybody.

'That's all very well,' she said, 'but where will I get the bacon and spices from?'

'Give six francs to Nanon, wife,' said Grandet, 'and remind me to go to the cellar to get some good wine.'

'But, Monsieur Grandet,' began the gamekeeper, who had prepared his speech with a view to getting the question of his wages settled, 'Monsieur Grandet . . .'

'Ta, ta, ta, ta,' said Grandet. 'I know what you want to say. You are a good fellow. We'll see about that tomorrow. I'm too busy today. Give him five francs, wife,' he said to Madame Grandet.

He hurried off. The poor woman was only too happy to buy peace for eleven francs. She knew that Grandet usually said nothing for a fortnight after taking back, coin by coin, the money he had given her.

'Here you are, Cornoiller,' she said, slipping ten francs into his hand. 'Some day we shall reward your services.'

Cornoiller had nothing to say. He left.

'Madame,' said Nanon, who had put on her black bonnet and picked up her basket. 'I need only three francs. Keep the rest. I'll manage alright on that.'

'Make a good dinner, Nanon. My cousin will be coming down,' said Eugénie.

'There is definitely something extraordinary going on,' said Madame Grandet. 'This is only the third time since our marriage that your father has asked anyone to dinner.'

About four o'clock, when Eugénie and her mother had finished laying the table for six, and the master of the house had brought up some bottles of those exquisite wines which provincials keep lovingly in their cellars, Charles came into the room. The young man was pale. His gestures, his face, his look, and the sound of his voice had a touching sadness about them. He was not simulating grief; he was really suffering, and the cloud spread over his features by sorrow gave him that interesting air that women find so attractive. Eugénie loved him even more for it. Perhaps, too, misfortune had brought him closer to her. Charles was no longer the rich, handsome young man living in a sphere beyond her reach, but a relative suddenly afflicted with terrible poverty. Poverty begets equality. Women have in common with angels the special care of suffering beings. Charles and Eugénie understood each other and communicated only with their eyes, for the poor, fallen dandy, the orphan, sat down in a corner and stayed there, calm and proud, without saying a word. But from time to time his cousin's gentle, affectionate glance shone on him, forcing him to leave his sad thoughts and venture with her into a land of hope for the future, where she was happy to go with him. At that moment, the town of Saumur was more excited about the dinner to which Grandet had invited the Cruchots than it had been the previous day by the sale of his harvest, an act which constituted a crime of high treason against the winegrowing community. If the scheming winegrower had given his dinner with the same idea in his head that cost Alcibiades' dog* his tail, he would perhaps have been a great man. But, as he felt too superior to the inhabitants of a town that he regularly took for a ride, he paid no attention to the opinions of Saumur.

The des Grassins soon learned of the violent death and probable bankruptcy of Charles's father. They decided to go and see their client that very evening in order to condole

93

with him in his misfortune and to show friendship, while at the same time they would discover the reasons which could have prompted him to invite the Cruchots to dinner in such circumstances.

At five o'clock precisely, President C. de Bonfons and his uncle the lawyer arrived, dressed up to the nines. The diners sat down to table and began by eating an uncommonly good meal. Grandet was solemn, Charles silent, Eugénie said not a word, Madame spoke no more than usual, so that the dinner was like a real funeral meal. When they rose from the table, Charles said to his aunt and uncle, 'With your permission, I'll go to my room. I must write a lot of sad letters.'

'By all means, nephew.'

When Charles had left the room and Grandet could assume that the young man was out of earshot and must be absorbed in his correspondence, he looked slyly at his wife.

'Madame Grandet, what we are going to talk about would be all Greek to you. It's half-past seven. You had much better tuck yourself up in your own little cubby-hole. Goodnight, Eugénie, my child.'

He kissed Eugénie, and the two women left the room. Then began the scene in which Père Grandet, more than at any other moment in his life, deployed the skill he had acquired in his dealings with men and which often earned for him the nickname of *old dog* from those whose skin he had bitten a little too sharply. If the Mayor of Saumur had had loftier ambitions, if fortunate circumstances, by allowing him to reach higher social spheres, had sent him to those congresses which deal with the affairs of nations, and if he had made use there of the genius that his own self-interest had developed in him, there is no doubt that he would have served the interests of France with glory. Yet perhaps it is just as likely that, away from Saumur, the old fellow would have cut but a sorry figure. Perhaps human minds are like certain animals that no longer breed if they are removed from their native climes.

'M-M-Monsieur le P-P-Président, y-y-you were s-s-saying . . .'

Grandet's stammer had been affected for so long that, like the deafness of which he complained in wet weather, it was thought to be genuine. At this point the two Cruchots found it so wearisome that, as they listened to him, they unconsciously distorted their faces as if in an effort to finish the words over which he deliberately stumbled.

Perhaps it would be useful to give the history of Grandet's stammer and deafness. No one in Anjou could hear Angevin French better or speak it more clearly than the cunning winegrower. Long ago, in spite of all his shrewdness, he had been deceived by a Jew. In their discussion, the Jew put his hand to his ear like an ear-trumpet, on the pretext of hearing better, and stuttered so much in his effort to find the right words, that Grandet, falling victim to his own humanity, felt obliged to suggest to the crafty Jew the words and ideas the Jew seemed to be looking for, to complete himself the arguments of the said Jew, to say what the accursed Jew should be saying, in short, to be the Jew and not Grandet. The cooper emerged from this strange contest having made the only agreement that he could complain of during the course of his business career. But if, financially speaking, he lost by it, morally he was taught a useful lesson and later he reaped its fruits. So, in the end, the old fellow blessed the Jew who had taught him the art of wearing out the patience of his business opponent and of keeping him so busy trying to express Grandet's thoughts that the opponent lost sight of his own. Now, no business transaction more than the one under consideration required the use of the deafness, stammering, and incomprehensible circumlocutions in which Grandet wrapped up his ideas. To begin with, he did not want to assume responsibility for his ideas; then, he wished to be in control of what he said and to leave his real intentions in doubt.

'Monsieur de Bon . . . Bon . . . Bonfons . . .' For the second time in three years, Grandet called the Cruchot nephew Monsieur de Bonfons. The President was entitled to think he was the crafty old man's chosen son-in-law.

'You-ou w-w-w-were saying, then, that b-b-bankr-rruptcies c-c-c-can, in c-c-c-certain cases, be pr-pr-pr-prevented b-by . . .'

'By the commercial courts themselves. That happens every day,' said Monsieur C. de Bonfons, grasping Père Grandet's idea, or thinking he guessed it, and trying helpfully to explain it to him. 'Listen.'

'I'm l-l-l-listening,' the old fellow replied humbly, with a mischievous look on his face like that of a child who appears to be paying great attention to his teacher while inwardly laughing at him.

'When a respected man in a good position, as was, for example, your late brother in Paris . . .'

'M-my brother, yes.'

'Is threatened with insolvency.'

'Th-th-that's c-c-called ins-s-solvency, then?'

'Yes. If his bankruptcy is imminent, the commercial court, which has jurisdiction over him, has the judicial power to nominate liquidators of his business. To liquidate is not the same as to go bankrupt; do you understand? If he goes bankrupt, a man is dishonoured, but if he goes into liquidation, his honour remains unscathed.'

'That's quite d-d-d-different, if it d-d-d-doesn't c-c-c-cost m-m-m-more,' said Grandet.

'But a liquidation can still be arranged, even without the help of the commercial court. For,' said the President, taking a pinch of snuff, 'how is a bankruptcy declared?'

'Yes, I've n-n-n-ever th-th-th-ought about it,' replied Grandet.

'First of all,' continued the magistrate, 'by the filing of a petition with the record office of the court, either by the businessman himself or by his officially registered agent. Now, if the businessman does not file a petition, if no creditor applies to the court for a judgement which declares the aforesaid businessman bankrupt, what would happen?'

'Y-y-yes, wh-wh-what indeed?'

'Then the deceased's family, his representatives, his heirs, or the man himself, if he is not dead, or his friends, if he has gone into hiding, arrange the liquidation. Do you

96

perhaps wish to liquidate your brother's business?' asked the President.

'Oh, Grandet,' exclaimed the lawyer, 'that would be a fine thing to do. There is honour still in our provincial towns. If you were to save your name, for it is your name, you would be . . .'

'Sublime,' said the President, interrupting his uncle.

'C-c-certainly', replied the old winegrower, 'm-m-my br-br-brother's n-n-name w-w-was Grandet, j-j-just like m-m-mine. Th-th-that's d-d-definitely the c-c-case. I d-d-don't s-s-say it isn't. And th-th-this l-l-liquidation m-m-might, in any c-c-case, b-b-be in ev-ev-ry w-w-way v-v-very advantageous to my n-n-nephew, and I'm f-f-fond of him. But I m-m-must l-l-look into it. I d-d-don't know the c-c-cunning f-f-fellows in P-p-paris. I l-l-live in S-s-saumur, you see. I have my v-v-vines, my d-d-ditches, my b-b-business to s-s-see to, I h-h-have n-n-never m-m-made out a b-b-bill. What is a bill? I h-h-have r-r-received m-m-many of them, I have never s-s-signed one. You g-g-get them, you d-d-discount them. Th-th-that's all I kn-kn-know about th-th-them. I've h-h-heard it s-s-said that you c-c-an b-b-buy b-b-back b-b-bills.'

'Yes,' said the President. 'You can buy bills on the market, less a certain percentage. Do you understand?'

Grandet cupped his hand behind his ear and the President repeated his statement.

'But,' replied the winegrower, 's-s-o th-th-ere's f-f-food and d-d-drink in all that. I kn-kn-know nothing, at m-m-my age, of all th-th-these m-m-matters. I m-m-must st-st-stay here to l-l-look after the gr-gr-grapes. The gr-gr-grapes p-p-pile up and it's the gr-gr-grapes we p-p-pay with. B-b-before all else, I m-m-must l-l-look after the h-h-harvest. I have important b-b-business affairs at Froidfond and c-c-onsiderable ones at that. I c-c-annot l-l-leave everything at h-h-home to g-g-go on a w-w-wild g-g-oose ch-ch-chase after c-c-complicated m-m-matters th-that I d-d-don't understand a w-w-word of. Y-y-you say that to l-l-liquidate, to st-st-stop the d-d-declaration of

97

b-b-bankruptcy, I ought to b-b-be in P-p-paris. S-s-since
I'm n-n-not a l-l-little b-b-bird, I c-c-can't be in t-t-two
p-p-places at once . . . And . . .'

'And I understand your position,' cried the lawyer. 'Well,
my old friend, you have friends, friends of long standing,
ready to devote themselves to you.'

'Come on, then,' the winegrower was thinking, 'make up
your minds!'

'And if someone were to go to Paris, and find your brother
Guillaume's largest creditor and say to him . . .'

'J-j-just a m-m-minute,' interrupted Grandet, 'say to
him—what? S-s-something like this: "M-m-monsieur G-g-
grandet of S-s-saumur this, M-m-monsieur G-g-grandet of
S-s-saumur that. He loves his brother, he loves his n-n-
nephew. Grandet is a g-g-good f-f-family m-m-man and he
has v-v-very g-g-good int-t-tentions. He has sold his g-g-
grape h-h-harvest for a g-g-good p-p-price. Don't declare a
b-b-bankruptcy, c-c-call a m-m-meeting of c-c-creditors,
appoint l-l-liquidators. Th-th-then G-g-grandet will s-s-see
what he c-c-can d-d-do. You'll g-g-get much more by l-l-
liquidating than by l-l-letting lawyers poke their noses into
it . . ." Eh, isn't that so?'

'Exactly so!' said the President.

'Because, you see, Monsieur de B-b-bonfons, I must look
into it all before m-m-making a d-d-decision. You c-c-can't
d-d-do what you c-c-can't d-d-do. In any b-b-business
involving large s-s-sums, you have to know wh-wh-
what you've g-g-got and wh-wh-at you'll h-h-have to
p-p-pay if you don't want to r-r-ruin yourself. Eh, isn't
that so?'

'Certainly,' said the President. 'My own opinion is that in
a few months' time you could buy up the debts for an agreed
sum and pay the whole thing by an amicable arrangement.
Oh yes, you can lead dogs a long way if you show them
a piece of bacon. If there hasn't been a declaration of
bankruptcy and you hold the creditors' claims' documents,
you become white as snow.'

'As s-s-snow', repeated Grandet, again cupping his hand

to his ear. 'I d-d-don't understand where s-s-snow c-c-comes into it.'

'But', shouted the President, 'just listen to me.'

'I'm l-l-listening.'

'A bill of exchange is a commodity that may rise and fall in value. That's a deduction from Jeremy Bentham's* theory of usury. He was a philosophical writer who proved that the prejudice which disapproved of money-lending was plain silly.'

'Oh, indeed!' said Grandet.

'Since, according to Bentham,' continued the President, 'money is a commodity and whatever represents money becomes a commodity as well, since it's well known that, subject as it is to the normal fluctuations of the market, the commodity-bill of exchange bearing a certain signature, like any article, is plentiful or scarce in the market-place, that it costs a lot or drops down to nothing, the court decrees . . . (But, oh dear, how stupid I am, forgive me), I think you could redeem your brother's debts for twenty-five per cent of their value.'

'Y-y-you c-c-call him J-j-jeremy Ben . . . .'

'Bentham, an Englishman.'

'That's a Jeremiah* who will save us a lot of lamentations in business,' said the lawyer with a laugh.

'The English are s-s-sometimes quite s-s-sensible,' said Grandet. 'So, ac-c-cording to B-b-bentham, if my b-b-brother's b-b-bills are w-w-worthless. So, I've g-g-got it r-r-right, haven't I? That seems clear to me . . . The creditors would be . . . no, wouldn't be. I've g-g-got it.'

'Let me explain it all to you,' said the President. 'In law, if you own the deeds to all the claims on the house of Grandet, your brother or his heirs owe nothing to anyone. Right.'

'Right,' repeated Grandet.

'In equity, if your brother's bills are negotiated on the market (do you fully understand what negotiated means?) at a loss of so much per cent, if one of your friends happens to be around and buys them up, the creditors not having been constrained by any violent means to give them up, then the estate of the late Grandet of Paris is honourably cleared of its debts.'

'That's true. B-b-business is b-b-business,' said the cooper. 'That's s-s-settled. But, still, y-y-you s-s-see, it's d-d-difficult. I have n-n-neither m-m-money nor t-t-time, nor t-t-time . . .'

'Yes. You can't manage to go. Well, I'm willing to go to Paris for you. (You'll pay my expenses; that's a trifle.) I'll see the creditors there. I'll talk to them, I'll postpone payment, and everything will be settled with a supplementary amount that you will add to what is realized by the liquidation, so that you can obtain possession of the bills.'

'B-b-but w-w-we m-m-must l-l-look into that. I c-c-can't, I d-d-don't w-w-want to c-c-commit myself without . . . If you c-c-can't, you c-c-can't. Y-y-ou understand?'

'That's fair.'

'M-m-y h-h-head's in a wh-wh-whirl w-w-with all th-th-this you've s-s-sprung on me. Th-th-this is the f-f-first t-t-time in my life that I am f-f-forced to th-th-think of . . .'

'Of course, you're not a legal expert.'

'I am a p-p-poor winegrower and know nothing about wh-wh-what y-y-you have just been saying. I m-m-must th-th-think about it.'

'Well,' resumed the President, getting ready as if to continue the discussion.

'Nephew . . .' interrupted the lawyer reproachfully.

'What is it, uncle?' answered the President.

'Let Monsieur Grandet explain what he intends to do. You are now proposing to undertake an important commission. Our dear friend must tell us explicit . . .'

A knock at the door which announced the arrival of the des Grassins family, their entry, and their greetings prevented Cruchot from finishing his sentence. The lawyer was pleased to be interrupted. Grandet was already looking at him askance, and his twitching wart indicated an inner storm. To begin with, the prudent lawyer did not think it fitting for the president of a county court to go to Paris to get the better of creditors and have a hand in a shady business which infringed the laws of strict honesty. Then, since he had not yet heard Père Grandet express the least inclination to pay anything at all, he trembled instinctively at seeing his nephew involved in the matter. So he took advantage of the des Grassins' arrival to take the President by the arm and draw him to the window recess.

'You've shown your hand enough, nephew. But that's sufficient devotion. Your wish to marry the daughter blinds you. Damn it all! You don't have to go at it like a crow knocking down nuts. Let me steer the boat now, you just help to keep it going. It's not really for you to compromise your dignity as a magistrate in such a . . .'

He did not finish; he heard Monsieur des Grassins say to the old cooper as he shook his hand, 'We have heard of the terrible misfortunes that have befallen your family, the collapse of Guillaume Grandet's firm and your brother's death. We have come to express our deepest sympathy with you at these sad events.'

'The only misfortune', said the lawyer, interrupting the banker, 'is the death of the younger Monsieur Grandet. Even then he wouldn't have killed himself if he had thought of calling on his brother for help. Our old friend, who is the soul of honour, expects to liquidate the debts of the Grandet firm in Paris. In order to spare him the trouble of a purely legal matter, my nephew, the President, is offering to set off immediately for Paris so as to arrange a deal with the creditors and make an appropriate settlement.'

These words, confirmed by the attitude of the wine-grower, who was stroking his chin, came as a complete surprise to the three des Grassins, who, on their way to Grandet's house, had criticized Grandet's avarice at length, almost accusing him of fratricide.

'Oh, I knew it,' exclaimed the banker, looking at his wife. 'What did I tell you on the way, Madame des Grassins? Grandet is honourable to the fingertips and would not allow the least slur on his name. Money without honour is a disease. There is honour in our provincial towns. That's

101

good, Grandet, very good. I'm an old soldier. I can't hide my thoughts. I say it bluntly. By Jove, that's sublime, that is!'

'W-w-well, the s-s-sublime c-c-costs a b-b-bit m-m-much,' replied Grandet as the banker shook his hand warmly.

'But, my good Grandet, with all due respect to Monsieur le Président,' continued des Grassins, 'this is a purely commercial matter and requires an experienced business-man. One needs to be an expert in returned bills, extra charges, and interest tables. I have to go to Paris on business. I could then undertake . . .'

'We sh-sh-should s-s-see then how we can t-t-try to arrange th-th-things t-t-together according to what is p-p-possible for us b-b-both and without c-c-committing m-m-myself to anything I w-w-wouldn't w-w-want to do,' said Grandet, stammering. 'For, you see, Monsieur le Président naturally asked me to pay his expenses.'

Grandet did not stammer over these last words.

'Oh,' said Madame des Grassins, 'but it's a pleasure to go to Paris. For my part, I would gladly pay to go there.'

And she signed to her husband as if to encourage him to snaffle this commission from their enemies, at any cost. Then she cast an ironic look at the two Cruchots, who cut a sorry figure. Grandet grabbed the banker by one of his coat buttons and drew him into a corner.

'I would have more confidence in you than in the President,' he said. 'Then, there's other fish to fry,' he added with a twitch of his wart. 'I want to invest in government bonds. I have some thousands of francs with which to buy government stock and I don't want to buy if they go higher than eighty francs. They say that the mechanism winds down at the end of every month. You know about that, don't you?'

'I certainly do! Well, so I'll have a few thousand or so livres to invest in the funds for you?'

'Not much to start with. Mum's the word! I want to play that game without anyone knowing anything about it.

102

Perhaps you would make a deal for me towards the end of the month. But don't say a word to the Cruchots about it; that would worry them. Since you're going to Paris, we can see at the same time what cards are trumps for my poor nephew.'

'Right, that's agreed. I'll go tomorrow by the mail-coach,' said des Grassins, raising his voice. 'And at—at what time shall I come for your final instructions?'

'At five o'clock, before dinner,' said the winegrower, rubbing his hands.

The two rival factions lingered, confronting each other, a few moments longer. Then, after a pause, des Grassins tapped Grandet on the shoulder, saying, 'It's good there are kind relatives like you.'

'Yes, I don't make a parade of it, but I *am* a kind r-r-relative,' replied Grandet. 'I loved my brother and I'll certainly prove it, if it d-d-doesn't c-c-cost . . .'

'We shall leave you now, Grandet,' said the banker, fortunately interrupting him before he could finish his sentence. 'If I am to leave earlier than I had intended, I must see to a few things first.'

'Certainly, certainly. I, too, in c-c-connection with you know what, I must r-r-retreat into my chamber of d-d-deliberations, as President Cruchot would say.'

'Damn it all! I'm not Monsieur de Bonfons any longer,' thought the magistrate sadly, and his face took on the expression of a judge bored by counsel's speech.

The leading members of the two rival families went out together. Neither side thought further about the treason Grandet had committed that morning against the wine-growers of the region; they were sounding each other out, though fruitlessly, in an effort to discover what was the other side's opinion about the old fellow's real intentions in this new matter.

'Are you coming to Madame d'Orsonval's with us?' des Grassins asked the lawyer.

'We'll go later,' replied the President. 'With my uncle's permission, I promised Mademoiselle de Gribeaucourt to call in for a few moments, and we'll go there first.'

'Goodbye for the moment, then, gentlemen,' said Madame des Grassins. But when the des Grassins had moved on a little away from the two Cruchots, Adolphe said to his father, 'They're blazing mad, aren't they?'

'Be quiet, dear. They can still hear us,' answered his mother. 'Anyway, your language is rather vulgar. It smacks of the law school.'

'Well, uncle,' exclaimed the magistrate when he saw that the des Grassins were out of earshot, 'I began by being President de Bonfons and at the end I was merely a Cruchot.'

'I could see that put you out, but the wind favoured the des Grassins. You are stupid, with all your brains! . . . Let them set sail on the strength of a *we shall see* from Père Grandet, and don't worry, my boy. Eugénie will be your wife all the same.'

In a short time, the news of Grandet's magnanimous decision had spread in three houses at once, and the whole town talked of nothing but his fraternal devotion. Everyone forgave him for selling his vintage in contempt of the sworn agreement made by the winegrowers; they admired his sense of honour and praised a generosity of which they had not thought him capable. It is in the French character to become enthusiastic, to get in a rage, or to feel passionately about the meteor of the moment, about the transient odds and ends of the present day. Have communities, have nations, no memory?

When Père Grandet had closed the door, he called Nanon. 'Don't let the dog loose, and don't go to sleep. We have work to do together. At eleven o'clock Cornoiller will be at the door with the old carriage from Froidfond. Listen for him coming so that you can stop him knocking, and tell him to come in very quietly. Police regulations forbid noise at night. Besides, the neighbourhood doesn't need to know that I'm about to go anywhere.'

Having given his orders, Grandet went back upstairs to his laboratory. Nanon could hear him there, moving about, rummaging, coming and going, but stealthily. Obviously he did not want to awaken his wife or his daughter, or above all to arouse the attention of his nephew; to begin with, he had sworn at him on noticing a light in his room. In the middle of the night, Eugénie, whose mind was full of her cousin, thought she heard the moan of a dying man, and for her the dying man was Charles. When she had left him, he was so pale, in such despair, perhaps he had killed himself. She quickly wrapped herself up in a long, hooded cloak and made to leave her room. At first a bright light, streaming through the cracks of her door, made her fear that the house was on fire, but she was soon reassured when she heard Nanon's heavy footsteps and the sound of her voice, which mingled with the whinnying of several horses.

'Is my father taking Charles away?' she wondered, opening her door a little so that she could see what was happening in the corridor, but cautiously enough to prevent it creaking.

Suddenly her eye met her father's. His look, though absent and unconcerned, froze her with terror. The old man and Nanon were yoked together by a big stick; its ends rested on their right shoulders and from it was suspended a strong rope, to which was attached a small barrel of the kind Père Grandet liked making in his bakehouse in his leisure moments.

'Good Lord, Monsieur, that's heavy!' whispered Nanon.

'What a pity it's only full of copper sous,' replied the old man. 'Take care not to knock against the candlestick.'

The scene was lit by a single candle, placed between two supports of the banisters.

'Cornoiller,' Grandet said to his gamekeeper *in partibus*,* 'did you bring your pistols?'

'No, Monsieur. Goodness me, what is there to be afraid of for a load of old coppers?'

'Oh, nothing,' said Père Grandet.

'Besides, we'll drive fast,' continued the gamekeeper. 'Your farmers have chosen their best horses for you.'

'Good, good. You didn't tell them where I was going?'

'I didn't know.'

'Good. Is it a strong carriage?'

105

'Strong, master? I should think so. It could carry thirty hundredweight. What do your wretched barrels weigh, then?'

'Oh, I know alright,' said Nanon, 'it's nearly eighteen hundredweight.'

'Hold your tongue, Nanon! You'll tell my wife I've gone to the country. I'll be back for dinner. Go at a good speed, Cornoiller. I must be at Angers before nine o'clock.'

The carriage set off. Nanon bolted the front door, untied the dog, and went to bed with a bruised shoulder. Nobody in the district suspected either Grandet's departure or the purpose of his journey. The old man's discretion was complete. No one ever saw a sou in that house full of gold. The old winegrower had learned from the morning's port gossip that gold had doubled in price as a result of the large number of ships being fitted out at Nantes, and that speculators had arrived at Angers to buy it. By simply borrowing horses from his farmers, he had put himself in a position to sell his gold and to bring back in Treasury bills, issued by the Receiver-General, the amount required to buy his government bonds, increased by his profit on the sale of his gold.

'My father's going away,' said Eugénie, who had heard everything from the top of the staircase.

Silence was restored in the house, and the distant sound of the carriage wheels, gradually dying away, could no longer be heard in sleeping Saumur. At that moment, Eugénie felt in her heart, even before the sound reached her ears, a moan which penetrated the dividing walls and came from her cousin's room. A band of light, as thin as the cutting edge of a sabre, shone from under his door and cut across the banisters of the old staircase.

'He's in pain,' she thought, going up two steps.

A second groan made her go up to the landing outside his room. The door was ajar and she pushed it open. Charles was sleeping, his head drooping over an arm of the old armchair; his hand had dropped his pen and was almost touching the floor. The jerky breathing occasioned by the young man's

106

posture suddenly frightened Eugénie and she quickly went into the room.

'He must be very tired', she said to herself, seeing a number of sealed letters. She read the addresses on them: To MM. Farry, Breilman, and Co., coachbuilders; To M. Buisson, tailor, etc. 'No doubt he has settled all his affairs so that he can leave France soon,' she thought. Her eyes fell upon two open letters. The first words of one of them, 'My dear Annette . . .', nearly made her faint. Her heart throbbed, her feet were riveted to the spot. 'His dear Annette, he loves, he is loved! There's no more hope! What does he say to her?' These thoughts went through her mind and her heart. She read the words everywhere, even on the window-panes, in letters of fire. 'Give him up already! No, I shan't read that letter, I ought to go away. Yet, what if I did read it?' She looked at Charles, took his head gently, and placed it against the back of the armchair; he submitted like a child who, even while asleep, still knows his mother and, without waking up, accepts her care and her kisses. Like a mother, Eugénie lifted the dangling hand and, like a mother, she gently kissed his hair.

'Dear Annette!' A demon screamed the two words in her ears.

'I know that I may be doing wrong, but I'll read the letter,' she said.

Eugénie turned her head away, for her high sense of honour reproached her. For the first time in her life, there was a conflict in her heart between good and evil. Until then she had not had to blush for any of her actions. Passion and curiosity won the day. At each sentence her heart grew heavier, and the keen emotion which stirred her as she read made her long even more for the joys of first love.

My dear Annette,

Only one thing on earth could have separated us, and that is the misfortune which has befallen me and which no human prudence could have foreseen. My father has killed himself; his fortune and mine are entirely lost. I am an orphan at an age when, with the upbringing I have had, I can be considered a child. Nevertheless, I

107

must emerge a man from the abyss into which I have fallen. I have just spent a part of tonight in working out my financial position. If I want to leave France an honest man, and there is no doubt about that, I haven't a hundred francs of my own with which to go and try my luck in the Indies or in America. Yes, my poor Anna, I shall go and seek my fortune in the most punishing climates. I am told that under those skies it comes surely and quickly. As for staying in Paris, I couldn't possibly. Neither my heart nor my face is made to put up with the insults, the coldness, the disdain, which can be expected by a man who is ruined, the son of a bankrupt. Good God! To think of owing two million! In Paris, I should be killed in a duel within a week. So I shan't go back there. Your love, the most tender and devoted that ever ennobled a man's heart, cannot draw me back. Alas, my beloved, I haven't enough money to go where you are, to receive a last kiss, a kiss from which I would draw the strength I need for my enterprise.

'Poor Charles, I was right to read it. I have money; I'll give it to him,' said Eugénie.

She wiped away her tears and resumed her reading.

Until now I had never thought about the hardships of poverty. If I have the hundred louis I need for the passage, I won't have a sou to spend on buying cheap goods to sell. But no, I won't have one louis, let alone a hundred; I won't know how much money I'll have left till after my debts are settled in Paris. If I have nothing, I shall go quietly to Nantes and work my passage out as an ordinary seaman. I shall begin my life abroad like other penniless, energetic young men who have returned rich from the Indies. Since this morning, I have faced my future realistically. It's worse for me than for anyone else— for me, who was spoiled by an adoring mother and cherished by the best of fathers, and who, on first going into society, experienced the love of an Anna! I have known only the flowers of life; such good fortune could not last. Yet, dear Annette, I have more courage than a carefree young man is expected to have, above all a young man used to the caresses of the most charming woman in Paris, cradled in the joys of family life, surrounded by smiling faces at home, and whose every wish was a law to his father . . . Oh, my father, Annette, he is dead . . . Well, I have thought carefully about my position, and about yours too. I have grown a lot older in twenty-four hours. Dear Anna, if, to keep me near you, in Paris, you were to sacrifice all your luxurious pleasures, your fine clothes, your box at the Opera, we still wouldn't have enough to pay for my extravagant way of life. And I couldn't accept so many sacrifices. So we part today for ever.

'He's leaving her. Oh, God, what bliss!'

Eugénie started with joy. Charles stirred and she turned cold with fright. But, fortunately for her, he did not wake up. She read on:

When shall I return? I don't know. Europeans age quickly in the climate of the Indies, especially if they work. Let's put ourselves in the situation of ten years from now. In ten years, your daughter will be eighteen, she will be your constant companion, and will always be spying on you. For you, society will be very cruel, your daughter perhaps even more so. We have seen examples of these society judgements and of young girls' ingratitude; let us profit from our experience. Keep in the bottom of your heart, as I shall in mine, the memory of these four happy years, and if you can, be faithful to your poor friend. I can't insist on that, however, because, you see, my dear Annette, I must adapt to my position; I must look at life from a conventional, middle-class point of view and calculate realistically. So I must think of marriage, which is a necessity of my new existence, and I will confess that here, in Saumur, in my uncle's house, I have found a cousin whose manners, face, mind, and heart you would like, and who, besides, seems to me to have . . .

'He must have been very tired to have stopped writing to her,' Eugénie thought when she saw the letter cut short in the middle of this sentence.

She was finding excuses for him! It was surely impossible for such an innocent girl to be aware of the cold-heartedness which permeated that letter. Ignorant, pure young girls, brought up in a religious atmosphere, find love everywhere as soon as they set foot in the magical realm of love. They walk through it surrounded by the heavenly light which is cast by their own hearts and which reflects its rays on their beloved. They see him glowing with the fires of their own emotion and ascribe to him their noble thoughts. A woman's mistakes nearly always stem from her belief in good news or from her confidence in truth. For Eugénie, the words, 'My dear Annette, my beloved', rang in her heart as the most charming language of love and were as sweet to her soul as the divine music of *Venite adoremus*,* played on the organ, had been to her ear in her childhood. Moreover, the tears in which Charles's eyes were still bathed were a testimony to all the noble qualities of heart which are bound to appeal to a young girl. How could she know that, if Charles loved his father so much and wept for him so sincerely, this affection stemmed less from the goodness of his heart than from his father's goodness to him? Monsieur and Madame Guillaume Grandet had gratified all their son's whims and had given him all the pleasures of wealth; he had thus never felt the need to make the appalling calculations most young Parisians are guilty of when, faced with the delights of Paris, they conceive desires and make plans which they regretfully see frustrated and delayed by their parents' being still alive. The father's lavish generosity had managed to sow disinterested filial affection in his son's heart. Nevertheless, Charles was a child of Paris, accustomed by Parisian ways and by Annette herself to calculate the consequences of every action; he was already old under the mask of youth. He had received the deplorable education of a society where more crimes are committed in thoughts and words than are punished judicially in the assize courts, where witticisms destroy the greatest ideas, and where one is deemed to be strong only in so far as one sees things as they are. And there, to see things as they are means to weigh a friend's purse every morning, to know how to exploit to your own advantage everything that happens, to express no spontaneous admiration for anything, neither works of art nor noble actions, and to ascribe self-interest as the motive for everything. After a thousand follies, the great lady, the beautiful Annette, forced Charles to think seriously. She spoke to him of his future position as she stroked his hair with her perfumed hand. As she adjusted one of his curls she made him consider the practical side of life; she made him effeminate and at the same time materialistic. It was a twofold corruption, but elegant and subtle and in good taste.

'You are foolish, Charles,' she would say. 'I'll find it a hard job to teach you the ways of the world. You behaved very badly to Monsieur des Lupeaulx. I know perfectly well that he's not a very admirable man, but wait till he's no longer in power; then you can despise him as much as you like. Do you know what Madame Campan* used to say to us? "Children, as long as a man is a minister, adore him; if he falls, help to drag him to the refuse-dump. In power, he is a kind of god; out of office, he is below Marat* in his sewer, because he is alive and Marat is dead. Life is a series of combinations, and you have to study and adapt to them if you are to succeed in maintaining a good position."'

Charles was too much a man about town, he had been too consistently indulged by his parents, too much flattered by society, to have noble feelings. The grain of gold which his mother had dropped into his heart had been drawn to a thread by Parisian life; he had used it all on the surface and it was being worn away by friction. But Charles was still only twenty-one. At that age the freshness of youth seems inseparable from a frank innocence of the heart. The voice, the look, the face seem to be in accord with the feelings. And so the sternest judge, the most sceptical lawyer, the harshest money-lender is always reluctant to believe that the heart is scheming and corrupt, like an old man's, when the eyes are still clear and the brow unwrinkled. Charles had never had occasion to apply the principles of Parisian morality and up to now he was unblemished through lack of experience. But, without being aware of it, he had been infected with selfishness. The seeds of Parisian economic practices, latent in his heart, were not to be slow in flowering as soon as he was no longer an idle spectator but had become an actor in the drama of real life. Few girls can resist the fair promise of such a handsome appearance as Charles's; but even if Eugénie had been as cautious and observant as some provincial girls are, could she have mistrusted her cousin when his manners, his words, and his deeds were still in harmony with his spontaneous feelings? By a chance, fatal for her, she witnessed the last manifestations

111

of genuine feeling in that young heart, and heard, as it were, the dying sighs of his conscience. So she put down the letter which, for her, seemed filled with love, and began happily to contemplate her sleeping cousin. For her, the dreams of youth could still be seen in his face, and there and then she vowed to love him for ever. Then she glanced at the other letter without attaching much importance to this further indiscretion; she began to read it, only to acquire new proofs of the noble qualities which, like all women, she ascribed to the man of her choice.

My dear Alphonse,

By the time you read this letter I shall have no more friends, but I must admit that though I have no faith in society people who use that word so readily, I have never doubted your friendship. So I entrust you with the settlement of my affairs and count on you to make the most of my remaining possessions. You must know my position by now. I have nothing left and am about to set off for the Indies. I have just written to everyone to whom I think I owe any money, and you will find enclosed as accurate a list as I can give from memory. My books, my furniture, my carriages, my horses, etc. will, I think, fetch enough to pay my debts. I want to keep for myself only those valueless trifles which will be suitable as a beginning of stock for trading. For the sale of my possessions, I shall send you, my dear Alphonse, a formal power of attorney, in case any objections are raised. Please send me all my arms, but keep Briton for yourself. Nobody will want to pay what that splendid animal is worth, I prefer to give him to you, like the ring a dying man usually leaves to the executor of his will. Farry, Breilman, and Co. have made me a very comfortable travelling carriage but they haven't delivered it yet. Ask them to keep it without requiring me to pay anything. If they refuse this arrangement, do nothing which might sully my reputation in my present situation. I owe the Englishman six louis, lost at cards; don't forget to give him . . .

'Dear cousin,' said Eugénie, putting down the letter and retreating quietly to her room with one of the lighted candles. It was not without a keen feeling of pleasure that she opened a drawer in an old oak chest, one of the finest pieces of the Renaissance period; the famous royal Salamander,* half obliterated, could still be seen on it. She took from the drawer a large red velvet purse, with golden tassels and an edging of worn gold braid, which she had inherited from her grandmother. Then, with great pride she felt the weight of her purse and enjoyed herself checking the total amount, now forgotten, of her little hoard. First she picked out twenty Portuguese coins, still bright as new, which had been struck in 1725, in the reign of John V. According to her father, they were worth five lisbonines at the present rate of exchange, so that each one was worth one hundred and sixty-eight francs, sixty-four centimes. But given the scarcity and beauty of the coins, which shone like little suns, their market value was a hundred and eighty francs. ITEM, five genovines or Genoese hundred-livre pieces, another rare coinage, worth eighty-seven francs at the exchange rate but a hundred francs to collectors of gold. They were given to her by old Monsieur La Bertellière. ITEM, three Spanish gold quadruples of the time of Philip V, struck in 1729, gifts from Madame Gentillet, who always used to say, as she gave them one at a time, 'That dear little canary, that little yellow coin, is worth ninety-eight livres! Take great care of it, sweetheart, it will be the flower of your collection.' ITEM, and her father prized these coins more than all the others (for the gold in them was a little over twenty-three carats), a hundred Dutch ducats, minted in 1756 and each worth almost thirteen hundred francs. ITEM, a great curiosity! . . . coins, looking like medals, of a kind particularly valued by misers, three rupees stamped with the sign of Libra, and five rupees with the sign of Virgo, all made of pure, twenty-four carat gold, the Grand Mogul's magnificent coinage, each piece of which was worth thirty-seven francs, forty centimes, by weight but at least fifty francs for connoisseurs who love handling gold. ITEM, the forty-franc napoleon she had received the previous day and had put casually in her red purse. Her treasure contained new coins in mint condition, real works of art that Grandet sometimes asked about and wanted to look at again, so as to point out to his daughter their intrinsic merits, like the beauty of the milling, the brightness of the flat surfaces, and the richness of the lettering whose sharp relief had not yet been worn down. But she did not think of their rarity, nor of her father's mania, nor of the risk she ran in giving away a treasure so dear to his heart; no, she was thinking of her cousin and finally came to realize, after making a few errors in arithmetic, that she possessed about five thousand eight hundred francs in real terms, which had a market value of nearly two thousand crowns. At the sight of her wealth, she clapped her hands in delight, like a child who is impelled to express her overflowing joy in spontaneous physical movement. So the father and the daughter had each coveted their fortunes, he so as to sell his gold, Eugénie to cast hers into an ocean of affection. She put the coins back into the old purse, took it in her hand, and, without hesitating, went upstairs again to her cousin's room. Her cousin's lonely poverty made her forget the time of night and the conventions. Moreover, her conscience was clear, her devotion and her happiness gave her strength. Just as she appeared at the door, holding the candle in one hand and her purse in the other, Charles woke up, saw his cousin, and gazed at her in amazement. Eugénie stepped forward, put the light on the table, and said in a voice filled with emotion, 'I want to ask your pardon, cousin, for a serious wrong I have done you, but God will forgive me for this sin if you will erase it.'

'What is it?' asked Charles, rubbing his eyes.

'I read those two letters.'

Charles blushed.

'How could I have done it?' she continued. 'Why did I come upstairs? I don't really know now. But I am tempted not to be too sorry I read those letters, since they have revealed your heart, your soul to me, and . . .'

'And what?' asked Charles.

'And your plans, your need for a sum of money . . .'

'My dear cousin . . .'

'Hush, hush, cousin, not so loud. We mustn't wake anyone up. Here,' she said, opening her purse, 'here are

114

the savings of a poor girl who doesn't need anything. Take them, Charles. This morning I did not know what money was. You have taught me. It is only a means to an end, that's all. A cousin is almost a brother and you can surely borrow your sister's purse.'

Eugénie, who was as much a woman as a girl, had not foreseen a refusal, but her cousin made no answer.

'Surely you're not refusing?' asked Eugénie, her heart beating so loudly that it could be heard in the deep silence.

Her cousin's hesitation humiliated her, but she became even more aware of the dire need of his situation and she went down on her knees.

'I won't get up till you take this money,' she said. 'For pity's sake, cousin, answer me . . . so that I know if you trust me, if you are generous, if . . .'

As he heard her noble, despairing cry, tears fell from Charles's eyes on to his cousin's hands. He grasped them to raise her to her feet. On feeling his hot tears, Eugénie snatched up her purse and emptied it out on to the table.

'The answer's yes, isn't it?' she said, weeping for joy. 'Have no fear, cousin, you will grow rich. This gold will bring you luck. One day you'll pay me back. In any case, we'll form a partnership. In fact, I'll accept any conditions you impose. But you shouldn't think so much of this gift.'

At last Charles was able to express his feelings.

'Yes, Eugénie, I should be very mean-spirited if I did not accept. But, nothing for nothing, trust for trust.'

'What do you mean?' she asked seriously.

'Listen, dear cousin, over there I have . . .' He broke off and pointed to a square box in a leather case standing on a chest of drawers. 'There you can see something which is as precious to me as life itself. That box is a present from my mother. Ever since this morning I have been thinking that if she could rise from her grave, she herself would sell the gold that, in her affection, she lavished on this dressing-case. But if *I* were to do it, I think it would be a sacrilege.'

Eugénie grasped her cousin's hand convulsively when she heard these last words. 'No,' he continued after a short pause, during which they looked at each other with tears in their eyes. 'No, I don't want to break it, nor to risk it on my travels. Dear Eugénie, I shall leave it in your care. Never has one friend entrusted anything more sacred to another. Judge for yourself.' He picked up the box, took it out of its leather case, opened it, and sadly showed his amazed cousin a dressing-case with fittings so beautifully worked in gold that they were worth much more than the weight of the metal. 'What you are admiring is nothing,' he said, pressing a spring which revealed an inner compartment. 'Here is something which, for me, is worth more than the whole world.' He took out two portraits, two masterpieces by Madame de Mirbel,* richly set in pearls.

'Oh, isn't she lovely! Is this the lady you were writing . . .?

'No,' he said with a smile. 'The lady is my mother, and here is my father. They are your aunt and uncle. Eugénie, I ought to go down on my knees to beg you to look after this treasure for me. If I were to die and lose your little fortune, this gold will compensate you. And it's only with you that I can leave these two portraits; you are worthy of looking after them. But destroy them, so that, after you, they don't fall into other hands . . .' Eugénie said nothing. 'Well, you'll say yes, won't you?' he added ingratiatingly.

On hearing her cousin's words, she looked at him for the first time with the eyes of a woman in love. It was one of those looks in which there is almost as much coquetry as deep feeling. He took her hand and kissed it.

'You are as pure as an angel. Between us, money will never matter, will it? Only feeling, which can give it some value, will be everything from now on.'

'You are like your mother. Was her voice as gentle as yours?'

'Oh, much more so.'

'Yes, for you,' she said, lowering her eyes. 'Come, Charles, go to bed. I insist. You are tired. Till tomorrow.'

She gently withdrew her hand from her cousin's. He took his candle and went with her to light the way to her room.

116

When they were both at the door, he exclaimed, 'Oh, why am I a ruined man?'

'It doesn't matter. I think my father is rich,' she replied.

'Poor child,' said Charles, with one foot inside the door of the room and his back against the wall. 'He wouldn't have let my father die, he wouldn't leave you in such a poverty-stricken dwelling. In fact, he'd live in a different style.'

'But he owns Froidfond.'

'And what is Froidfond worth?'

'I don't know, but he has Noyers, too.'

'Some miserable farm.'

'He has vines and meadows . . .'

'They're not worth much,' said Charles contemptuously. 'If your father had an income of even twenty-four thousand livres, would your room be as cold and bare as this is?' he asked, stepping with his other foot into the room. So that's where my treasures will be kept,' he said, pointing to the old chest, in order to conceal what he was thinking.

'Go to sleep,' she said, preventing him from going into her untidy room.

Charles retreated and they smiled goodnight at each other. They both fell asleep dreaming the same dream, and from then on Charles's mourning began to be relieved by a few rosy prospects. The next morning Madame Grandet found her daughter walking with Charles before breakfast. The young man was still sad, naturally so for an unfortunate who had, as it were, reached the rock bottom of his sorrows and who, measuring the depth of the abyss into which he had fallen, had fully realized the difficulty of his future life.

'My father won't be back before dinner-time,' said Eugénie, noticing her mother's anxious expression.

It was easy to see in Eugénie's face and manner, and in the unusual gentleness acquired by her voice, the fellow-feeling that existed between her and her cousin. They were ardently wedded in their hearts, perhaps even before they were fully aware of the strength of the feelings that united them. Charles stayed in the living-room, where his sad feelings

117

were respected. Each of the three women had a lot to do. Grandet had forgotten about his business appointments, so that there was a large number of callers. The roofer, the plumber, the mason, the carpenter, building labourers, vineyard workers, farmers, all came, some to settle the amount to be charged for repairs, others to pay rents or receive payments. So Madame Grandet and Eugénie had to come and go, to reply to the interminable chatter of the workmen and the country folk. Nanon stored the payments in kind in her kitchen. She always waited for her master's orders to know what was to be kept for the house and what was to be sold at the market. Like many country landowners, the old man used his poor quality wine and spoiled fruit in his own household. About five o'clock in the afternoon, Grandet came back from Angers; he had made fourteen thousand francs from the sale of his gold, and in his wallet he had Treasury bills which would bear interest until the time came for him to pay for his government bonds. He had left Cornoiller at Angers to look after the exhausted horses and to bring them back slowly after allowing them a good rest.

'I've been to Angers, wife,' he said. 'I'm hungry.'

Nanon called out to him from the kitchen, 'Haven't you eaten anything since yesterday?'

'Nothing at all,' replied the old man.

Nanon brought in the soup. As the family sat down to table, des Grassins came in to take his client's instructions. Père Grandet had not even noticed his nephew.

'Don't interrupt your meal, Grandet,' said the banker. 'We'll talk as you eat. Do you know the price of gold at Angers? They've been going there to buy it because of the work at Nantes. I am going to send some.'

'Don't send any,' replied Grandet. 'They've got enough already. We are such close friends that I couldn't let you waste your time.'

'But gold is fetching thirteen francs, fifty centimes there.'

'Say rather, *was* fetching.'

'Where the devil did it come from?'

'I went to Angers last night,' Grandet replied, quietly.

The banker gave a start of surprise. Then the two men began a whispered conversation during which they looked at Charles several times. A second start of surprise escaped des Grassins, no doubt at the point when the former cooper told the banker to invest a sum for him that would bring in an income of a hundred thousand livres.

'Monsieur Grandet,' said the banker, turning to Charles, 'I am going to Paris, and if there's anything I can do for you . . .'

'Nothing, thank you, Monsieur,' replied Charles.

'Thank him more warmly than that, nephew. Monsieur is going to settle the affairs of the firm of Guillaume Grandet.'

'Would there be any hope, then?' asked Charles.

'But aren't you my nephew? Your honour is ours. Is your name not Grandet?' exclaimed the cooper with a well-simulated pride.

Charles got up, threw his arms round Père Grandet, kissed him on both cheeks, turned pale, and left the room. Eugénie looked admiringly at her father.

'Well, goodbye, my dear des Grassins. I'm much obliged to you. Just cajole those fellows to do our bidding.' The two diplomats shook hands and the former cooper saw the banker to the door. Then, when he had shut it, he sank back into his chair and said to Nanon, 'Give me some blackcurrant cordial.' But he was too excited to sit still. He got up, looked at the portrait of Monsieur de la Bertellière, and began to sing and to do what Nanon called 'a little dance'.

In the French Guards,
I had a kind papa.

Nanon, Madame Grandet, and Eugénie looked at each other in silence. The winegrower's delight always terrified them when it reached its climax. The evening was soon over. For one thing, Père Grandet wanted to go to bed early, and when he went to bed, everyone else had to, just as when Augustus drank, Poland got drunk.* And then Nanon, Charles, and Eugénie were no less weary than the master of the house. As for Madame Grandet, she slept, ate, drank, and walked according to her husband's wishes. Nevertheless, during the two hours allowed for digestion, the cooper, more jovial than he had ever been, uttered many of his own characteristic aphorisms, one of which is enough to indicate the quality of his wit. When he had drunk his blackcurrant cordial, he looked at the glass.

'You've no sooner put your lips to a glass than it's empty. That's the human lot. You can't have your cake and eat it. You can't use your money and keep it in your purse. If you could, life would be too beautiful.'

He was good-humoured and kindly. When Nanon came in with her spinning-wheel, he said, 'You must be weary. Leave your hemp alone.'

'Oh, but why? I would be bored,' answered the servant.

'Poor Nanon! Would you like some blackcurrant cordial?'

'Oh, I won't say no to blackcurrant cordial. Madame makes it much better than the apothecaries do. The stuff they sell is like medicine.'

'They put too much sugar in. It has no flavour left,' said the old man.

When the family assembled at eight o'clock the next morning for breakfast, they looked for the first time like a picture of real domestic intimacy. Misfortune had quickly forged a bond between Madame Grandet, Eugénie, and Charles, and even Nanon instinctively sympathized with them. All four of them began to form one single family. As for the old winegrower, his avarice was satisfied and he was sure of seeing the dandy's departure without having to pay anything for him except the journey to Nantes, so he was almost indifferent to his nephew's presence in the house. He left the two children, as he called Charles and Eugénie, free to do as they liked under the eye of Madame Grandet, in whom, moreover, he had complete confidence as far as behaviour and morality were concerned. He was entirely occupied with seeing to the alignment of his meadows and ditches bordering the main road, with his poplar plantations by the Loire, and with the winter work in his vineyards and at Froidfond. The springtime of love then began for Eugénie. Since the midnight scene when she had given her savings to her cousin, her heart had followed the gift. They shared the same secret and looked at each other with expressions of mutual understanding. It strengthened their feelings, drawing them more closely and intimately together, and so putting the two cousins, as it were, outside ordinary life. Did not the fact that they were cousins authorize a gentleness in the voice and a tenderness in the eyes? And so Eugénie found happiness in making her cousin forget his grief in the childlike joys of a budding love affair. Are there not charming similarities between the beginning of love and the beginning of life? Do we not lull a child with sweet songs and kind looks? Do we not tell him marvellous tales which gild his future? Does not hope always unfold its radiant wings for him? Does he not shed alternate tears of joy and sorrow? Does he not pick quarrels about trifles, about pebbles with which he tries to build a shaky palace, about bunches of flowers, no sooner cut than forgotten? Is he not eager to advance time, to get ahead in life? Love is our second metamorphosis. Childhood and love were the same thing for Eugénie and Charles. Their love was a first passion with all its childish ways, all the dearer to their hearts because of the surrounding sadness. To begin with, their love struggled against the trappings of mourning, but this made it only more in keeping with the provincial simplicity of the dilapidated house. As he exchanged a few words with his cousin by the well in that silent courtyard, as they sat in the little garden on a mossy bench till sunset, saying sweet nothings to each other or silently absorbed in the cloister-like tranquillity that reigned between the ramparts and the house, Charles came to realize the sanctity of love. His great lady, his dear Annette, had acquainted him only with its troubles and storms, but now he was abandoning passion as it is in Paris, flirtatious, vain, and showy, in favour of pure, sincere love. He grew fond of the old house, whose ways he

121

no longer found so ridiculous. He would come downstairs first thing in the morning so as to be able to have a few minutes' chat with Eugénie before Grandet came to give out the day's provisions, but when the old man's footsteps were heard on the stairs, he would retreat into the garden. The mildly criminal nature of this early morning tryst, a secret even from Eugénie's mother, with Nanon pretending not to notice it, gave the most innocent love in the world the excitement of forbidden pleasures. Then, after lunch, when Père Grandet went to inspect his land and farms, Charles would stay with the mother and daughter and experience delights he had never known before, in holding out his hands for them to wind their skeins of thread on, in watching them at work, in listening to their chatter. The simplicity of this almost monastic life, which revealed to him the beauty of souls who knew nothing of the outside world, affected him keenly. He had thought such a way of life was impossible in France and that it existed only in Germany, and even then not outside legend and Auguste Lafontaine's* novels. Soon Eugénie was for him an ideal figure like Goethe's Marguerite,* but a Marguerite without the sin. And so, from day to day, his looks and words filled the poor girl's heart with joy and she abandoned herself deliciously to the current of love. She clutched at her happiness like a swimmer who clutches at a willow branch so that he can pull himself out of a river and rest on the bank. Did not the grief of an imminent departure already sadden the happiest hours of those fleeting days? Every day some little event reminded them of the approaching separation. For instance, three days after des Grassins had gone to Paris, Charles was taken by Grandet to the magistrate's court, with all the solemnity provincials attach to such acts, in order to sign a renunciation of all claims to his father's estate. A terrible repudiation! A kind of family apostasy. He went to Maître Cruchot to obtain two powers of attorney, one for des Grassins, the other for the friend commissioned to sell his belongings. Then he had to comply with the formalities required to obtain a passport

122

for leaving the country. Finally, when the simple mourning clothes Charles had ordered from Paris arrived, he sent for a Saumur tailor and sold his now useless wardrobe. Père Grandet was particularly pleased by this action.

'Ah, now you're dressed like a man who is setting out to make his fortune,' he said when he saw Charles dressed in a frock-coat of coarse, black cloth. 'Good, very good!'

'I assure you, sir,' replied Charles, 'that I fully appreciate my present circumstances.'

'What's that?' asked the old man, whose eyes lit up at the sight of a handful of gold which Charles showed him.

'Monsieur, I have collected up my studs and rings and all the useless articles I possess which might have some value, but since I don't know anyone in Saumur, I wanted to ask you this morning to . . .'

'To buy them from you?' asked Grandet, interrupting him.

'No, uncle, to tell me the name of an honest man who . . .'

'Give them to me, nephew. I'll go upstairs and value the gold, and come back and tell you what it's worth to the nearest centime. Jewellery gold,' he said, examining a long chain, 'eighteen to nineteen carats.'

The old man held out his big hand and took the pile of gold away.

'Cousin,' said Charles, 'allow me to give you these two clasps, which you could use to attach ribbons to your wrists. That would make a bracelet of a style that's very fashionable just now.'

'I accept them without hesitation, cousin,' she said, giving him a look of private understanding.

'Here is my mother's thimble, aunt. I have been keeping it carefully in my dressing-case,' said Charles, handing a pretty gold thimble to Madame Grandet, who had been wanting one for ten years.

'I can't possibly thank you enough, nephew,' said the old mother, her eyes filling with tears. 'When I say my prayers, morning and evening, I shall add one to my prayers for

123

travellers, the most fervent of all, especially for you. If I were to die, Eugénie would keep this jewel for you.'

'That's worth nine hundred and eighty-nine francs, seventy-five centimes, nephew,' said Grandet, opening the door. 'But to save you the trouble of selling it, I'll give you the money in livres.'

Among the people of the Loire valley, the words 'in livres'* mean that six-livre pieces are to be accepted for six francs without deduction.

'I hesitated to suggest that,' replied Charles, 'but I didn't like the idea of selling all my jewellery in the town you live in. As Napoleon used to say, dirty linen shouldn't be washed in public. Thank you for being so obliging.' Grandet scratched his ear and there was a moment's silence. 'Dear uncle,' continued Charles, looking at him uneasily, as if he were afraid of wounding his susceptibilities, 'my cousin and my aunt have each been kind enough to accept a little memento from me. Would you, in your turn, be so good as to accept these cuff-links, which are now useless to me. They will remind you of a poor boy who, though far away from you, will certainly think of those who, from now on, are all the family he has.'

'My dear boy, you must not strip yourself of all your belongings like that . . . What did he give you, wife?' he asked, turning to her eagerly. 'Ah! a gold thimble. And you, little girl? Well, well, diamond clasps. Yes, I'll take your cuff-links, my boy,' he continued, shaking Charles's hand. 'But . . . you must let me pay . . . your, yes . . . your passage to the Indies. Yes, I should like to pay for your passage. Besides, my boy, you see, when I valued your jewellery, I only took account of the value of the gold, and the workmanship may well add something to that. So, that's agreed. I'll give you fifteen hundred francs . . . in livres. Cruchot will lend me them, for I haven't a brass farthing here unless Perrotet, who is in arrears with his rent, pays up. Yes, that's what I'll do; I'll go and see him.'

He took up his hat, put on his gloves, and went out.

'You are going away, then,' said Eugénie, with a look in which sadness and admiration were mingled.

'I must,' he said, bowing his head.

For some days, Charles's bearing, manners, and speech had become those of a man in deep sorrow, who, though he feels weighed down by immense obligations, draws new courage from his misfortunes. He no longer deplored his lot, he had become a man. Never had Eugénie esteemed her cousin's character more highly than when she saw him come downstairs in his suit of coarse, black cloth, which so well became his now pale face and his sad expression. That day, the two women also put on mourning and they went with Charles to a requiem mass at the parish church for the soul of the late Guillaume Grandet.

At lunch, Charles received letters from Paris and read them right away.

'Well, cousin, are you pleased with the way your affairs are going?' whispered Eugénie.

'Never ask questions like that, my dear,' replied Grandet. 'Goodness me, I don't tell you about *my* business afairs. Why are you poking your nose into your cousin's? Leave the boy alone.'

'Oh, I have no secrets', said Charles.

'Ta, ta, ta, nephew, you'll have to learn to bridle your tongue in business.'

When the two lovers were alone in the garden, Charles led Eugénie to the old bench under the walnut tree, saying as they sat down, 'I was right about Alphonse. He has behaved admirably. He has conducted my affairs discreetly and honourably. I owe nothing in Paris. All my belongings have been sold well and he has used the three thousand remaining francs to buy a trading stock of cheap European novelties which can be sold at an excellent profit in the Indies. He has forwarded my packages to Nantes, where a ship for Java is being loaded. In five days' time, Eugénie, we must say goodbye to each other, perhaps for ever, but at any rate, for a long time. My trading stock and ten thousand francs sent by two of my friends are a very small beginning. I can't think of returning for several years. My dear cousin, don't link your life to mine. I might die. Perhaps you will have the opportunity of being comfortably settled in life . . .'

'Do you love me?' she asked.

'Oh, yes, indeed I do,' he replied in a tone which revealed the depths of his feeling.

'I shall wait for you, Charles. Oh dear! My father's at his window,' she said, pushing her cousin away as he came nearer to kiss her.

She fled under the archway and Charles followed her there. When she saw him, she retreated to the foot of the staircase and opened the folding door. Then, without really knowing where she was going, Eugénie found herself near Nanon's closet in the darkest part of the passage. There, Charles, who had followed her, took her hand, drew it to his heart, put his arm round her waist, and pressed her gently to him. Eugénie resisted no longer, she received and gave the purest, the sweetest, but also the most wholehearted of kisses.

'Dear Eugénie, a cousin is better than a brother. He can marry you,' said Charles.

'Amen,' said Nanon, opening the door of her cubby-hole.

The two startled lovers fled into the living-room, where Eugénie took up her work and Charles began to read the litanies of the Virgin in Madame Grandet's prayer-book.

'Well, I never!' said Nanon. 'We're all saying our prayers.'

As soon as Charles had announced the date of his departure, Grandet became very active so as to give the impression that he was much concerned about his nephew. He displayed liberality in everything that cost nothing, was active in finding a packer, said that the man wanted to charge too much for his packing-cases, and then insisted on making them himself, using old pieces of wood.

He got up early in the morning to plane, trim, smooth, and nail down his planks, and he made some very fine cases, in which he packed all Charles's belongings. He undertook to send them down the Loire by boat, to insure them, and to dispatch them for Nantes in good time.

Since the kiss exchanged in the passage, the hours fled by with terrifying speed for Eugénie. Sometimes she wanted to follow her cousin. Anyone who has experienced that most compelling of all passions, a passion whose duration is daily shortened by age, or time, or a mortal illness, or any of the fatalities that afflict mankind, will understand the anguish that Eugénie suffered. She would often weep as she walked in the garden, which, like the courtyard, the house, and the town, seemed too confined for her now; in her imagination she was pressing on ahead over the vast expanses of the sea. At last, the day before Charles's departure arrived. In the morning, while Nanon and Grandet were out, the precious casket with the two portraits was solemnly installed beside the now empty purse in the only drawer of the chest that could be locked. This treasure was not put away without many tears and kisses. When Eugénie placed the key in her bosom, she did not have the heart to prevent Charles from kissing the spot.

'The key will always stay there, my dear.'

'And my heart will always be with it there, too.'

'Oh, Charles, you mustn't say that,' she said, but not at all crossly.

'Aren't we married?' he replied. 'I have your word. Accept mine.'

'Yours for ever,' they both said and repeated.

No purer promise was ever made on earth. Eugénie's innocent sincerity had momentarily sanctified Charles's love. Breakfast the next morning was sad. In spite of the gold-embroidered gown and gilt cross which Charles had given her, even Nanon, who was free to express her feelings, had tears in her eyes.

127

'The poor, dear little gentleman, going away off to sea. May God guide him.'

At half past ten, the family set off to go with Charles to the stage-coach for Nantes. Nanon had untied the dog and locked the door, and insisted on carrying Charles's overnight bag. All the tradesmen in the old street were at the doors of their shops to see the procession go by, and Maître Cruchot joined them in the square.

'You mustn't cry, Eugénie,' said her mother.

'Nephew, you are going away poor, come back rich', said Grandet at the inn door, kissing Charles on both cheeks. 'You will find your father's honour in safe keeping. I, Grandet, take responsibility for that. For the rest, it's up to you . . .'

'Oh, uncle, you make the bitterness of my departure more bearable. Isn't that the finest present you could give me?'

Not understanding the words of the old cooper whom he had interrupted, Charles shed tears of gratitude on his uncle's sun-tanned face, while Eugénie gripped her father's hand and her cousin's as tightly as she could. Only the lawyer was smiling in admiration of Grandet's subtlety, for he alone had understood what the old man meant. The four Saumur townsfolk, with several people standing around them, stayed by the coach until it left. Then, when it had disappeared over the bridge and could only be heard in the distance, the winegrower called out, 'Have a good journey!' Fortunately Maître Cruchot was the only one who heard this remark. Eugénie and her mother had gone to a part of the quay from where they could still see the coach, and were waving their white handkerchiefs. Charles replied by waving his.

'Mother, I wish I could have God's power for a single moment,' said Eugénie when Charles's handkerchief was out of sight.

In order not to interrupt the course of events which took place within the Grandet family, we must cast a glance ahead at the operations which were undertaken on Grandet's behalf in Paris by des Grassins. A month after the banker's departure, Grandet was in possession of a certificate for government stock, bringing in an income of a hundred thousand livres a year, bought at eighty francs a share. The information contained in the inventory at his death shed no light at all on the means adopted by his suspicious mind for changing his gold into the sum needed to buy the stock itself. Maître Cruchot thought that Nanon, without being aware of it, was the faithful agent of the transfer of capital. About that time, the servant was away for five days, on the pretext of going to attend to something at Froidfond, as if the old man was capable of leaving any business unfinished. As for the affairs of the firm of Guillaume Grandet, all the cooper's expectations were realized.

As everyone knows, very precise information about the great fortunes of Paris and of the departments is kept at the Bank of France. The names of the des Grassins and of Félix Grandet of Saumur were well known there and enjoyed the esteem given to financial celebrities whose fortunes are based on extensive, unmortgaged landed properties. So the arrival of the Saumur banker, with instructions, it was said, to liquidate the Grandet firm of Paris honourably, sufficed to spare the dead merchant's shade the shame of protested bills.* The seals were lifted in the presence of the creditors, and the family lawyer proceeded, in due form, to make an inventory of the estate. Next, des Grassins called a meeting of the creditors, who unanimously elected the Saumur banker, together with François Keller, head of a rich banking house and one of the main creditors, as liquidators. They were entrusted with all the powers necessary to safeguard both the family honour and the creditors' claims. These transactions were facilitated by the credit accorded to Grandet of Saumur and by the hope that it inspired in the minds of the creditors through the agency of des Grassins. Not one of the creditors made any objection. No one thought of transferring his claim to the profit and loss account, and they all said to themselves, 'Grandet of

Saumur will pay.' Six months elapsed. The Parisians had withdrawn the bills in circulation and put them away underneath the other papers in their files. That was the first result the cooper wanted to achieve. Nine months after the first meeting, the two liquidators distributed forty-seven per cent to each creditor. This sum was realized by the sale of securities, properties, and sundry goods and chattels belonging to the late Guillaume Grandet, a sale conducted with scrupulous fairness. The liquidation was carried out with the most punctilious honesty. The creditors were happy to acknowledge the admirable, indisputable honour of the Grandet family. When these praises had circulated for an appropriate period of time, the creditors asked for the rest of their money. They were obliged to write a collective letter to Grandet.

'Here it comes,' said the former cooper, throwing the letter into the fire. 'Have patience, good friends.'

In reply to the proposals contained in the letter, Grandet of Saumur asked that all documents concerning claims against his brother's estate should be lodged with a lawyer, along with receipts for the payments already made. The pretext for this was that it would clarify the accounts and allow an accurate statement of the liabilities of the estate to be drawn up. This request raised innumerable problems. Usually, a creditor is a kind of maniac. One day he is ready to agree to a settlement, the next he is breathing fire and brimstone, a little later he will agree to anything. Today his wife is in a good mood, his youngest child has cut his teeth, everything is going well at home, and he doesn't want to lose a penny; tomorrow it will be raining, he won't be able to go out, he will be depressed, so he'll say yes to any proposal which would settle a matter. The day after tomorrow he will require guarantees and at the end of the month he will demand your head, the brute! A creditor is like the house sparrow on whose tail small children are encouraged to try to put a pinch of salt. But the creditor turns the comparison against his debtors when he can't lay hands on any part of what is due to him. Grandet had studied the varying moods of creditors, and his brother's conformed to all his expectations. Some became angry and refused point-blank to lodge their claims with the lawyer. 'Good! it's going well,' said Grandet, rubbing his hands as he read the letters which des Grassins wrote to him about the business. Others agreed to lodge their claims only on condition that these were clearly stated, that they renounced none of their rights, and that they even reserved to themselves the right of declaring a bankruptcy. There was more correspondence, after which Grandet of Saumur agreed to all the stipulated conditions. By means of this concession, the more benevolent creditors made the more tough-minded see reason. The claims were lodged, but not without some grumbling. 'The old fellow is laughing at you and at us,' they said to des Grassins. Twenty-three months after Guillaume Grandet's death, many merchants, caught up in the activity of business life in Paris, had forgotten what the Grandet estate owed them or thought of it only to say, 'I'm beginning to think the forty-seven per cent is all I'll get out of that.' The cooper had counted on the power of time, who, he said, is a good chap. At the end of the third year, des Grassins wrote to Grandet that, by paying ten per cent of the two million, four hundred thousand francs still owed by the firm of Grandet, he had persuaded the creditors to hand over their claims to him. Grandet replied that the lawyer and stockbroker whose dreadful bankruptcies had caused his brother's death, *they* were still alive and might have become solvent again; they should be sued so that something could be got out of them, which would reduce the amount of the deficit. At the end of the fourth year, the deficit was finally and duly fixed at the sum of twelve hundred thousand francs. Then there were negotiations, lasting for six months, between the liquidators and the creditors and between Grandet and the liquidators. To cut a long story short, being strongly pressed to pay up, about the ninth month of that year, Grandet of Saumur wrote, in reply to the two liquidators, that his nephew, who had made a fortune in the Indies, had declared the intention of paying his father's debts in full. He could not take it on himself to wind up the business by paying the creditors less than their due without consulting his nephew; he was waiting for a reply. Towards the middle of the fifth year, the creditors were still being held at bay by the words *in full*, let fall from time to time by the sublime cooper, who would chuckle to himself and never mention 'those Parisians!' without a cunning smile and an oath. But a fate unheard of in the annals of commerce was reserved for the creditors. When the course of this story requires them to reappear, they will still be in the position in which Grandet had kept them. When government stock reached a hundred and fifteen, Père Grandet sold out and withdrew from Paris two million, four hundred thousand francs in gold, which he added to the six hundred thousand francs of compound interest earned from his investment and kept in his little kegs. Des Grassins remained in Paris for two reasons. First of all, he was elected a deputy. Then, though father of a family but bored with the dull life of Saumur, he became infatuated with Florine, one of the prettiest actresses at the Théâtre de Madame; the temperament of the quartermaster latent in the banker had revived. There is no point in discussing his behaviour; in Saumur it was considered profoundly immoral. His wife was lucky enough to be mistress of her own property and she had enough ability to manage the business in Saumur, which she continued in her own name so as to repair the inroads made into her fortune by Monsieur des Grassins' folly. The Cruchot party did all they could to exploit the quasi-widow's false position, so that she made a very bad match for her daughter and had to give up any hope of a marriage between Eugénie Grandet and her son. Adolphe joined his father in Paris and, so it's said, turned out very badly. The Cruchots were triumphant.

'Your husband has no sense,' Grandet would say whenever he advanced Madame des Grassins a loan (on security). 'I am very sorry for you. You are a good little woman.'

132

'Ah, Monsieur,' replied the poor lady, 'who would have thought that the day he left your house to go to Paris, he was going headlong to his ruin?'

'Heaven is my witness, Madame, that up to the last moment I did all I could to stop him going. Monsieur le Président was very anxious to take his place, and if he was so keen to go, now we know why.'

And so Grandet had no obligation to des Grassins.

Family Sorrows

In every situation, women have more cause for grief than men and suffer more. A man has his strength and the exercise of his powers. He is active, he comes and goes, he is busy, he thinks, he plans for the future and finds consolation in it. That is what Charles did. But a woman stays at home; she remains face to face with her sorrow, with nothing to distract her from it; she plumbs the depths of the abyss it has opened up, and often fills it with her prayers and tears. That is what Eugénie did. She was starting out on her destiny. To feel, to love, to suffer, to be devoted, will always be the theme of women's lives. Eugénie was to experience a woman's lot to the full, but without its consolations. Her moments of happiness, had they been collected like nails scattered on a wall (in Bossuet's* sublime words), were not one day to fill the hollow of her hand. Sorrows never keep one waiting, and for her they soon arrived. The day after Charles's departure, the Grandet household returned to its usual ways and looked the same to everyone, except to Eugénie, who suddenly found it very empty. Without telling her father, she insisted that Charles's room should stay as he had left it. Madame Grandet and Nanon were willing accomplices in the maintenance of this *status quo*.

'Who knows if he won't come back sooner than we think?' she said.

'Oh, I'd like to see him back here,' replied Nanon. 'I was getting quite used to him. He was so nice, a perfect gentleman, almost as pretty as a girl with his curly hair.' Eugénie looked at Nanon. 'My goodness, Mademoiselle, your eyes are fit to make you lose your soul. Don't look at a body like that.'

From that day on, Mademoiselle Grandet's good looks took on a new character. The solemn thoughts of love which slowly pervaded her soul, the dignity of a woman who is

134

loved, gave her features the kind of radiance which painters represent by a halo. Before her cousin's arrival, Eugénie could be compared to the Virgin before the conception; when he had gone, she was like the Virgin mother; she had conceived love. These two Marys, so different from each other and so well depicted by some Spanish painters, constitute one of the most brilliant of the images in which Christianity is so rich. The day after Charles's departure, she went to mass—she had vowed to go every day—and on the way home she bought a map of the world from the town's bookseller. She pinned it up near her mirror so that she could follow her cousin's route to the Indies and feel, evening and morning, almost as if she were in the ship which was taking him there, as if she could see him, ask him a thousand questions, and say to him, 'Are you alright? Aren't you unhappy? Are you really thinking of me when you see that star, whose beauty and purpose you taught me to appreciate?' Then, in the morning, she would sit pensively under the walnut tree on the worm-eaten bench covered with grey moss, where they had said so many nice and silly things to each other, where they had built castles in the air about the pretty home they would have. She thought of the future as she looked at the narrow patch of sky visible between the walls, then at the section of the old wall and at the roof under which was Charles's room. In short, her love was that solitary, genuine, lasting love which pervades every thought and becomes the substance, or, as our ancestors would have said, the stuff, of life. When her father's so-called friends came to play cards in the evening, she was cheerful, she hid her feelings, but all morning she would talk about Charles with her mother and Nanon. Nanon had realized that she could sympathize with her young mistress's suffering without failing in her duty to her old master, and she would say to Eugénie, 'If I'd had a man of my own, I'd have followed him . . . down to hell. I'd have . . . oh, I don't know what . . . oh well, I'd have worked myself to death for him. But . . . there's been no one. I'll die without knowing what it's like to live. Would you believe it, Mademoiselle, but that old Cornoiller, who's a good fellow all the same, hovers around my skirts because of my savings, just like the folks who sniff at the master's pile when they come here courting you? I can see that, because I'm still pretty smart, even though I'm as big as a house. Ah! Well, Mam'zelle, I like that, even though it's not love.'

And so two months went by. This domestic life, which used to be so monotonous, had been enlivened by the tremendous interest of the secret which bound the three women more closely together. For them, Charles was still there, coming and going beneath the grimy living-room rafters. Morning and evening, Eugénie would open the dressing-case and gaze at her aunt's portrait. One Sunday morning, her mother surprised her as she was busy trying to discern Charles's features in the face in the picture. Madame Grandet was then initiated into the terrible secret of how Eugénie had received the dressing-case and given her treasure in exchange.

'You gave him the whole lot!' said her mother, appalled. 'But what will you say to your father, on New Year's Day, when he wants to see your gold?'

A fixed look came into Eugénie's eyes, and for half the morning the two women were in a state of mortal terror. They were so agitated that they missed the time for high mass and could only go later to the military mass.* In three days, the year 1819 would end. In three days, a terrible drama would begin, a bourgeois tragedy without poison, dagger, or bloodshed, but, as far as the actors were concerned, more cruel than all the tragedies enacted in the renowned house of Atreus.*

'What will become of us?' Madame Grandet asked her daughter, letting her knitting fall to her lap.

For two months the poor mother had been so worried that the woollen sleeves she needed for the winter were not yet finished. This fact, though purely domestic and apparently quite unimportant, had sad consequences for her. Without her warm sleeves, she unfortunately caught a nasty chill after a violent sweat brought on by one of her

136

husband's terrible rages.

'I was thinking, my poor child, that if you had confided your secret to me, we would have had time to write to Paris to Monsieur des Grassins. He might have been able to send us gold coins that looked like yours. And, although Grandet knows them well, perhaps . . .'

'But where would we have got so much money?'

'I would have pledged my own property. Besides, Monsieur des Grassins would have certainly . . .'

'It's too late now,' replied Eugénie in a dull, strained voice, interrupting her mother. 'Tomorrow morning, we have to go and wish him a happy New Year in his room, don't we?'

'But, my dear, why shouldn't I go and see the Cruchots?'

'No, no. That would put me in their power and make us dependent on them. Besides, I have made up my mind. I did what was right and I don't regret anything. God will protect me. May his holy will be done. Oh, if you had read his letter, mother, you would have thought only of him.'

The next morning, the first of January 1820, the abject terror which had gripped mother and daughter suggested to them the most natural excuse for not making their ceremonious visit to Grandet in his room. The winter of 1819 to 1820 was one of the severest of the time. Snow lay thick on the roofs.

As soon as Madame Grandet heard her husband moving about in his room, she said to him, 'Grandet, do ask Nanon to light a little fire in my room. It's so bitterly cold that I'm freezing under my blankets. I have reached an age when I need to take a little care. Besides,' she continued after a short pause, 'Eugénie can come here to dress. The poor girl might catch a chill dressing in her own room in such weather. Then we'll go down and wish you a happy New Year by the living-room fire.'

'Ta, ta, ta, ta, what a chatterbox! What a way to begin the year, Madame Grandet! You've never talked so much in your life. I don't suppose you've eaten a piece of bread dipped in wine, have you?' There was a moment's silence. 'Well,' continued the old fellow, probably not displeased by his wife's suggestion, 'I'll do as you ask, Madame Grandet. You're really a good woman and I don't want any harm to come to you because of your age, although, on the whole, the La Bertellières are a tough lot . . . Eh, isn't that so?' he called out after a pause. 'Still, we inherited their money, so I forgive them.' And he coughed.

'You're very gay this morning, Monsieur,' said the poor woman gravely.

'Oh, I'm always gay . . .

> Gay, gay, the cooper's gay,
> Mend your washtub any day!

he sang, as he came into his wife's room, fully dressed. 'Yes, by gum, it really is cold this morning. We'll have a good breakfast, wife. Des Grassins has sent me some *pâté de foie gras* with truffles. I'm going to meet the coach to collect it. He's very likely put a double napoleon in with it for Eugénie,' the cooper whispered in his wife's ear. 'I've no gold left, wife. I still had a few old coins left; I can tell *you* that. But I had to use them for business.' And to celebrate New Year's Day, he kissed her on the forehead.

'Eugénie,' cried her devoted mother, 'I don't know which side your father slept on, but he's in a good mood this morning. It's alright, we'll manage.'

'What's come over the master this morning?' asked Nanon as she came into the room to light the fire. 'First, he said, "Good morning, a happy New Year, old girl! Go and light a fire in my wife's room; she's cold." And I was struck dumb when I saw him hold out his hand to give me a six-franc piece which is hardly clipped at all. Here, Madame, just look at it. Oh, what a fine man he is, after all. There are some men who, the older they get, the harder they get. But he's becoming as sweet as your blackcurrant cordial, and improves with age. He's a real perfect, real good man . . .'

The secret reason for Grandet's good humour lay in the complete success of his speculation. After deducting the amount the cooper owed him for discounting Dutch bills worth a hundred and fifty thousand francs, and for

138

the advances required to complete the purchase of a hundred thousand livres of government stock, Monsieur des Grassins was sending Grandet, by the stage-coach, thirty thousand francs in écus,* the remainder of his half-yearly dividend, and had informed him of the rise in value of government stocks. They stood then at 89; at the end of January, the most prominent capitalists were buying them at 92. For the last two months, Grandet had been making twelve per cent on his capital; he had discharged his liabilities and would receive, from now on, fifty thousand francs every six months without having to pay taxes or spend money on expenses. At last he understood the importance of stock, an investment for which provincial people show a deep aversion, and he saw that, after five years, he would be master of a capital of six million, which had been amassed without much trouble and, added to the value of his landed property, would constitute a colossal fortune. The six francs he had given to Nanon were perhaps the payment for an immense service that the servant had unwittingly rendered her master.

'Oh, oh, where's Père Grandet off to, dashing along so early in the morning as if to put out a fire?' wondered the tradesmen as they opened their shops. Then, when they saw him coming back from the quay, followed by a porter from the coach-office carting well-filled sacks on a wheelbarrow, one of them said, 'Water always flows to the river. The old chap was going for his écus.' 'They roll in from Paris, from Froidfond, and from Holland,' said another. 'He'll buy up the whole of Saumur before he's done,' exclaimed a third. 'He doesn't worry about the cold. He's always attending to his business,' a woman said to her husband. 'Hey, Monsieur Grandet, if those get in your way, I'll take them off your hands,' said a cloth-merchant, his next-door neighbour.

'Bah, they're only pennies,' replied the winegrower.

'Silver ones,' murmured the porter.

'If you want me to do anything for you, keep your mouth shut,' said the old man to the porter, as he opened the door.

'Oh, the old fox, I thought he was deaf,' thought the porter. 'It looks as if he can hear when the weather's cold.'

'Here's twenty sous for your New Year present, and mum's the word! And now be off!' said Grandet. 'Nanon will bring back your barrow.'

'Nanon, have the womenfolk gone to mass?'

'Yes, Monsieur.'

'Come on, get going! To work!' he called, loading her with bags. In a moment the écus had been carried up to his room and he had locked himself in. 'Knock at my door when breakfast's ready. Take the barrow back to the coach-office.'

The family did not have breakfast till ten o'clock.

'Your father won't ask to see your gold in this room,' Madame Grandet said to her daughter as they came in from mass. 'In any case, you can pretend to feel the cold. Then we'll have time to replenish your purse before your birthday.'

As Grandet came downstairs he was planning to change his Parisian écus into good, solid gold without delay, and thinking of his admirably successful speculation in government bonds. He had decided to invest his earnings in this way until the stock rose to a hundred francs. These thoughts were disastrous for Eugénie. As soon as he came in, the two women wished him a happy New Year, his daughter putting her arms round his neck affectionately, Madame Grandet with grave dignity.

'Ah, my child,' he said, kissing his daughter on both cheeks. 'I am working for you, you know. I want you to be happy. You need money to be happy. Without money, nothing doing! Look, here's a new napoleon. I've had it sent from Paris. My goodness me, there's not a scrap of gold in the house, except for yours. You're the only one that has any gold. Show me your gold, my pet.'

'Oh no! It's too cold. Let's have breakfast,' answered Eugénie.

'Oh well, we'll see it afterwards, eh? That will help our digestions. Old des Grassins has sent us this, in spite of

140

everything,' he continued. 'So eat up, children, it doesn't cost us a penny. He's doing well, des Grassins; I'm pleased with him. The old bird's looking after Charles's business, and for nothing, what's more. He's managing the late lamented Grandet's affairs very well. Ooh, ooh!' he said with his mouth full, after a pause. 'That's good. Have some, wife. That'll feed you for at least two days.'

'I'm not hungry. I'm not at all well, you know that.'

'Oh well, you can eat your fill without fear of bursting your barrel. You are a La Bertellière, a woman with a sound constitution. You are just a bit yellow today, but I like yellow.'

A prisoner condemned to death, awaiting an ignominious public execution, is probably less terrified than Madame Grandet and her daughter were at the prospect of what would happen after this family breakfast was over. The more gaily the winegrower spoke and ate, the more their hearts sank. Yet the daughter had one support in this crisis; she drew strength from her love.

'For him, for him, I would die a thousand deaths,' she said to herself.

At this thought, she looked at her mother, her eyes blazing with courage.

'Clear all that away,' Grandet said to Nanon when, about eleven o'clock, breakfast was over. 'But leave us the table. We'll be able to survey your little treasure more comfortably,' he said, looking at Eugénie. 'Little —believe me, it's certainly not that. The actual value of what you have is five thousand nine hundred and fifty-nine francs. Add the forty you got this morning, that makes six thousand francs, all but one. Well, I'll give you one franc to make up the sum myself, because you see, little girl . . . But why are you listening to us, Nanon? Be off with you and get on with your work,' said the old man. Nanon disappeared. 'Listen, Eugénie, you must give me your gold. You won't refuse your old papa, little girl, will you?' The two women said nothing. 'I haven't any gold myself now. I had some, but it's all gone. I'll give you six thousand francs in livres, in exchange for it, and you'll invest them following my instructions. You mustn't think about your "dozen" any more. When you get married—and that will be quite soon—I'll find you a husband who can give you the finest dozen that anyone's heard of in the whole district. Listen to me, little girl. There's a fine opportunity available. You can invest your six thousand francs in government stock, and every six months you'll have nearly two hundred francs in interest, without taxes or expenses, and unaffected by hail, frost, or flood, or any of the things that eat up income from land. Perhaps you're reluctant to part with your gold, are you, little girl? Bring it me, all the same. I'll collect gold coins for you, ducats from Holland, Portuguese moidores and genovines, and the Mogul's rupees, and, together with what I'll give you on your birthdays, in three years you'll have recovered half of your nice little treasure in gold. What do you say to that, little girl? Lift up your head. Go on, go and get it, my pet. You ought to give me a hearty kiss of thanks for telling you all these secrets and mysteries about the life and death of money. For truly, money lives and breeds like men; it comes and goes, it toils, it begets more of its kind.'

Eugénie got up, but after taking a few steps towards the door she turned round suddenly, looked straight at her father, and said, 'I have none of *my* gold left.'

'You have none of your gold left!' exclaimed Grandet, rearing like a horse who hears a cannon fired ten steps away from him.

'No, I have none left.'

'You are mistaken, Eugénie.'

'No.'

'By my father's pruning-hook!'

When the cooper swore like that, the rafters shook.

'Heaven help us! How pale Madame's gone!' cried Nanon.

'Grandet, your rage will be the death of me,' said the poor woman.

'Ta, ta, ta, ta, in your family, you never die!—Eugénie, what have you done with your coins?' he shouted, turning to her in a fury.

'Monsieur,' said the girl, bending over Madame Grandet, 'my mother's very ill. Look at her, don't kill her.'

Grandet was alarmed by the pallor that had spread over his wife's previously sallow face.

'Nanon, help me to go to bed,' said the mother faintly, 'I am dying.'

Nanon gave her arm to her mistress at once and Eugénie did the same, but it was not without great difficulty that they managed to get her up to her room, for she nearly fainted at every step. Grandet was left alone. After a few moments, however, he went up seven or eight steps and called out, 'Eugénie, when your mother's in bed, come downstairs.'

'Yes, father.'

She reassured her mother and came down right away.

'You're going to tell me where your gold is, my girl,' said Grandet.

'Father, if you give me presents that I can't do as I like with, take them back,' answered Eugénie coldly, taking the napoleon from the mantelpiece and holding it out to him.

Grandet pounced on the napoleon and slipped it into his waistcoat pocket.

'I'll certainly never give you anything again, not even that,' he said, clicking his thumb-nail against his front teeth. 'So you despise your father; so you don't trust him; so you don't know what the word father means. If he's not everything to you, he's nothing. Where's your gold?'

'Father, I love and respect you in spite of your anger, but I must very humbly point out to you that I'm twenty-two years old. You've told me often enough for me to know by now that I am of age. I have disposed of my money as I chose to, and you can rest assured that it is well invested . . .'

'Where:

143

'That's an inviolable secret,' she said. 'Don't you have your secrets?'

'Am I not head of my family? Can't I have my business affairs?'

'And this is *my* business affair.'

'It must be a bad affair if you can't tell your father about it, Mademoiselle Grandet.'

'It is excellent and I can't tell my father about it.'

'At least tell me, when did you give your gold away?' Eugénie shook her head. 'You still had it on your birthday, hadn't you?' Love had made Eugénie as cunning as avarice had made her father, and she again shook her head. 'I've never seen such obstinacy, nor such robbery,' said Grandet, his voice rising in a crescendo which gradually rang through the house. 'What, here, in my own house, someone has taken your gold! The only gold in the house! And I'm not to know who? Gold is an expensive commodity. The best of girls can make mistakes, can give away all sorts of things. That happens in the upper classes and even in middle-class families. But to give away gold! For you did give it to someone, didn't you?' Eugénie remained unmoved. 'Has anyone ever seen such a daughter? Can you be a child of mine? If you invested it, you must have a receipt . . . .'

'Was I free, yes or no, to do what I liked with it? Was it mine?'

'But you are a child.'

'I am of age.'

Dumbfounded by his daughter's logic, Grandet turned pale, stamped his foot, and swore. Then, finding words at last, he shouted, 'Accursed serpent of a daughter! Oh, you bad lot, you know I love you and you take advantage of it. She's cutting her father's throat! Good Lord, you must have thrown your fortune at the feet of that good-for-nothing with his fine leather boots. By my father's pruning-hook, I can't disinherit you, by my casks! But I curse you, your cousin, and your children! You'll see no good come from all this, do you hear? If it was to Charles that . . . But no, it's not possible. What, that vicious little dandy rob me . . .' He looked at his daughter, who stood there cold and silent. 'She won't budge; she won't bat an eyelid. She's more of a Grandet than I am. You didn't give your gold away for nothing, at least? Come on, did you?' Eugénie looked at her father with an ironic glance which exasperated him. 'Eugénie, you are in my house, in your father's house. If you are to stay here, you must obey my orders. The church commands you to obey me.' Eugénie bowed her head. 'You hurt me in what I hold most dear,' he continued. 'I don't want to see you until you do as I say. Go to your room. You will stay there until I allow you to leave it. Nanon will bring you bread and water. You heard me, go!'

Eugénie burst into tears and fled to her mother's bedside. Grandet paced several times round his garden in the snow without noticing the cold, and then, suspecting that his daughter must be with his wife, and delighted to catch her disobeying his orders, he hurried upstairs, as agile as a cat. He entered his wife's room to find Eugénie with her face buried in her mother's bosom and Madame Grandet stroking her daughter's hair.

'Don't worry, my poor child. Your father will calm down.'

'She no longer has a father,' said the cooper. 'Was it really you and me, Madame Grandet, who produced a daughter as disobedient as this one? A pretty upbringing she's had, and a religious one at that! Well, you're not in your room. Off with you, to prison, to prison, Mademoiselle.'

'Do you want to deprive me of my daughter, Monsieur?' asked Madame Grandet, her face flushed with fever.

'If you want to keep her, take her away; clear out of the house, both of you. Damn it all, where's the gold? What's become of the gold?'

Eugénie got up, looked proudly at her father, and went to her room. The old man locked her in.

'Nanon,' he called, 'put out the fire in the living-room.' Then he came and sat down in an armchair by the fireplace in his wife's room, saying, 'I'm sure she's given it to that penniless seducer, Charles; he was only after our money.'

In her love for her daughter, threatened with such danger, Madame Grandet found enough strength to remain apparently unmoved, deaf and dumb.

'I know nothing of all this,' she replied, turning her face to the wall to escape her husband's glittering eyes. 'Your violence makes me so ill that, if I trust my own feelings, I shall leave this room only when I'm carried out feet first. You ought to have shown more consideration for me at this time, Monsieur. I have never caused you any trouble; at least, I don't think I have. Your daughter loves you. I believe her to be as innocent as a new-born child. So don't distress her; reconsider your decision. The cold is very sharp, and you might make her seriously ill.'

'I shall neither see her nor speak to her. She will stay in her room on bread and water till she has obeyed her father. What the devil, the head of a family ought to know what happens to the gold in his house. She owned perhaps the only rupees in France, and then there were the Genoese coins and the Dutch ducats.'

'Monsieur, Eugénie is our only child, and even if she had thrown them in the river . . .'

'Thrown them in the river!' cried the old man. 'Thrown them in the river! Are you mad, Madame Grandet? What I've said, I've said; you know that. If you want peace restored in the house, make your daughter confess, worm it out of her. Women understand each other better about that sort of thing than we men do. Whatever she's done, I won't eat her. Is she afraid of me? Even if she had covered her cousin in gold from head to foot, he's on the high seas, isn't he? We can't run after him . . .'

'Well, Monsieur . . .' As she started to reply, Madame Grandet noticed her husband's wart twitching terribly, for her tense, nervous state or her affection for her daughter had sharpened her awareness. She changed what she was going to say without changing her tone. 'Well, Monsieur, have I more authority over her than you have? She said nothing to me, she takes after you.'

146

'My goodness, you've got the gift of the gab this morning. Ta, ta, ta, ta, I believe you're defying me. Maybe you're in league with her.'

He stared hard at his wife.

'Really, Monsieur Grandet, if you want to kill me, you have only to go on like this. I tell you, Monsieur, and were it to cost me my life I would say it again: you are unjust to your daughter; she is more reasonable than you are. That money belonged to her. She could only have made a good use of it, and God alone has a right to know what deeds of charity we do. Monsieur, I beg you, restore Eugénie to your favour . . . In that way you will reduce the effect your anger has had on me, and perhaps you will save my life. My daughter, Monsieur, give me back my daughter.'

'I'm clearing out,' he said. 'I can't bear to stay in my own house. The mother and daughter argue and talk as if . . . Brooouh! Pouah! You've given me a cruel New Year present, Eugénie,' he called. 'Yes, yes, you may well cry! What's the good of going to communion six times every three months, if you secretly give your father's gold to a good-for-nothing who'll eat your heart out when you've only that left to give him. You'll see what your Charles is worth with his morocco leather boots and his innocent looks. He has neither heart nor soul, since he dares carry off a poor girl's savings without her parents' consent.'

When the front door was closed, Eugénie came out of her room and went to her mother's bedside.

'You are brave for your daughter,' she said.

'You see where wrongdoing leads us, my child . . . You made me tell a lie.'

'Oh, I shall ask God to punish only me.'

'Is it true', asked Nanon in dismay, as she came into the room, 'that now Mademoiselle's to be on bread and water for the rest of her days?'

'What does it matter, Nanon?' asked Eugénie calmly.

'And do you think I'll eat *frippe** when the daughter of the house is eating dry bread? No, no.'

'Don't say a word about all this, Nanon,' said Eugénie.

147

'I'll keep my mouth shut, you'll see.'

Grandet dined alone for the first time in twenty-four years.

'So you're a widower now, Monsieur,' Nanon said to him. 'It's not at all nice being a widower with two women in the house.'

'I wasn't speaking to you. Hold your tongue or I'll send you packing. What's in the saucepan that I hear simmering on the stove?'

'It's some fat that I'm melting down . . .'

'Some people will be coming in this evening. Light the fire.'

The Cruchots, Madame des Grassins, and her son arrived at eight o'clock and were surprised to see neither Madame Grandet nor her daughter.

'My wife is not very well. Eugénie is sitting with her,' said the old winegrower, his face showing no emotion.

An hour went by in trivial conversation, and then Madame des Grassins, who had gone up to see Madame Grandet, came downstairs again. Everyone asked her, 'How is Madame Grandet?' 'Not at all well, not at all,' she said. 'The state of her health seems to me very worrying. At her age, one must take the greatest care, Papa Grandet.'

'We'll see,' replied the winegrower abstractedly.

They all wished him goodnight. When the Cruchots were out in the street, Madame des Grassins said, 'Something's happened at the Grandets. The mother's in a very bad way without realizing it. The daughter's eyes are red, as if she had been crying for a long time. I wonder if they want to marry her off against her will.'

When the winegrower was in bed, Nanon tiptoed silently in her stocking-feet to Eugénie's room and showed her a pâté made in a casserole.

'Look, Mademoiselle,' said the good soul, 'Cornoiller gave me a hare. You eat so little that the pâté will last you for fully eight days. And in this frost it doesn't risk going bad. At least you won't be kept on dry bread. That's not good for you at all.'

'Poor Nanon,' said Eugénie, pressing her hand.

'I made it very tasty and very light, and *he* didn't notice anything. I got the bacon and the bay leaves out of my six francs. I've a right to do as I like with my own money.' Then the servant fled, thinking she heard Grandet moving.

During a period of several months, the winegrower came regularly to see his wife at different hours of the day. He did not mention his daughter's name, or see her, or make the slightest reference to her. Madame Grandet did not leave her room, and her condition deteriorated from day to day. Nothing made the old cooper give way. He remained as immovable, harsh, and cold as a pillar of granite. He continued to come and go according to his usual habits. But he no longer stammered, talked less, and was harder in business dealings than he had ever been. Quite often he made a slip in his calculations.

'Something's up at the Grandets,' the Cruchot party and the Grassinites were saying. 'What's happened in the Grandet household?' was a stock question that people regularly asked each other at all the Saumur evening gatherings. Eugénie went to church as usual, escorted by Nanon. If Madame des Grassins said a few words to her on the way out, she replied evasively and without satisfying the curiosity of the banker's wife. After two months, however, it was impossible to conceal the secret of Eugénie's imprisonment either from the Cruchots or from Madame des Grassins. There came a time when no pretexts were adequate to explain her continual absence. Then, without anyone knowing who had given away the secret, the whole town learned that, since New Year's Day, on her father's orders, Mademoiselle Grandet had been locked up in her room, on bread and water, and without a fire, and that Nanon made delicacies for her and brought them to her at night; it was even known that the girl could see and care for her mother only when her father was out of the house. Grandet's behaviour was then very severely censured. The whole town, as it were, outlawed him; they recalled his double-dealing and his hard bargains, and excommunicated him. When he passed by, everyone pointed at him and whispered. When his daughter went down the winding street with Nanon, to mass or vespers, all the inhabitants, filled with curiosity, went to their windows to study the rich heiress's face and bearing, which expressed angelic sweetness and melancholy. Her imprisonment, her father's disgrace, were nothing to her. Could she not see the map of the world, the little bench, the garden, the section of the wall? Did she not savour on her lips the honey left by love's kisses? For some time she was unaware of the gossip about her in the town, just as her father was. Devout and pure in God's sight, her conscience and her love helped her to endure her father's vengeful anger with patience. But one deep sorrow silenced all the others. Her tender, gentle mother, whose soul, as she neared the grave, gave forth a beautifying radiance, was sinking day by day. Eugénie often reproached herself for being the innocent cause of the malady that was slowly consuming her mother. Although Madame Grandet tried to allay her daughter's remorse, it bound her even more closely to her love. Every morning, as soon as her father had gone out, she would come to her mother's bedside and Nanon would bring her breakfast there. But poor Eugénie, sad and feeling her mother's suffering, would draw Nanon's attention to Madame Grandet's face with a silent gesture, weep, and not dare to mention her cousin.

Madame Grandet had to be the first to say, 'Where is *he*? Why does *he* not write?'

Neither mother nor daughter had any idea of distance.

'Let's think of him and not talk about him, mother,' Eugénie would reply. 'You are ill; you come before everything.'

Everything meant *him*.

'My dears, I am not sorry that my life is over,' Madame Grandet would say. 'God has been good to me in enabling me to look forward joyfully to the end of my sorrows.'

There was a Christian piety in all Madame Grandet's words. When, during the first months of the year, her husband came to breakfast with her and paced up and down her room, she would always make the same remarks, repeated with an angelic gentleness but with the firmness of

150

a woman to whom approaching death gave a courage she had lacked in her lifetime.

'Monsieur, I thank you for the interest you take in my health,' she would say when he had made the most conventional of inquiries, 'but if you wish to alleviate the bitterness of my last moments and lighten my suffering, restore your favour to our daughter. Act like a Christian husband and father.'

On hearing these words, Grandet would sit down near the bed and behave like a man who, seeing a shower of rain coming on, calmly takes shelter under an archway. He would listen to his wife in silence and make no reply. To the most touching, the most affectionate, the most pious entreaties, he would reply, 'You're a little pale today, my poor wife.' To judge from his stony brow and set lips, one would think he had completely forgotten his daughter. He was not even moved by the tears which, after his vague, almost unvarying replies, would course down his wife's white face.

'May God forgive you, Monsieur, as I forgive you myself,' she would say. 'One day you will need mercy.'

Since his wife's illness he had not dared to pronounce his terrible 'Ta, ta, ta, ta, ta!' But his tyranny had not been disarmed by that gentle angel whose plain features became more beautiful day by day under the influence of the spiritual qualities that blossomed in her face. She was all soul. The genius of prayer seemed to purify and soften the harsher features of her face and make it glow. Who has not observed the phenomenon of the transfiguration of the faces of the saintly, where, in the end, the qualities of the soul triumph over the most roughly hewn features and imprint on them the special animation that comes from the nobility and purity of elevated thoughts? The sight of the change wrought by the suffering that was destroying the last shreds of human life in this woman had an effect, though but a slight one, on the old cooper, who remained as hard as nails. He no longer talked contemptuously, but maintained an imperturbable silence which preserved his superior position as head of the family. If his faithful Nanon appeared in the market, jeers and complaints about her master would whistle round her ears. But although public opinion loudly condemned Père Grandet, the servant defended him out of family loyalty.

'Well,' she would say to the old man's detractors, 'don't we all become harder as we grow older? Why do you expect him not to get a bit more crotchety like everyone else? Keep your lying mouths shut. Mademoiselle lives like a queen. She's alone, well, that's her own choice. Besides, my master and mistress have good reasons.'

Finally, one evening, towards the end of spring, Madame Grandet, overcome by sorrows even more than by illness, and having failed, in spite of her pleading, to reconcile Eugénie and her father, confided her secret woes to the Cruchots.

'To put a girl of twenty-three on bread and water! . . .' exclaimed President de Bonfons, 'and without cause. But that constitutes *excessive cruelty; she can take action against him, both in and on . . .*'

'Come, nephew,' said the lawyer, 'drop your legal jargon. Don't worry, Madame. I'll put an end to the imprisonment from tomorrow.'

On hearing her name mentioned, Eugénie came out of her room.

'Gentlemen,' she said, coming forward proudly, 'I beg you not to concern yourselves with the matter. My father is master in his own house. As long as I live in his house, I must obey him. His conduct should not be subject to the approval or disapproval of other people; he is answerable only to God. In the name of our friendship I ask you to observe the utmost silence about this. To blame my father is to attack our own reputation. I am grateful to you, gentlemen, for the interest you are taking in me, but you would oblige me even more if you would put an end to the offensive rumours that are circulating in the town and that I've learned of accidentally.'

'She's right,' said Madame Grandet.

'Mademoiselle, the best way to stop people from gossiping is to have your liberty restored,' replied the old lawyer respectfully. He was struck by the beauty which seclusion, melancholy, and love had given to Eugénie's face.

'Well, my dear, let Monsieur Cruchot look after the matter, since he answers for its successful outcome. He knows your father and understands how to deal with him. If you want to see me happy for the short time I have left to live, you and your father must be reconciled at all costs.'

The next day, Grandet, following a habit he had adopted since Eugénie's imprisonment, took a few turns round his little garden. He had selected for his walk the moment when Eugénie was doing her hair. When the old man reached the big walnut tree, he would hide behind its trunk and stay for a few moments to look at his daughter's long tresses; he was no doubt wavering between the thoughts inspired by his temperamental obstinacy and the desire to embrace his child. He would often linger, sitting on the little bench of rotten wood where Charles and Eugénie had sworn eternal love to each other, while she for her part would look at her father out of the corner of her eye or watch him in her mirror. If he got up and began walking again, she would gladly sit at the window and begin to examine the section of the wall where the prettiest flowers climbed and from whose crevices hung maidenhair fern, convolvulus, and a yellow or white succulent plant called sedum, that grows abundantly among the vines at Saumur and Tours. It was a fine June day. Maître Cruchot came early and found the old winegrower sitting on the little bench, his back against the dividing wall, watching his daughter.

'What can I do for you, Maître Cruchot,' he asked, when he caught sight of the lawyer.

'I've come to talk business with you.'

'Aha! Have you a little gold to give me in exchange for silver coin?'

'No, no. It's not a money matter, it's about your daughter Eugénie. Everyone's talking about her and you.'

'What business is it of theirs? A charcoal burner's master in his own house . . .'*

'Agreed. A man is free to kill himself too, or, what's more, to throw his money out of the window.'

'What do you mean by that?'

'It's that your wife is very ill, my friend. In fact, you ought to call in Monsieur Bergerin. Her life is in danger. If she were to die without getting proper attention, I don't think you'd be very easy in your mind about it.'

'Ta, ta, ta, ta! You know what's wrong with my wife. These doctors, once they set foot in your house, they come five or six times a day.'

'Well, Grandet, you'll do as you think best. We are old friends. There isn't a man in all Saumur who is more concerned for all your interests than I am. So I had to say that to you. Now, come what may, you are a mature adult, you know how to conduct your own business, let it pass. Anyway, that's not the matter that brought me here. Perhaps it's something more serious for you. After all, you don't want to kill your wife. She's too useful to you. Just think of the situation you'd be in with regard to your daughter if Madame Grandet were to die. You would have to give an account of your assets to Eugénie, since you and your wife are joint owners of your property. Your daughter would have the right to demand her share in your fortune, to sell Froidfond. In short, she will have the inheritance from her mother and you cannot have it.'

These words were like a thunderbolt to the old man, who was not as knowledgeable about the law as he might be on business matters. He had never thought that his jointly owned property might be sold by auction.

'So I advise you to treat her gently,' concluded Cruchot.

'But do you know what she did, Cruchot?'

'What?' asked the lawyer, eager to receive a confidence from Père Grandet and curious to know the cause of the quarrel.

'She gave away her gold.'

'Well, wasn't it hers?' asked the lawyer.

'That's what they all say to me,' said the old man, letting his arms fall with a tragic gesture.

'And for a trifle are you going to put obstacles in the way of the concessions that you will ask her to make when her mother dies?' continued Cruchot.

'Oh, so you call six thousand francs in gold a trifle, do you?'

'Well, my old friend, do you know what the inventory and division of your wife's estate will cost, if Eugénie insists on them?'

'How much?'

'Two, or three, or perhaps four hundred thousand francs. You see, it will have to be put up for auction and sold, so that its real value can be ascertained, whereas if you come to an understanding . . .'

'By my father's pruning-hook!' cried the winegrower, sitting down again and turning pale. 'We'll see about that, Cruchot.'

After a moment of agonized silence, the old man looked at the lawyer and said, 'Life is very hard. It is full of sorrows. Cruchot,' he continued solemnly, 'you wouldn't deceive me, would you? Swear to me on your honour that what you're telling me is legally sound. Show me the Code.* I want to see the Code.'

'My poor friend,' replied the lawyer, 'don't I know my job?'

'So it's really true. I shall be despoiled, betrayed, murdered, pillaged by my own daughter.'

'She is her mother's heiress.'

'What's the use of having children, then? Oh, but I love my wife. Fortunately she's tough. She's a La Bertellière.'

'She hasn't a month to live.'

The cooper struck his forehead, walked down the garden, came back to Cruchot, and, giving him a terrible look, said, 'What is to be done?'

'Eugénie might purely and simply renounce all claim to her mother's estate. You don't want to disinherit her, do you? But if you wish to obtain an arrangement of that kind, don't be harsh with her. What I'm telling you, my friend, is against my own interest. What does my job consist of?

155

. . . Liquidations, inventories, sales, divisions of property
. . .'

'We shall see, we shall see. Let's talk no more about that, Cruchot. You're wringing my very heart. Did you get any gold?'

'No, but I have some old louis, about ten, which I'll give you. My good friend, make your peace with Eugénie. You know, all Saumur is accusing you.'

'The scoundrels.'

'Come, come. Government bonds have gone up to 99. Be content, then, for once in your life.'

'To 99, Cruchot?'

'Yes.'

'Well, well, 99!' said Grandet, going as far as the street door with the old lawyer. Then, too excited by what he had just heard to stay at home, he went up to his wife's room and said to her, 'Well, mother, you can spend the day with your daughter. I'm going to Froidfond. Be good, both of you. It's our wedding anniversary, dear wife. Look, here's ten écus for your Corpus Christi altar. You've wanted to have one for a fairly long time, so treat yourself. Enjoy yourselves, be happy, and get well. Long live happiness!' He threw ten six-franc pieces on to his wife's bed, took her head in his hands, and kissed her on the forehead. 'Dear wife, you are feeling better, aren't you?'

'How can you think of receiving in your house the God who forgives when you banish your daughter from your heart?' she said in a voice filled with emotion.

'Ta, ta, ta, ta,' said the father soothingly, 'we'll see about that.'

'Heaven be praised! Eugénie!' cried her mother, flushing with joy. 'Come and kiss your father! He forgives you!'

But the old man had gone. He was off to his vineyards as fast as his legs could carry him, trying as he went to set his shattered ideas in order. Grandet was just beginning his seventy-sixth year. During the last two years especially, his avarice had increased, as human obsessions always do. It has been observed that misers, ambitious men, and all those whose lives have been devoted to one dominant interest, devote their feelings more particularly to one symbol of their passion. For Grandet, the sight of gold, the possession of gold, had become his monomania. His tyrannical tendency had developed in proportion to his avarice, and to give up the control of the smallest part of his property on his wife's death seemed to him a thing *against nature*. To disclose his financial situation to his daughter, to make an inventory of all his possessions, both personal estate and land, to have them put up for auction! . . .

'It would be like cutting one's own throat,' he said out loud in the middle of a vineyard as he examined his vines. Finally he made up his mind and went back to Saumur at dinner-time, having decided to give in to Eugénie, to coax and humour her so that he could die regally, holding the reins of his millions till his last gasp. The old man, who, as it happened, had taken his front-door key with him, went stealthily upstairs to his wife's room just at the very moment when Eugénie had brought the beautiful dressing-case and put it on her mother's bed. In Grandet's absence, the two women were giving themselves the pleasure of detecting Charles's features in the portrait of his mother.

'It's just his forehead and mouth,' Eugénie was saying as the winegrower opened the door. When she saw the look that her husband cast at the gold, Madame Grandet called out, 'God have pity on us!'

The old man leapt at the dressing-case as a tiger pounces on a sleeping child. 'What's that?' he said, carrying off the treasure and taking it over to the window. 'Solid gold! Gold!' he exclaimed. 'Lots of gold! That must weigh a couple of pounds. Aha! Charles gave you that in exchange for your fine coins. Well, why didn't you tell me? That's good business, little girl! You are my very own daughter, I acknowledge that.' Eugénie was trembling from head to foot. 'This is Charles's, isn't it?' continued the old man.

'Yes, father, it isn't mine. That case is a sacred trust.'

'Ta, ta, ta! He took your fortune. You must restore your own little hoard.'

'Father! . . .'

The old man wanted to take out his knife in order to prise out one of the sections of gold, and so he had to put the dressing-case on a chair. Eugénie rushed forward to retrieve it, but the cooper, who had his eye both on his daughter and on the case, put out his arm and pushed her back so violently that she fell on to her mother's bed.

'Monsieur, Monsieur,' called out her mother, sitting up in bed.

Grandet had taken out his knife and was preparing to prise out the gold.

'Father,' cried Eugénie, throwing herself on her knees and struggling towards him with her hands raised in supplication, 'father, in the name of the Virgin and of all the Saints, in the name of Christ who died on the cross, in the name of your eternal salvation, father, in the name of my life, don't touch that box! That dressing-case is neither yours nor mine. It belongs to an unfortunate relative who entrusted it to me, and I must give it back to him, intact.'

'Why were you looking at it, if it was entrusted to you? Looking is worse than touching.'

'Father, don't damage it, or you will dishonour me. Father, do you hear?'

'Monsieur, for pity's sake!' said her mother.

'Father!' shrieked Eugénie so loudly that Nanon rushed upstairs, terrified. Eugénie gripped hold of a knife that lay within her reach and armed herself with it.

'Well?' said Grandet unmoved, with a cold smile.

'Monsieur, Monsieur, you're killing me,' said the mother.

'Father, if your knife so much as scratches a fraction of that gold, I will stab myself with this one. You have already made my mother fatally ill; now you are going to kill your daughter as well. Go ahead now; if you strike, so will I.'

Grandet held his knife over the dressing-case, looked at his daughter, and hesitated.

158

'Would you be capable of doing such a thing, Eugénie?' he asked.

'Yes, Monsieur,' said her mother.

'She would do as she says,' cried Nanon. 'Do be reasonable, Monsieur, for once in your life.' For a moment the cooper looked from the gold to his daughter and back. Madame Grandet fainted. 'There, do you see, Monsieur? Madame is dying,' cried Nanon.

'Come, child, let's not quarrel about a box. Take it then,' exclaimed the cooper suddenly, throwing the dressing-case on to the bed. 'Nanon, go and fetch Monsieur Bergerin. Come, mother,' he said, kissing his wife's hand, 'it's nothing, come now. We've made it up. Isn't that so, little girl? No more dry bread. You'll eat whatever you like. Ah! She's opening her eyes. Well, mother, dear little mother, good little mother, it's alright. Look here, I'm giving Eugénie a kiss. She loves her cousin; she can marry him if she wants to; she can keep the little box for him. But you must live for a long time, my poor sick wife. Come, turn your head. Listen, you'll have the most beautiful altar that has ever been made in Saumur.'

'My God, how can you treat your wife and daughter like that?' said Madame Grandet, faintly.

'I shan't do it again,' cried the cooper. 'You'll see, my dear wife.' He went to his office and came back with a handful of louis, which he scattered on the bed. 'Here, Eugénie, here, wife, these are for you,' he said, fingering the coins. 'Come now, cheer up, wife. Get well, you will want for nothing, neither will Eugénie. Here's a hundred gold louis for her. You won't give these away, Eugénie, will you?'

Madame Grandet and her daughter looked at each other in amazement.

'Take them back, father. All we need is your affection.'

'Oh well, that's alright,' he said, pocketing the louis. 'Let's be good friends. Let's all go downstairs to the living-room for dinner and play lotto every evening for two sous' stakes. Have a good time! What about it, wife?'

'Alas, I should like to, since that might please you,' said the dying woman, 'but I can't get up.'

'Poor mother,' said the cooper, 'you don't know how much I love you. And you, too, daughter.' He took her in his arms and kissed her. 'Oh, how nice it is to kiss one's daughter after a quarrel, little girl! Look, you see, little mother, we are quite united now. There, go and put that away,' he said to Eugénie, pointing to the case. 'Go on, don't be afraid. I'll never mention it to you again.'

Monsieur Bergerin, the most distinguished doctor in Saumur, soon arrived. After the consultation, he told Grandet firmly that his wife was very ill, but that complete peace of mind, a light diet, and very careful nursing might prolong her life till the end of the autumn.

'Will that cost a lot? Will she need medicines?' asked the old man.

'Not much medicine, but a great deal of care,' replied the doctor, who could not restrain a smile.

'And, Monsieur Bergerin,' continued Grandet, 'you are an honourable man, aren't you? I have confidence in you. Come and see my wife whenever and as often as you think is advisable. Preserve my good wife's life for me. I love her dearly, you see, though I may not show it, because, with me, everything goes on inside and upsets me within. I have sorrows. Sorrows entered my house with my brother's death; for him I am spending sums in Paris amounting to . . . in short, the very eyes out of my head. And there's no end to it. Goodbye, Monsieur. If my wife can be saved, save her, though it should mean I have to spend a hundred or even two hundred francs.'

In spite of Grandet's fervent wishes for his wife's health —the uncertainty about the disposal of her fortune was like a preliminary death for him—in spite of his readiness on every occasion to accede to the slightest wishes of his astonished wife and daughter, in spite of Eugénie's most devoted care, Madame Grandet was rapidly approaching death. Each day she became weaker and was fading away, as do most women of her age who are attacked by illness

She was as fragile as the autumn leaves on the trees. Like a leaf shot through and tinged with gold by the sunlight, she shone in the rays of light from heaven. It was a death worthy of her life, a wholly Christian death; is that not to say it was sublime? In October 1822, her virtues, her angelic patience, and her love for her daughter shone out more than ever. She expired without uttering the slightest complaint. A spotless lamb, she went to heaven, regretting nothing in this world but the gentle companion of her bleak life; for Eugénie, her last glance seemed to foretell countless ills. She trembled at leaving that ewe-lamb, as pure as herself, alone in a selfish world which would want to rip off her fleece and grab her treasure.

'My child,' she said, just before she died, 'there is no happiness except in heaven. You will know that one day.'

The day after Madame Grandet's death, Eugénie found new reasons for clinging to the house where she had been born, where she had suffered so much, and where her mother had just died. She could not look at the window and the raised chair in the living-room without shedding tears. She thought she had misunderstood her old father's nature when she found herself the object of his most tender care. He would come to take her down to breakfast on his arm; he would look at her with an almost benevolent eye for hours on end; in fact he cherished her as if she had been made of gold. The old cooper was so little like himself, was so anxiously solicitous in his daughter's presence, that Nanon and the Cruchot party, who saw his weakness, attributed it to his great age and so feared that his mental powers were declining. But the day the family put on mourning, after a dinner to which Maître Cruchot, who alone knew his client's secret, was invited, the reason for the old man's conduct became clear.

'My dear child,' he said to Eugénie when the table had been cleared and the doors carefully shut, 'now you are your mother's heir and we have some little matters of business to settle between us. Isn't that so, Cruchot?'

'Yes.'

'But do we have to talk about them today, father?'

'Yes, yes, little girl. I can't go on in my present state of uncertainty. You wouldn't want to distress me, would you?'

'Oh, father!'

'Well, we must settle everything this evening.'

'What do you want me to do, then?'

'But, little girl, that's not for me to say. You tell her, Cruchot.'

'Mademoiselle, your father would rather not divide or sell his property, nor pay enormous taxes on the ready money he may happen to have in hand. So, to avoid having to do that, we'd have to do without making an inventory of all the assets which today you and your father hold in common . . .'

'Cruchot, are you quite sure of all that to talk in this way in front of a child?'

'Let me say what I have to say, Grandet.'

'Yes, yes, my friend. Neither you nor my daughter want to rob me. Isn't that right, little girl?'

'But, Monsieur Cruchot, what do I have to do?' asked Eugénie, impatiently.

'Well,' said the lawyer, 'you would have have to sign this deed, by which you would renounce your inheritance from your mother and allow your father the use during his lifetime of all the property you hold in common and of which he guarantees you the full ownership.'

'I don't understand a word of what you are saying,' replied Eugénie. 'Give me the deed and show me the place where I have to sign.'

Père Grandet looked from the deed to his daughter and from his daughter to the deed, a prey to such violent emotion that he wiped away some beads of sweat from his brow.

'Little girl,' he said, 'I would rather you didn't sign that deed, which would cost a lot to register, but instead purely and simply renounced your inheritance from your poor, dear, late mother and relied on me for the future. I would make you a good, substantial allowance of a hundred francs a month. Look, you could afford as many masses as you wanted to be said for anyone you choose. What about it? A hundred francs a month in livres!'

'I'll do whatever you like, father.'

'Mademoiselle,' said the lawyer, 'it is my duty to point out that you are divesting yourself . . .'

'My goodness,' she said, 'I don't care about that.'

'Be quiet, Cruchot. That's settled, that's settled,' cried Grandet, taking his daughter's hand and tapping it with his own. 'You won't go back on your word, Eugénie? You're an honest girl, aren't you?'

'Oh, father! . . .'

He kissed her effusively and hugged her so tightly that he nearly stifled her.

'There, child, you restore life to your father. But you're only giving him back what he gave you, so now we're quits. That's how business ought to be done. Life is a business transaction. Bless you! You're a good girl who loves her father. Do as you like now. I shall see you tomorrow then, Cruchot,' he said, looking at the horrified lawyer. 'You will see that the deed of renunciation is properly drawn up at the office of the clerk of the court.'

The next day, about noon, the declaration was signed and Eugénie had divested herself of all her inheritance. Yet, in spite of what he had said, the old cooper had still not given his daughter a sou of the hundred francs a month which he had solemnly promised her. So when Eugénie mentioned it to him, half jokingly, he could not help blushing. He went hurriedly upstairs to his study, came down again, and gave her about a third of the jewellery which he had got from his nephew.

'Here you are, child,' he said in a sarcastic tone, 'would you like these instead of your twelve hundred francs?'

'Oh, father! Are you really giving them to me?'

'I'll give you the same amount again next year,' he said, throwing them into her apron lap. 'So, in a short time, you will have all *his* trinkets,' he added, rubbing

163

his hands, happy to be able to profit from his daughter's feelings.

Although the old man was still in good health, he nevertheless felt the need of initiating his daughter into the secrets of his domestic arrangements. For two successive years he made her order the household supplies in his presence, and receive the rents in kind. Slowly and one by one, he taught her the names and the extent of his vineyards and farms. As the third year approached, he had got her so used to all his miserly ways, he had so obviously made them her own habits, that he was not afraid to leave the pantry keys in her possession, and he appointed her mistress of the house.

Five years went by, unmarked by any outstanding event in the monotonous existence of Eugénie and her father. The same acts were performed unvaryingly, with the mechanical regularity of the old clock. Mademoiselle Grandet's profound melancholy was a secret to no one. But though everyone had an idea of the cause, she never uttered a word which might justify the suspicions entertained by all social circles in Saumur about the state of the rich heiress's heart. Her only society was made up of the three Cruchots and some of their friends, whom they had gradually introduced into the house. They taught her how to play whist and came in every evening for a rubber.

In the year 1827, her father, feeling the weight of the infirmities of age, was obliged to initiate her into the secrets of his landed property and told her that, if she had any difficulties, she should consult Cruchot the lawyer, whom he knew to be an honest man. Then, finally, towards the end of that year, at the age of eighty-two,* the old man was stricken by an attack of paralysis which developed rapidly. Monsieur Bergerin said there was no hope for him. Realizing that she would soon be alone in the world, Eugénie drew closer to her father and clung more tightly to this last link of affection. In her mind, as in the minds of all women in love, love was the whole world, and Charles was not there. She was sublime in

164

the care and attention she gave to her old father, whose faculties were beginning to decline, but whose avarice remained instinctively undiminished. So he died as he had lived.

First thing in the morning he had himself wheeled to a spot between the fireplace in his room and the door to his office, which was no doubt filled with gold. He would sit there without moving, but his eyes would turn anxiously from any caller to the iron-lined door. He required an explanation of the faintest sound he could hear, and to the lawyer's great amazement he would hear his dog yawning in the courtyard. He would rouse himself from his apparent stupor on the day and at the time when he had to receive farm rents, settle accounts with the vinedressers, or give receipts. Then he would move his wheelchair to a place opposite his office door. He would tell his daughter to open it and see to it that she, herself, secretly put away the money bags, one on top of another, and shut the door. Then he would return silently to his place as soon as she had given him back the precious key, which he kept in his waistcoat pocket, where he would finger it from time to time. Meanwhile his old friend the lawyer, feeling certain that, if Charles Grandet did not return, the rich heiress was bound to marry his nephew the President, redoubled his care and attention. Every day he came to put himself at Grandet's service, went at his bidding to Froidfond, to the farms, the meadows, or the vineyards, sold the crops, and changed all the proceeds into gold and silver, which was secretly added to the piles in the office. The death struggle came at last and the old man's strong frame wrestled with destruction. He wanted to remain sitting by his fire in front of his office door. He pulled off all the blankets that were wrapped round him and rolled them up, saying to Nanon, 'Put them away, put them away; they might be stolen.' Whenever he could open his eyes, where all that remained of his life had taken refuge, he would turn them straight away to the door of the office where his treasure lay, and say to his daughter,

'Are they there? Are they there?' in a kind of panic-stricken voice.

'Yes, father.'

'Look after the gold. Put some gold in front of me.'

Eugénie would spread out some louis for him on a table and he would stay for hours with his eyes glued to the coins like a child who, as soon as he first starts to see, gazes blankly at one and the same thing. And like a child, he would give a feeble smile.

'That warms me,' he would say sometimes, and a blissful expression would appear on his face.

When the parish priest came to administer the last rites, Grandet's eyes, which for some time had appeared lifeless, lit up at the sight of the cross, the candlesticks, and the silver holy-water basin. He stared hard at them and his wart twitched for the last time. When the priest brought the silver crucifix near to his lips so that he could kiss the image of Christ, he made a terrifying movement to grasp it, and this final effort cost him his life. He called Eugénie, whom he could not see though she was kneeling in front of him and bathing his already cold hand with her tears.

'Father, give me your blessing', she begged.

'Take good care of everything. You will have to account to me for it all in the next world,' he said, proving by these last words that Christianity must be the misers' religion.

So Eugénie Grandet found herself alone in the world, in the old house, having only Nanon to whom she could look with the certainty of being listened to and understood. Nanon was the only being who loved her for herself and with whom she could talk of her sorrows. For Eugénie, Big Nanon was a providence and now no longer a servant but a humble friend.

After her father's death, Eugénie learned from Maître Cruchot that she had an income of three hundred thousand livres from property in the Saumur district, six million francs invested in three per cent government bonds (bought at sixty francs a share and now worth seventy-seven), a further two million francs in gold, and a hundred thousand in silver crowns, without counting arrears that were due to be paid. The estimated total value of her possessions amounted to seventeen million francs.

'But where is my cousin?' she wondered.

On the day Maître Cruchot presented his client with the account of her inheritance, now clear and free of all liabilities, Eugénie was left alone with Nanon. They were sitting on either side of the fireplace in the room which now seemed so empty, where everything was a reminder of the past, from the raised chair where her mother used to sit, to the glass from which Charles had drunk.

'Nanon, we are alone . . . .'

'Yes, Mademoiselle, and if I knew where he was, the sweet young gentleman, I'd go on foot to fetch him.'

'The sea lies between us,' said Eugénie.

While the poor heiress was weeping thus, in the company of her old servant, in that cold, dark house which was her whole universe, from Nantes to Orléans people talked of nothing but Mademoiselle Grandet's seventeen million. One of her first acts was to give an annuity of twelve hundred francs to Nanon, who, as she already had six hundred francs a year of her own, became a rich match. In less than a month she changed her state from spinster to married woman, under the protection of Antoine Cornoiller, who was appointed head keeper of Mademoiselle Grandet's land and property. Madame Cornoiller had an immense advantage over her contemporaries. Although she was fifty-nine years old, she did not look more than forty. Her coarse features had resisted the assaults of time and, thanks to her monastic way of life, she could defy old age, with her ruddy complexion and iron constitution. Perhaps she had never looked better than she did on her wedding-day. Her plainness had its own advantages and she looked big, strong, and rounded, with an expression of happiness on her indestructible face which made some people envy Cornoiller's lot.

'Her colour's fast,' said the draper.

'She could still have children,' said the salt merchant. 'She's been as well preserved as if she'd been kept in brine, if I may say so.'

'She's rich, and that fellow Cornoiller's done very well for himself,' said another neighbour.

As she came out of the old house and went down the winding street to the parish church, Nanon, who was loved by the whole neighbourhood, received nothing but good wishes. As a wedding present, Eugénie gave her three dozen knives, forks, and spoons. Cornoiller, amazed at such munificence, spoke of his mistress with tears in his eyes; he would have let himself be cut in pieces for her. Now that she had become Eugénie's trusted housekeeper, Madame Cornoiller experienced a happiness that, for her, was equal to that of having a husband. At last she had a pantry of her own to open and lock up, and food supplies to give out in the morning as her late master used to do. Then she had two servants to rule over, a cook and a maid, whose duty it was to mend the household linen and make Mademoiselle Grandet's dresses. It goes without saying that the cook and the maid selected by Nanon were real *treasures*. So Mademoiselle Grandet had four servants whose devotion to her was boundless. And the farmers hardly noticed the old man's death, so strictly established were the customs and practices of his administration, which were scrupulously adhered to by Monsieur and Madame Cornoiller.

AT THE age of thirty, Eugénie had not yet experienced any of the joys of life. Her sad, bleak childhood had been passed in the company of a mother whose bruised and slighted feelings had caused her constant suffering. As she joyfully took leave of life, Madame Grandet pitied Eugénie for having to go on living, and the mother left in her daughter's heart a little touch of remorse and unending regret. Eugénie's first and only love was a source of sadness to her. Having spent a brief few days with her lover, she had given him her heart between two kisses secretly exchanged. Then he had gone, putting a whole world between them. This love, abhorred by her father, had nearly cost her her mother's life and had brought her only sorrow mingled with faint hope. Thus, till now, she had spent herself in aspiring towards happiness but gaining nothing with which to renew her strength. In the life of the spirit, as in that of the body, there is a breathing-in and a breathing-out; the soul needs to absorb the feelings of another soul, to assimilate them, to return them enriched. Without that wonderful human phenomenon, there is no life for the heart; it suffers from lack of air and fades away. Eugénie was beginning to suffer. For her, money was neither power nor consolation; her existence lay only in love, religion, and faith in the future. Love explained to her the meaning of eternity. Her heart and the Gospels showed her two worlds to look forward to. Day and night she was immersed in two boundless thoughts, which for her, perhaps, were one and the same. She withdrew into herself, loving and believing herself to be loved. For seven years her passion had utterly absorbed her. Her treasures were not the millions with the interest piling up, but Charles's dressing-case, the two portraits hanging at her bedside, the jewels bought back from her father, proudly displayed on a bed of cotton-wool in a drawer of the chest, her aunt's thimble which her mother had used and which she used every day religiously to work at embroidery, a Penelope's web* undertaken only to put on her finger the memory-laden trinket. It did not seem likely that Mademoiselle Grandet would want to marry during her period of mourning. Her genuine piety was well known. And so the Cruchot family, wisely guided in its policy by the old Abbé, contented itself with laying siege to the heiress and surrounding her with the most affectionate attentions. Her living-room was filled every evening with a company composed of the most ardent and devoted partisans of the Cruchots, who did their best to sing the praises of the mistress of the house in every key. She had her physician in ordinary, her grand almoner, her chamberlain, her first mistress of the wardrobe, her prime minister, above all her chancellor, a chancellor who wanted to keep her informed about everything. If the heiress had wanted a train-bearer, they would have found one for her. She was a queen, and the most skilfully flattered of all queens. Flattery never emanates from the great-hearted. It is the prerogative of the mean-minded, who manage to diminish themselves still further, the better to insinuate themselves into the life of the person around whom they revolve. Flattery implies self-interest. Thus the people who came every evening and filled Mademoiselle Grandet's living-room (they now called her Mademoiselle de Froidfond) were remarkably successful in showering her with praise. This chorus of praise, which was something new to Eugénie, made her blush at first. But however clumsy the compliments were, little by little her ear became so well used to hearing her beauty praised, that if some newcomer had thought her plain, she would have felt the aspersion much more keenly than eight years before. Then, in the end, she came to like the compliments, which she laid secretly at her idol's feet, and gradually she became used to being treated as a queen and to seeing her court filled every evening.

Monsieur le Président de Bonfons was the hero of the little circle, where his wit, his looks, his learning, and his kindliness were continually praised. One of the company would say that the President had greatly increased his fortune in the last seven years, that Bonfons was worth at least ten thousand francs a year and, like all the Cruchot property, was surrounded by the heiress's vast estates.

'Do you know, Mademoiselle,' one of the regular visitors would say, 'that the Cruchots have an income of forty thousand livres?'

'To say nothing of their savings,' an old Cruchot partisan, Mademoiselle de Gribeaucourt, would add. 'Recently a gentleman from Paris came and offered Monsieur Cruchot two hundred thousand francs for his practice. He ought to sell it, if he can be appointed to a judgeship.'

'He wants to succeed Monsieur de Bonfons as president of the county court and is taking suitable steps,' replied Madame d'Orsonval, 'for Monsieur le Président will become a councillor and president of the court of appeal. He is so gifted, he is bound to get on.'

'Yes, he's an exceptionally talented man,' another visitor would say. 'Don't you think so, Mademoiselle?'

Monsieur le Président had tried to adapt himself to the part he wished to play. In spite of his forty years and his swarthy, unattractive face, which was wizened, like most lawyers' faces, he dressed like a young man, sported a cane, abstained from snuff in Mademoiselle de Froidfond's house, and always arrived there wearing a white cravat and a shirt whose wide, frilled front made him look as if he were related to the turkey family. He would talk in familiar tones to the beautiful heiress and call her 'our dear Eugénie'. In short, apart from the number of people present, the substitution of whist for lotto, and the absence of Monsieur and Madame Grandet, the scene at the start of this part of the story was almost the same as that of years ago. The pack was still pursuing Eugénie and her millions, but it had increased in size, barked more loudly, and encircled its prey according to a strategic plan. If Charles had arrived from the far Indies, he would still have found the same people pursuing the same interests.

Madame des Grassins, to whom Eugénie was unfailingly cordial and kind, continued to vex the Cruchots. Then, as in the past, the figure of Eugénie was the centre of attention; as in the past, Charles would still have reigned supreme. Nevertheless, some progress had been made. The bouquet which the President used to present to Eugénie on her birthday had become a daily gift. Every evening he would bring the rich heiress a large and magnificent bouquet that Madame Cornoiller would ostentatiously put in a vase and secretly throw away in a corner of the yard as soon as the visitors had gone. In the early spring, Madame des Grassins tried to disturb the contentment of the Cruchot party by speaking to Eugénie of the Marquis de Froidfond, whose ruined family fortunes could be restored if the heiress were willing to give him back his estate by a marriage contract. Madame des Grassins dwelt on the importance of the peerage and the title of marquis, and taking Eugénie's disdainful smile for a sign of approval, she went about saying that Monsieur le Président Cruchot's marriage was not as certain as people thought.

'Although Monsieur de Froidfond is fifty,' she would say, 'he doesn't look any older than Monsieur Cruchot. He's a widower, he has children, that's true. But he's a marquis, he'll be a peer of France, and these days you won't easily find a marriage of that quality. I know for certain that when Père Grandet joined all his property to the Froidfond estate, he intended to graft his own family on to the Froidfond family tree. He often told me so. He was an astute old fellow.'

'How can it be, Nanon, that in seven years he won't have written to me once?' said Eugénie one evening as she went to bed.

While all this was happening at Saumur, Charles was making his fortune in the Indies. From the start, his trading stock had sold very well. He had quickly realized a sum of six thousand dollars. Crossing the line* had made him lose many prejudices. He became aware that the best way to make his fortune, in the tropics as well as in Europe, was

172

to buy and sell men. So he went to the African coast and engaged in the slave trade, and combined his trade in men with that of the most profitable merchandise that could be sold on the different markets where his interests led him. He was so active in business that he had no time for anything else. He was dominated by the thought of returning to Paris with all the splendour of a great fortune, and of securing an even more brilliant position than the one from which he had fallen. He knocked around in many lands and came in contact with many kinds of men; he noticed their differing customs, with the result that his own views altered and he became sceptical. He no longer had fixed ideas of right and wrong, for he saw that what was regarded as a crime in one country was deemed a virtue in another. From unremitting contact with selfish interests, his heart grew cold; his feeling for others contracted and withered away. The blood of the Grandets fulfilled its destiny. Charles became hard and ruthless in the pursuit of gain. He sold Chinamen, negroes, swallows' nests, children, theatrical performers. He engaged in money-lending on a large scale. His habit of defrauding the customs made him less scrupulous about defrauding men. He went to Saint-Thomas* to buy at a very low price goods stolen by pirates, and then took them to places where they were in short supply. If, on his first voyage, Eugénie's pure, noble face accompanied him, like the image of the Virgin which Spanish sailors put on their ships, and if he attributed his first successes to the magic influence of the vows and prayers of that sweet girl, later on, negresses, mulattoes, whites, Javanese women, dancing girls, orgies of every kind, and adventures in different countries completely wiped out the memory of his cousin, of Saumur, the house, the bench, and the kiss snatched in the passage. He remembered only the little garden surrounded by old walls, because there he had started on his risky life of adventure. But he repudiated his family. His uncle was an old cad who had swindled him out of his jewellery. Eugénie filled no place in his heart or thoughts; she had a place in his business affairs as a creditor for six

173

thousand francs. This way of life and these ideas explain Charles Grandet's silence. In the Indies, in Saint-Thomas, on the African coast, in Lisbon and the United States, the speculator had assumed the pseudonym of Sepherd so as not to compromise his real name. Carl Sepherd could, without risk, appear everywhere as a tireless, bold, greedy man, who, determined to make his fortune *quibuscumque viis*,* was then in a hurry to have done with villainy so that he could be an honourable man for the rest of his life. By the use of these methods he made his fortune swiftly and brilliantly, and so in 1827 he returned to Bordeaux, on the *Marie-Caroline*,* a fine brig belonging to a Royalist firm. He owned nineteen hundred thousand francs, contained in three strongly bound barrels of gold-dust, on which he hoped to make a profit of seven or eight per cent by having it made into gold coins in Paris. On the brig there was also a gentleman-in-ordinary to His Majesty King Charles X, Monsieur d'Aubrion, a kindly old man, who had been foolish enough to marry a lady of fashion, whose fortune was in property in the West Indies. In order to compensate for Madame d'Aubrion's extravagances, he had gone to the Indies to sell her estates there. Monsieur and Madame d'Aubrion, of the Aubrion de Buch family, whose last Captal* had died just before 1789, were now reduced to an income of about twenty thousand livres a year. They had a rather ugly daughter, whom the mother wanted to marry off without a dowry, since her fortune was barely enough to live on in Paris. That was an undertaking whose success would have seemed very questionable to all society people, in spite of the skill they attribute to women of fashion. So Madame d'Aubrion herself, when she looked at her daughter, was almost in despair of encumbering anyone at all with her, even a man who was besotted with the idea of an aristocratic connection.

Mademoiselle d'Aubrion was as elongated as a dragonfly. She was thin and spare, with a supercilious mouth, dominated by a blunt, over-long nose, which was normally yellowish but became quite red after meals, a kind of vegetable phenomenon that is more unpleasant in a pale, bored face than in any other. In fact, she was just the daughter that a mother of thirty-eight, still beautiful and with pretensions of her own, could wish for. But to counterbalance these shortcomings, the Marquise d'Aubrion had given her daughter a very distinguished bearing, had put her on a diet which kept her nose provisionally at a reasonable flesh colour, had instructed her in the art of dressing with taste, had endowed her with pleasing manners, and had taught her to cast those melancholy glances which arouse a man's interest and make him think that he is about to find the angel so long sought in vain. She had shown her how to manage her foot, how to bring it forward at the right moment for its smallness to be admired, just when the nose had the impertinence to turn red. In short, she had made her daughter into a very satisfactory match. By means of wide sleeves, padded bodices, full-skirted, carefully trimmed dresses, and a tight-laced corset, she had obtained such curious feminine attributes that she ought to have exhibited them in a museum for the instruction of mothers. Charles became very friendly with Madame d'Aubrion, who had the precise intention of becoming friendly with him. Some people even maintain that, during the voyage, Madame d'Aubrion did not neglect any means of ensnaring such a rich son-in-law. When they landed at Bordeaux in June 1827, Monsieur, Madame, and Mademoiselle d'Aubrion and Charles stayed in the same hotel and set off for Paris together. The Hôtel d'Aubrion was heavily mortgaged; Charles was to free it. The mother had already said how pleased she would be to give up the ground floor to her son-in-law and daughter. As she did not share Monsieur d'Aubrion's prejudices about the aristocracy, she had promised Charles Grandet that she would obtain from the good King Charles X a royal ordinance authorizing him, Grandet, to bear the name and assume the arms of the Aubrions and, by purchasing the entail to the Aubrion property worth sixty thousand livres a year, succeed to the title of Captal de Buch and Marquis d'Aubrion. By combining their resources and living in amity together, and with the help of a few sinecures, they could muster over a hundred thousand livres a year at the Hôtel d'Aubrion.

'And when you have an income of a hundred thousand livres, a name, a family, and a position at court (for I'll get you appointed a gentleman of the bedchamber), you can rise as high as you like,' she would say to Charles. 'So you can make your choice; you can be Master of Requests in the Council of State, prefect, embassy secretary, or even ambassador. Charles X is very fond of d'Aubrion; they have known each other since childhood.'

During the voyage, this woman had made Charles crazy with ambition and he had come to cherish all the hopes that had been skilfully aroused in him by apparently confidential heart-to-heart talks. Thinking that his father's affairs had all been settled by his uncle, he saw himself immediately safe in port in the Faubourg Saint-Germain,* where everyone, at that time, wanted to gain entry, and reappearing there, in the shadow of Mademoiselle Mathilde's blue-blooded nose, as Comte d'Aubrion, just as the Dreux family* reappeared one day under the name of Brézé. Charles, dazzled by the prosperity of the Restoration* that he had left tottering, and in the grip of ideas of aristocratic splendour, retained undiminished in Paris the enthusiasm that had been aroused in him on board ship. He determined to do all he could to attain the high position that his selfish mother-in-law had indicated to him. So his cousin was nothing more to him than a speck in this brilliant vista. He saw Annette again. As a woman of the world, Annette strongly advised her old friend to make the marriage and promised him her support in all his ambitious undertakings. Annette was delighted to encourage Charles to marry an ugly, uninteresting girl, especially as his stay in the Indies had made him even more attractive. His complexion had become tanned, his manner had become firm and decisive like that of a man accustomed to make decisions, to dominate, and to succeed. Charles breathed more easily in Paris when he saw he could play a part there. Des Grassins, hearing of Charles's return, his approaching marriage, and his wealth, went to see him to discuss the three hundred thousand francs required to pay his father's debts.

He found the young man closeted with a jeweller, who was showing him designs for the jewels he had ordered for Mademoiselle d'Aubrion's wedding present. Although Charles had brought magnificent diamonds back from the Indies, the settings, the silverware, and the solid but useless ornaments for the young couple's new home still came to more than two hundred thousand francs. Charles received des Grassins, whom he did not recognize, with the impertinence of a fashionable young man who had killed four men in separate duels in the Indies. Monsieur des Grassins had already tried to see him three times. Charles listened to him coldly. Then he answered without having properly taken in what he had said.

'My father's affairs are not mine. I am obliged to you, Monsieur, for the trouble you have been good enough to take and from which I cannot benefit. I haven't amassed almost two million by the sweat of my brow to chuck them at the heads of my father's creditors.'

'And if your father were to be declared bankrupt in a few days' time?'

'In a few days' time, I shall be called Comte d'Aubrion, Monsieur. So you can understand that that will be completely indifferent to me. Besides, you know better than I do that when a man has an income of a hundred thousand livres, his father has never become bankrupt,' he added, shepherding Monsieur des Grassins politely towards the door.

At the beginning of August of that year, Eugénie was sitting on the little wooden bench in the garden, where her cousin had sworn eternal love and where she would come for breakfast when the weather was fine. It was a particularly fresh and lovely morning, and the poor girl was

177

taking pleasure in retracing in her memory all the events, great and small, of her love affair and the catastrophes that had followed it. The sun lit up the picturesque section of the wall, now completely cracked and almost in ruins, but the heiress capriciously forbade anyone to touch it, though Cornoiller often told his wife that one day someone would be crushed beneath it.

Just then, the postman knocked at the door and handed a letter to Madame Cornoiller, who came into the garden, shouting, 'Mademoiselle, a letter!'

She gave it to her mistress, saying, 'Is it the one you were waiting for?'

These words echoed in Eugénie's heart as loudly as their real echo rang out between the walls of the courtyard and the garden.

'Paris! It's from him. He's come back.'

Eugénie turned pale and, for a moment, held the letter in her hand. She was shaking so much that she could not break the seal and read it. Big Nanon stood looking on, her hands on her hips, and joy seemed to emanate like smoke from the furrows in her sunburnt face.

'Do read it, Mademoiselle . . .'

'Oh, Nanon, why has he come back to Paris, when he went from Saumur?'

'Read it and you'll find out.'

Eugénie, trembling, broke the seal. A cheque, drawn on the firm of *Madame des Grassins et Corret*, fell out of the envelope. Nanon picked it up.

'My dear cousin . . .'

'He doesn't call me Eugénie any more', she thought and her heart sank.

'*Vous* . . .'*

'He used to say *tu*!'

She folded her arms, not daring to read any further, and large tears came into her eyes.

'Is he dead?' asked Nanon.

'He would not write, if he were,' said Eugénie.

She read the letter to the end. Here it is.

178

My dear cousin,

I am sure you will be pleased to learn of the success of my ventures. You brought me luck, I have become rich and I have followed my uncle's advice. I have just heard of his death and of my aunt's from Monsieur des Grassins. The death of our parents is in the course of nature and we must follow on after them. I hope you have recovered from your loss by now. I know from my own experience that nothing resists the passage of time. Yes, dear cousin, unfortunately for me, the time for illusions is over. Well, that's how it is! As I travelled through many countries, I reflected about life. I was a child when I went away, I have returned a man. Today I am aware of many things that I used not to think about at all. You are free, cousin, and I am still free. It looks as if there is nothing to prevent the realization of our little plans. But I have too honourable a nature to conceal the state of my affairs from you. I haven't forgotten that I have a commitment to you. In all my long journeys, I have always remembered the little wooden bench . . .

Eugénie jumped up as if she had been sitting on hot coals, and then sat down on one of the courtyard steps.

. . . the little wooden bench where we swore eternal love to each other, the grey living-room, my attic bedroom. And I have not forgotten the night when, with delicacy and kindness, you made my future easier. Yes, these memories have kept up my spirits and I told myself that you were always thinking of me as I often thought of you at the hour we agreed. Did you really look at the clouds at nine o'clock? Yes, you did, didn't you? So I don't want to betray a friendship which I hold sacred. No, I must not deceive you. At the moment, a marriage has been proposed to me which accords with all the views I have come to hold on the subject. Love in marriage is a pipe-dream. Today my experience tells me that when one marries, one must obey all society's laws and satisfy all the social conventions. There is already a difference in age between us which may affect your future, dear cousin, more than mine. I shall say nothing about your mode of life, or your upbringing, or your habits, which are quite alien to Parisian life and would probably not fit in with my future plans. One of my intentions is to maintain a large establishment and to entertain in a big way, and I seem to remember that you like a gentle,

179

quiet life. No, I shall be more frank and let you decide about my situation. You are entitled to know it and you shall have the right to be judge of it. Today I have an income of eighty thousand livres. This fortune allows me to marry into the d'Aubrion family, whose heiress, a young lady of nineteen, will bring me, as a dowry, her name, a title, the post of honorary gentleman of the bedchamber to His Majesty, and a very brilliant position in society. I shall confess to you, my dear cousin, that I don't care in the least for Mademoiselle d'Aubrion, but, by marrying her, I guarantee to my children a social situation whose advantages will, one day, be incalculable. With each day that passes, royalist ideas are coming back more into favour. So, in a few years' time, my son, who will have become Marquis d'Aubrion, owner of an inherited estate yielding an income of forty thousand livres, will be able to have any State office that he cares to choose. We owe it to our children. You see, cousin, how frankly I am revealing to you the state of my heart, my hopes, and my fortune. It is possible that after seven years of separation you, for your part, have forgotten our childish dreams. But _I_ have not forgotten either your kindness or my promises. I remember them all, even those given most lightly and that a less conscientious young man than I, one with a less youthful and upright heart, wouldn't even think of any more. By telling you that I am thinking of making a marriage which is one of convenience only, and that I still remember our childish love affair, I am putting myself entirely in your hands; I am making you mistress of my fate and saying to you that if I must renounce my social ambitions, I shall gladly content myself with the simple, pure happiness of which you gave me such a touching picture . . .

'Tum, ti, tum.—Tum, ti, ta.—Tan, ti, tum. Boom! —Boom, ti, ta.—Tan, ti, tum . . ., etc.', Charles had sung to the tune of _Non più andrai_,* as he signed his name.

'My goodness me, that's standing on a lot of ceremony,' he said to himself. And he had looked for the cheque and added the following.

P.S. I enclose with my letter a cheque payable to you, drawn on the firm of des Grassins, for eight thousand francs; that covers the capital and the interest on the amount you were kind enough

180

to lend me. I am expecting the arrival from Bordeaux of a chest which contains a few objects which I hope you will allow me to send you as a token of my eternal gratitude. You can return my dressing-case by the stage-coach to the Hôtel d'Aubrion, Rue Hillerin-Bertin.

'By the stage-coach!' said Eugénie. 'Something for which I would have given my life a thousand times!'

Appalling and utter disaster! The ship was sinking without leaving a rope or a plank on the vast ocean of hope. Some women, realizing they have been abandoned, rush to tear their beloved from a rival's arms, kill her, and flee to the ends of the earth, the scaffold, or the grave. There is, to be sure, a certain grandeur in that; the motive of the crime is a sublime passion which disarms human justice. Others bow their heads and suffer in silence. They go their way, cut to the heart but resigned, weeping and forgiving, praying and remembering until their last breath. That is love, true love, the love of angels, the proud love that lives on grief and dies of it. Such was Eugénie's feeling after reading the horrible letter. She raised her eyes to heaven, thinking of her mother's last words. As sometimes happens to people who are dying, Madame Grandet had had a penetrating, clear vision of the future. Then, Eugénie, remembering that prophetic life and death, foresaw her whole destiny at a glance. All that was left to her was to unfold her wings, reach out to heaven, and live in prayer until the day of her deliverance.

'My mother was right,' she said, weeping. 'I can only suffer and die.'

She returned slowly to the living-room from the garden. Contrary to her usual habit, she did not go through the corridor. But she retraced the memory of her cousin in the grey old living-room; on its mantelpiece there was still a particular saucer which she used every morning at breakfast, as well as the old Sèvres sugar-bowl. That morning was to be a solemn and eventful one for her.

Nanon announced the parish priest. This priest, a relative of the Cruchots, worked for the interests of President de Bonfons. Some days previously, the old Abbé had made him agree to speak to Mademoiselle Grandet of her obligation, from the purely religious point of view, to get married. When she saw her pastor, Eugénie thought he had come for the thousand francs she gave every month to the poor. But the priest began to smile.

'Today, Mademoiselle, I have come to talk to you about a poor girl everyone in Saumur is concerned about; through lack of charity towards herself, she is not leading a Christian life.'

'Oh dear, Monsieur le Curé, you have come at a time when I can't possibly think of others; I am so occupied with my own troubles. I am very unhappy. My only refuge is the church. The church has an embrace large enough to contain all our sorrows, and her compassionate feelings are so abundant that we may draw on them without fear of exhausting the supply.'

'Well, Mademoiselle, in looking after this girl, we shall be looking after you. If you wish to work for your salvation, there are only two paths you can follow, either to leave the world or to follow its laws, to obey your earthly destiny or your heavenly one.'

'Oh, your voice speaks to me just when I wanted to hear a voice. Yes, God is directing you here, Monsieur. I want to say farewell to the world and live for God alone in silence and seclusion.'

'You must think carefully, my daughter, before making such an extreme decision. Marriage is a life, the veil is a death.'

'Well, let it be death, a speedy death, Monsieur le Curé,' she said with a frightening eagerness.

'Death! But you have great obligations to society to fulfil, Mademoiselle. Are you not the mother of the poor to whom you give clothing and wood in winter and work in summer? Your great wealth is a loan that you must repay, and you have always piously accepted it as such. To bury yourself in a convent would be selfish. As for remaining an old maid, you ought not to. Besides, could you manage your enormous fortune by yourself? You might perhaps lose it. You would soon be engaged in countless lawsuits and you would be involved in interminable difficulties. Believe your pastor. A husband would be useful to you. You ought to look after what God has given you. I am speaking to you as a beloved lamb of my flock. You love God too sincerely not to work for your salvation in the world. You are one of its finest ornaments and you set it a saintly example.'

At this moment, Madame des Grassins was announced. Her visit was inspired by a desire for vengeance and by deep despair.

'Mademoiselle,' she began. 'Oh, you are here, Monsieur le Curé. I say no more. I was coming to talk business with you, but I see you are having an important consultation.'

'Madame,' said the curé, 'I leave the field free for you.'

'Oh, Monsieur le Curé,' said Eugénie. 'Come back in a few minutes. I need your help badly just now.'

'Yes, my poor child, certainly you do,' said Madame des Grassins.

'What do you mean?' asked Mademoiselle Grandet and the curé together.

'I know about your cousin's return and his marriage to Mademoiselle d'Aubrion. A woman doesn't keep her wits in her pocket.'

Eugénie blushed and said nothing. But she decided that, in future, she would assume an impassive expression as her father had always done.

'Well, Madame,' she replied at last, ironically. 'My wits are no doubt in my pocket, but I don't understand. Speak out freely in front of Monsieur le Curé. As you know, he is my confessor.'

'Well, Mademoiselle, here is what des Grassins has written to me. Read it for yourself.'

Eugénie read the following letter.

My dear wife,

Charles Grandet has come back from the Indies. He has been in Paris for a month . . .

'A month!' thought Eugénie, letting her hand fall to her side.

After a pause, she took up the letter again.

. . . I had to call on him twice before I was admitted to speak to the future Vicomte d'Aubrion. Although all Paris is talking of his marriage, and the banns have been published . . .

'So he was writing to me at the very moment when . . .', Eugénie said to herself. She did not finish her thought. She did not exclaim 'the scoundrel', as a Parisian girl would have done. But although it was not expressed, her contempt was none the less complete.

. . . the marriage is far from being certain. The Marquis d'Aubrion will not give his daughter to the son of a bankrupt. I called to tell him of the trouble that his uncle and I had taken with his father's affairs, and of the clever devices by which we had managed to keep the creditors quiet up till now. The impudent young puppy had the cheek to say to me, to *me*, who have devoted myself night and day for five years to looking after his interests and his honour, that *his father's affairs were not his*. A commercial lawyer would be entitled to ask him for fees of thirty to forty thousand francs, at the rate of one per cent of the total debt. But, wait a minute! Twelve hundred thousand francs are quite legally due to his creditors, and I am going to have his father declared bankrupt. I got involved in the business on the word of that old crocodile, Grandet, and I made promises in the name of the family. If Monsieur le Vicomte d'Aubrion does not care much about his honour, I am concerned for mine. So I'm going to explain my position to the creditors. Still, I have too much respect for Mademoiselle Eugénie, with whom in happier times we had hoped to be closely connected, to take any action before you have spoken to her about the matter . . .

At this point Eugénie handed the letter back coldly to Madame des Grassins, without reading further.

'Thank you,' she said to Madame des Grassins. 'We shall see . . .'

'As you said that, your voice was just like your late father's,' said Madame des Grassins.

'Madame, you have eight thousand, one hundred francs in gold to pay out to us,' said Nanon.

'That's true. Do me the favour of coming with me, Madame Cornoiller.'

'Monsieur le Curé, would it be a sin to remain a virgin while being married?' asked Eugénie with a dignified composure inspired by the thought she was about to express.

'That's a question of conscience to which I don't know the answer. If you want to know what the illustrious Sanchez* thinks about it in his treatise *De Matrimonio,* I can tell you tomorrow.'

After the curé had gone, Mademoiselle Grandet went up to her father's office and spent the day there, alone. She would not even come down at dinner-time, in spite of Nanon's entreaties. She appeared in the evening in time for the arrival of the usual circle of visitors. The Grandet living-room had never been as full as it was that evening. The news of Charles's return and of his foolish treachery had spread through the whole town. But although the visitors looked and listened with great attention, their curiosity was not satisfied. Eugénie, expecting them to be very inquisitive, did not allow any of the painful emotions that were ravaging her to appear on her calm face. She turned with a smile to those who wanted to show their sympathy by commiserating looks or words. In fact she concealed her distress with a veil of politeness. About nine o'clock, the games of whist were coming to an end and the players were leaving their tables, paying their debts, and discussing the last hands as they joined the circle who were sitting chatting. Just as all the company got up to go, there was a dramatic incident that reverberated throughout Saumur and from there to the whole district and the four surrounding prefectures.

'Please stay behind for a moment,' Eugénie said to

Monsieur de Bonfons when she saw him take his walking-stick.

At these words, there was no one in that numerous company who did not feel excited. The President turned pale and had to sit down.

'The millions will go to the President,' said Mademoiselle de Gribeaucourt.

'It's obvious. President de Bonfons is going to marry Mademoiselle Grandet,' exclaimed Madame d'Orsonval.

'That's the best trick of the evening's whist,' said the Abbé.

'It's a splendid grand slam,' said the lawyer.

Everyone had his comment to make, everyone cracked his joke about it; they all saw the heiress, high up on her millions as on a pedestal. The drama begun nine years ago was coming to a conclusion. To ask the President to stay behind, in front of all Saumur, was surely to announce that she wished to make him her husband. In small towns, the conventions are so strictly observed that a breach of this kind is equivalent to the most solemn of promises.

'Monsieur le Président,' said Eugénie agitatedly, when they were alone, 'I know what you find attractive about me. Swear to leave me free for the whole of my life, to claim none of the rights which marriage gives you over me, and my hand is yours. Oh,' she continued, seeing him go down on his knees, 'I haven't finished yet. I must not deceive you, Monsieur. I have an inextinguishable love in my heart. Friendship will be the only feeling I can offer my husband. I do not want to hurt him, nor to contradict the dictates of my own heart. But you will have my hand and my fortune only if you do me a very great service.'

'I am ready to do anything,' said the President.

'Here are fifteen hundred thousand francs, Monsieur le Président,' she said, drawing a certificate for one hundred shares in the Bank of France from her bodice. 'Leave for Paris, not tomorrow, not tonight, but this very minute. Go to Monsieur des Grassins, find out from him the names of all my uncle's creditors, call them to a meeting, pay everything that the estate can possibly owe them, capital and interest at five per cent from the day the debt was incurred until the repayment date, and finally see that you get a receipt for everything in proper legal form. You are a magistrate; I am relying entirely on you in this matter. You are an honourable man, a gentleman. On the strength of your word, I shall set out on the dangerous voyage of life under the protection of your name. We shall bear with each other's failings. We have known each other for such a long time; we are almost relations. You wouldn't want to make me unhappy.'

The President fell at the rich heiress's feet, trembling with the violence of his joy.

'I shall be your slave,' he said.

'When you get the receipt, Monsieur,' she continued, looking at him coldly, 'you will take it with all the relevant documents to my cousin Grandet and you will give him this letter. On your return, I shall keep my word.'

As for the President, he understood that he owed Mademoiselle Grandet to a disappointment in love, so he hurried to carry out her orders with all possible speed, in case there should be any reconciliation between the two lovers.

When Monsieur de Bonfons had gone, Eugénie collapsed into her chair and burst into tears. Everything was finally settled. The President took the mail-coach and was in Paris the next evening. The morning after his arrival, he went to see des Grassins. He called the creditors to a meeting at the lawyer's office where the claims were deposited, and not one of them failed to attend. They may have been creditors but, to give them their due, they were all on time. There, President de Bonfons, in the name of Mademoiselle Grandet, paid them the capital and all the interest that was due. For the business world of Paris, the payment of the interest was one of the most astonishing events of the day. When the receipt had been registered and des Grassins rewarded for his trouble by a gift of fifty thousand francs which Eugénie had provided for him, the President went to the Hôtel d'Aubrion. There he found Charles just as he was returning to his rooms, in an utterly despondent state after an interview with his future father-in-law. The old Marquis had just declared that his daughter would be given to Charles only when all Guillaume Grandet's creditors had been paid.

The President first of all gave him the following letter.

Dear cousin,

Monsieur le Président de Bonfons has undertaken to give you the receipt for all the sums owed by my uncle, and also a receipt acknowledging that I received the money from you. I heard talk of bankruptcy! . . . It occured to me that the son of a bankrupt would perhaps not be able to marry Mademoiselle d'Aubrion. Yes, cousin, you judged my temperament and my habits correctly. I am sure I have nothing in common with high society; I know nothing of its intrigues or its manners, and could not give you the pleasures you look for there. Be happy, according to the social conventions to which you sacrifice our early love. To make your happiness complete, all I can give you is your father's honour. Farewell. You will always have a faithful friend in your cousin

EUGÉNIE

The President smiled at the exclamation that the ambitious young man could not suppress as he received the legally receipted documents.

'We shall both announce our marriages at the same time,' he said.

'Ah! So you're going to marry Eugénie. Well I'm pleased; she's a good girl. But', he continued, struck by a sudden enlightening thought, 'she must be rich then!'

'Four days ago, she had nearly nineteen million,' replied the President in a bantering tone, 'but today she has only seventeen left.'

Charles, dumbfounded, stared at the President.

'Seventeen . . . mill . . .'

'Seventeen million, yes, Monsieur. When we are married, Mademoiselle Grandet and I together will have an income of seven hundred and fifty thousand livres.'

'My dear cousin,' said Charles, recovering a little of his self-assurance, 'we shall be able to further each other's interests.'

'Quite so,' said the President. 'I have here, as well, a little case, which I am also to give only to you,' he added, putting the box containing the dressing-case down on the table.

'Well, my dear,' said Madame la Marquise d'Aubrion, coming in and taking no notice of Cruchot, 'don't pay any attention to what Monsieur d'Aubrion, poor man, has just told you. The Duchesse de Chaulieu has been turning his head. I repeat, there is nothing to prevent your marriage . . .'

'Nothing, Madame,' replied Charles. 'The three million which were formerly owed by my father were paid yesterday.'

'In cash?' she asked.

'The lot, interest and capital, and I am going to restore his good name.'

'What nonsense!' cried the future mother-in-law. 'Who is this person?' she whispered to Charles as she noticed Cruchot.

'My man of business,' he murmured in reply.

The Marquise inclined her head disdainfully towards Monsieur de Bonfons and left the room.

'We are furthering each other's interests already,' said the President as he took his hat. 'Goodbye,—cousin.'

'He's laughing at me—that Saumur cockatoo. I'd like to ram six inches of steel into his body.'

But the President had gone. Three days later, back in Saumur, he announced his marriage to Eugénie. Six months later, he was appointed Councillor to the Court-Royal at Angers. Before leaving Saumur, Eugénie had melted down the gold of the jewels which had been dear to her heart for so long. Together with the eight thousand francs from her cousin, she used them for a gold monstrance, which she presented to the parish church where she had prayed so often for *him*. In fact, she divided her time between Angers and Saumur. Her husband, who had shown devotion to the

Government in a political affair, became President of the Chamber* and finally, after a few years, First President. He impatiently awaited the next general election so that he could win a seat in the Chamber of Deputies.* He was already aspiring towards the peerage, and then . . .

'Then he'll be cousin to the King,' said Nanon, Big Nanon, Madame de Cornoiller, respected Saumur house-wife, when Eugénie told her of the heights to which her mistress was about to rise.

Nevertheless, Monsieur le Président de Bonfons (he had finally dispensed with the family name of Cruchot) did not succeed in realizing any of his ambitious plans. He died eight days after being appointed deputy* for Saumur. God, who sees everything and never strikes unjustly, was no doubt punishing him for his calculations and for the legal skill with which, *accurante Cruchot*,* he had drawn up his marriage contract. In it the husband and wife gave each other, *in the event of their not having children, all their property, both landed and personal, without exception or reservation, in absolute ownership, dispensing even with the formality of an inventory, the omission of the said inventory not to be to the detriment of their heirs or assigns, it being understood that the aforesaid donation, etc.* This clause may explain the profound respect which the President always showed for Madame de Bonfons's wishes and for her desire to live in solitude. Women referred to Monsieur le Premier Président as one of the most delicately considerate of men. They pitied him and went as far as to blame Eugénie for her grief and for her devotion to her first love, as only they can blame a woman, with apparently innocuous but very cruelly barbed remarks. 'Madame la Présidente de Bonfons must really be very ill to leave her husband on his own. Poor little thing! Will she soon get well? What's the matter with her? Is it gastritis, or perhaps cancer? Why doesn't she see a doctor? She's been looking yellow for some time now; she ought to go and consult a specialist in Paris. How is it that she doesn't want to have a child? They say she's very fond of her husband, so why not give him an heir, with the position that he holds? You know, that's frightful, and if it's just because of some whim, then she's much to be blamed. Poor President!'

Eugénie had the refined sensibility that a solitary person acquires from continual meditation and from the acute vision with which he perceives the things that come within his orbit. Moreover, her sorrow and the experiences attendant upon it had taught her to see clearly into the hearts of others. So she knew that the President wished for her death in order to be the sole owner of their enormous fortune, which had been increased still further by the estates of his uncle the lawyer and his uncle the Abbé, whom God had seen fit to call to himself. The poor recluse pitied the President. Providence avenged her for the shocking, calculated indifference of a husband who respected the hopeless passion she fed on, as the strongest guarantee of his own interests. To give life to a child, that would surely put an end to the selfish hopes, the delightful ambitions, cherished by the First President. And God continued to shower quantities of gold on his prisoner who cared nothing for gold. She longed for heaven and lived, with saintly thoughts, pious and good, continually giving secret help to those in distress.

Madame de Bonfons was a widow at the age of thirty-three, with an income of eight hundred thousand livres a year. She was still beautiful, but with the beauty of a woman approaching forty. Her face is pale, composed, and calm. She speaks gently and thoughtfully, her manner is unaffected. She has all the nobility of grief, the saintliness of one whose soul is unsullied by contact with the outside world. But she has also the rigid outlook of an old maid and the narrow vision that comes from the restricted life of a provincial town. In spite of her income of eight hundred thousand livres, she lives as poor Eugénie Grandet used to live. She lights her fire only on the days when her father used to allow the fire to be lit in the living-room, and puts it out according to the rules in force when she was young. She always dresses as her mother did. The house at Saumur, sunless, devoid of warmth, gloomy, and always in the shade, reflects her life. She looks after her accumulating income carefully and would perhaps appear to be mean, did she not give the lie to slander by the noble use she makes of her fortune. Foundations for pious and charitable purposes, an old-age home, Christian schools for the children, a richly endowed public library, testify, year by year, against the charge of avarice with which some people reproach her. The churches of Saumur owe their embellishments to her. Madame de Bonfons, though she is jokingly called *Mademoiselle*, inspires a reverent respect everywhere. Her noble heart, which was moved only by the tenderest feelings, was thus fated to be exploited by the calculations of the self-interested. Money was destined to impart its cold glitter to her angelic life and to inspire a mistrust of feeling in a woman who was all feeling.

'You are the only one who loves me,' she would say to Nanon.

Eugénie's hand tends the hidden wounds in any family. Her path to heaven is marked by a succession of good deeds. The greatness of her soul lessens the effect of the narrowness of her upbringing and of the ways of her early life. Such is the story of a woman who, made to be a magnificent wife and mother, has neither husband nor children nor family. In the last few days, there has been talk of a new marriage for her. The people of Saumur are gossiping about her and the Marquis de Froidfond, whose family are beginning to besiege the young widow as the Cruchots used to do in the past. People say that Nanon and Cornoiller are on the side of the Froidfonds, but nothing can be further from the truth. Neither Big Nanon nor Cornoiller is smart enough to understand the corruptions of the world.

PARIS, SEPTEMBER 1833

EXPLANATORY NOTES

2 *Maria*: Maria du Fresnay had been married for four years to a man twenty years her senior, when, in 1833 at the age of twenty-four, she was expecting her first child, of whom Balzac was sure he was the father. She has been identified as the naïve, sweet young woman who, according to a letter written by Balzac to his sister in 1833, came to him saying, 'Love me for a year and I shall love you all my life.'

4 *a member of the League*: the Holy League was formed in 1576 by Duke Henry of Guise to defend the Catholic religion against the Protestants. During the Reformation, Saumur was one of the most active centres of Protestantism in France.

4 *Henri IV*: the conflict between Catholics and Protestants led to civil war, in which the Leaguers were defeated by Henry of Navarre, who in 1589 became King of France. For the sake of national unity he abjured Protestantism and adopted Catholicism, the religion of the majority of the French people.

6 *church property*: after the French Revolution of 1789, the state confiscated church property and put it up for sale.

7 *national property*: this term included both confiscated church property and property confiscated from aristocrats who had left France after the 1789 Revolution.

7 *émigrés*: the term applied to all those who had 'emigrated', i.e. left France after the 1789 Revolution.

7 *Republican armies*: the 1789 Revolution was followed by a war waged by French émigrés, helped by foreign powers, against the armies of the French Republic set up by the Revolution.

7 *Consulate*: from 1799 to 1804 France was governed by three 'consuls', of whom Napoleon Bonaparte was the chief.

7 *Empire*: Napoleon was proclaimed Emperor in 1804. The Empire lasted from 1804 till his defeat and the Restoration

of the Bourbon monarchy in 1814–15.

7   *with 'de' before his name*: the owner of such a name would be a member of the landed aristocracy.

7   *Legion of Honour*: an order instituted by Napoleon to reward people of merit and distinction.

9   *five louis*: i.e. half the amount for which Grandet sold his casks.

10   *Rothschilds*: the prosperity of the Rothschild family began in the early 19th century. Its founder, Meyer-Anselm Rothschild, died in 1812.

10   *Laffitte*: Jacques Laffitte (1767–1844), a French banker and politician.

13   *Medici . . . Pazzi*: two famous rival families in 15th-century Florence. The Pazzi conspired against the Medici in 1478, but their conspiracy failed and they were executed.

14   *Talleyrand*: Charles de Talleyrand-Périgord (1754–1838), a clever and unscrupulous French diplomat.

14   *the red cap of the Revolutionaries*: some extreme supporters of the 1789 Revolution wore a red cap which became an emblem of the Revolution.

17   *Civil Wars*: cf. note to 'Henri IV' on p.4

23   *Catherine de Médicis*: a daughter of the Italian, Lorenzo de Medici, she married in 1533 Henri, Duc d'Orléans, who in 1547 became Henri II, King of France.

26   *A charcoal burner is mayor in his own house*: the French word 'maire' here replaces 'maître', the normal form of the proverb, which means that a man is master in his own house. The President's clumsy pun alludes to Grandet's career during the Revolution, when he was mayor of Saumur.

28   *Austerlitz*: the site in 1805 of one of Napoleon's most celebrated victories.

30   *lotto*: a game like bingo.

35   *Buisson*: a well-known Parisian tailor, a friend and creditor of Balzac.

37   *Encyclopédie méthodique*: a large encyclopaedia in 201 volumes (1781–1832).

38 *Moniteur*: a daily newspaper, which first appeared in 1789.

38 *Westall*: Richard Westall (1765–1836), a celebrated English painter in water-colours.

38 *English keepsakes*: volumes of extracts from contemporary authors, illustrated with engravings and bound in silk or morocco. They were published annually in England from about 1820 to 1850 and were fashionable Christmas and New Year presents. The fashion spread abroad and especially in France.

38 *the Findens*: William Finden (1787–1852), a successful English engraver, was joined by his brother Edward to help him cope with the volume of work.

43 *Chantrey's statue*: Francis Chantrey (1782–1841), a celebrated English sculptor.

46 *Farewell to the baskets, the harvest's over*: a popular saying, meaning that someone else has obtained what we have been striving for.

47 *Faublas*: *Les Amours du chevalier de Faublas* (1790) by Louvet de Couvray was a popular novel of the time, distinguished by its immorality.

47 *Les Liaisons dangereuses*: (1782), by Choderlos de Laclos, another widely read novel of the period, well known for its immorality as well as its literary merit.

56 *Venus de Milo*: this famous statue was discovered in 1820, bought by the French Government, and placed in the Louvre.

56 *Phidias' Jupiter*: Phidias (490–432 BC) was regarded as the greatest sculptor of ancient Greece, and his statue of Jupiter at Olympia as his greatest work. It was destroyed by fire in AD 475. In 1815 a French author, Quatremère de Quincey, tried to describe the statue in a work about ancient Greek sculpture and included a coloured plate in his text.

60 *a duty in the days of the Empire*: during the Napoleonic wars, the blockade of France caused a steep rise in the price of sugar.

66 *Hungarian sisters*: Hungarian twins (1701–23) who were joined at birth, like the later, more famous Siamese twins.

69 *Bréguet*: Abraham-Louis Bréguet (1747–1823), a celebrated French watchmaker.

71 *Chaptal*: Jean-Antoine Chaptal (1756–1832) was a celebrated French chemist. There is no record in his works of the invention of a coffee-pot, though Balzac in his novels makes several references to one.

77 *Two million*: in the first edition, Guillaume Grandet's debt was given as three million, and in the Charpentier edition as two. In the Furne edition, it became four million, but Balzac omitted to make the change at this point.

78 *novenas*: prayers which are said in church for nine consecutive days. A fee has to be paid to the priest; hence Grandet's response to Eugénie's proposal.

81 *Balthazar*: the last King of Babylon. At a feast, during which he desecrated holy vessels pillaged from the Temple in Jerusalem, he saw the words *Mene, Mene, Tekel, Upharsin* being written on the wall. The prophet Daniel interpreted these words as heralding the destruction of Balthazar. That same night, Balthazar was killed and Darius the Mede took over his kingdom (cf. Daniel 5).

85 *per fas et nefas*: a Latin phrase meaning 'by any means, legal or illegal'.

87 *bonhomme*: there is no real equivalent in English for 'bonhomme'. Balzac here explains his own use of the term, which has been rendered in this translation as 'old man' or 'old fellow'.

93 *Alcibiades' dog*: Alcibiades (*c*.450–404 BC) was a brilliant young Athenian general, admired for his talents and disliked for his scandalous behaviour. There is a story that he docked the fine tail of his handsome dog and, when told that people criticized him for it, said: 'That's just what I want; while they talk of this, they will not say anything worse about me.'

99 *Jeremy Bentham*: (1748–1832). His *Defence of Usury* advocated the abolition of laws limiting interest on money-lending, because money-lending was socially useful.

99 *Jeremiah*: a pun on the name of the biblical prophet Jeremiah, deemed to be the author of the Book of Lamentations.

196

105 *in partibus*: the Latin phrase *in partibus infidelium* was applied originally to a bishop appointed to a diocese in a pagan country, and then to one who has, for some reason, no diocese to administer. Here it means that Cornoiller is Grandet's gamekeeper without receiving the wages he should be entitled to.

110 *Venite adoremus*: refrain of a well-known hymn, *Adeste fideles* (Oh come, all ye faithful), often sung at Christmas-time.

111 *Madame Campan*: during the first part of her life Madame Campan (1752–1822) had an official position at the court of Marie Antoinette. After the Revolution she opened a girls' school, and later Napoleon appointed her head of a school for the daughters of officers. When, after the fall of Napoleon, the Bourbons were restored to the throne of France, she was reproached with having betrayed the friendship she had enjoyed with Marie Antoinette.

111 *Marat*: Jean-Paul Marat (1744–93), organizer of the September massacres during the French Revolution, was murdered in his bath by Charlotte Corday. In 1794 his remains were buried at the Panthéon in Paris with great pomp, but in 1795 they were removed and placed in the Sainte-Geneviève cemetery, while his heart was paraded through Paris, insulted, and thrown into a sewer in the Rue Montmartre.

112 *Salamander*: a kind of lizard which was the heraldic design of King Francis I of France (1494–1547). It is to be found on many works of art made during his reign.

116 *Madame de Mirbel*: (1746–1849), a fashionable painter of the period.

119 *when Augustus drank, Poland got drunk*: a line of verse written by Frederick the Great (1712–86), King of Prussia, about Frederick-Augustus III (1696–1763), King of Poland.

122 *Auguste Lafontaine*: (1759–1831), a popular German writer, whose novels, containing sentimental scenes of family life, were all translated into French.

122 *Goethe's Marguerite*: the heroine of Goethe's *Faust* (1806, translated into French by Gérard de Nerval in 1828), a simple, virtuous girl, seduced by Faust and convicted of infanticide. In literature, she became a symbol of the innocent victim of love.

197

124   *in livres*: according to a decree of 1810, the six-livre coin was worth 5fr.80.

129   *protested bills*: bills which are not honoured.

134   *Bossuet*: (1627–1704), Bishop of Meaux, a great orator and preacher. In a sermon 'On the brevity of life', he talks of his moments of happiness being like nails scattered at intervals along a long wall. Although they cover a considerable extent, if gathered together they would not fill his hand.

136   *military mass*: a low mass attended by cadets from the cavalry school at Saumur.

136   *Atreus*: King of Mycenae, famous in Greek mythology for his hatred of his brother Thyestes and the vengeance he took on him. He killed Thyestes' children and caused their limbs to be served up to their father at a banquet. He was killed by another son of Thyestes. The descendants of Atreus were notorious for the terrible crimes which were committed within the family. The most celebrated were Agamemnon, leader of the Greeks against Troy, who sacrificed his daughter Iphigenia and was murdered by his wife Clytemnestra, and his brother Menelaus, King of Sparta, whose wife Helen was abducted by Paris and so the cause of the Trojan War.

139   *écus*: i.e. in silver coin.

147   *frippe*: cf. p.59.

153   *A charcoal burner's master in his own house*: cf. note to p.26.

155   *Code*: refers to the relevant section of French law which was systematized into five 'codes' during the Napoleonic regime.

164   *at the age of eighty-two*: we are told at the beginning of the novel that Monsieur Grandet was 57 in 1806. This means that in 1827 he should have been 78, not 82. Balzac is careless in his chronology.

170   *Penelope's web*: Penelope was the wife of Ulysses, Greek hero of the Trojan War. During his long absence from home, she put off numerous suitors by promising to select one of them as soon as she had finished a piece of tapestry she was weaving, but each night she undid what she had

done during the day. Hence she is often used as a symbol of conjugal fidelity.

172 *Crossing the line*: the line here referred to is the equator. It was a naval tradition to duck in a tub on deck sailors who crossed the line for the first time.

173 *Saint-Thomas*: an island in the West Indies.

174 *quibuscumque viis*: 'in any way at all'.

174 *Marie-Caroline*: the first name of the Duchesse de Berry, whose husband, second son of King Charles X of France, was assassinated in 1820. It is thus an appropriate name for a ship belonging to a Royalist firm.

174 *Captal*: 'Captal' was a title which used to be given to the heads of certain aristocratic families before 1789, in particular of the Buch family in the region of Bordeaux (cf. p.175).

176 *Faubourg Saint-Germain*: the quarter of Paris where the old aristocratic families had their town-houses.

176 *Dreux family*: the Dreux and the Brézé were two distinct aristocratic families until 1686, when the Comte de Dreux exchanged his marquisate of La Galissonnière for the estate and marquisate of Brézé.

176 *Restoration*: the period from the defeat of Napoleon in 1814, comprising the reigns of Louis XVIII and Charles X, who had to abdicate after the 1830 Revolution, is known as the Restoration. The short period in 1815 known as the 'Hundred Days', during which Napoleon returned to France before his defeat at Waterloo, is of course excluded.

178 *Vous*: it is not possible to render into modern English the difference between 'vous', the more formal mode of address, and 'tu', the word used in talking to intimate friends, family, children, and animals. The use of 'tu' is now much more widespread than it was in 19th-century France. In Eugénie's day, its use would suggest a degree of intimacy in the relationship between Eugénie and Charles, while the use of 'vous' immediately indicates to Eugénie that, although they are cousins, there is no longer in Charles's mind a special relationship between them. The extended use of 'tu' in modern French can be compared to the extended use of first names in modern English.

180 *Non più andrai*: an air sung by Figaro in Mozart's opera *The Marriage of Figaro*.

185 *Sanchez*: Thomas Sanchez (1550–1610), a Jesuit who wrote a confessors' manual, celebrated for its precise information. Its full title is *Disputationes de sancto matrimonii sacramento*.

190 *Chamber*: in French towns where there is a lot of legal work, each court is subdivided into sections called 'chambers'. Each of these has a president, the first president being the head of the whole court.

190 *Chamber of Deputies*: the French equivalent of the British House of Commons.

190 *deputy*: the French equivalent of a Member of Parliament.

190 *accurante Cruchot*: a Latin expression meaning that a legal document had been drawn up by a particular lawyer.

THE WORLD'S CLASSICS

A Select List

HANS ANDERSEN: Fairy Tales
Translated by L. W. Kingsland
Introduction by Naomi Lewis
Illustrated by Vilhelm Pedersen and Lorenz Frølich

JANE AUSTEN: Emma
Edited by James Kinsley and David Lodge

Mansfield Park
Edited by James Kinsley and John Lucas

J. M. BARRIE: Peter Pan in Kensington Gardens & Peter and Wendy
Edited by Peter Hollindale

WILLIAM BECKFORD: Vathek
Edited by Roger Lonsdale

CHARLOTTE BRONTË: Jane Eyre
Edited by Margaret Smith

THOMAS CARLYLE: The French Revolution
Edited by K. J. Fielding and David Sorensen

LEWIS CARROLL: Alice's Adventures in Wonderland
and Through the Looking Glass
Edited by Roger Lancelyn Green
Illustrated by John Tenniel

MIGUEL DE CERVANTES: Don Quixote
Translated by Charles Jarvis
Edited by E. C. Riley

GEOFFREY CHAUCER: The Canterbury Tales
Translated by David Wright

ANTON CHEKHOV: The Russian Master and Other Stories
Translated by Ronald Hingley

JOSEPH CONRAD: Victory
Edited by John Batchelor
Introduction by Tony Tanner

DANTE ALIGHIERI: The Divine Comedy
Translated by C. H. Sisson
Edited by David Higgins

VIRGIL: The Aeneid
Translated by C. Day Lewis
Edited by Jasper Griffin

HORACE WALPOLE: The Castle of Otranto
Edited by W. S. Lewis

IZAAK WALTON and CHARLES COTTON:
The Compleat Angler
Edited by John Buxton
Introduction by John Buchan

OSCAR WILDE: Complete Shorter Fiction
Edited by Isobel Murray

The Picture of Dorian Gray
Edited by Isobel Murray

VIRGINIA WOOLF: Orlando
Edited by Rachel Bowlby

ÉMILE ZOLA:
The Attack on the Mill and other stories
Translated by Douglas Parmée